Varangian

Varangian

Book 3 in the Aelfraed Series

By
Griff Hosker

Varangian

Published by Griff Hosker 2013
Copyright © Griff Hosker Fourth Edition

The author has asserted their moral right under the Copyright, Designs and Patents Act, 1988, to be identified as the author of this work.

All Rights Reserved. No part of this publication may be reproduced, copied, stored in a retrieval system, or transmitted, in any form or by any means, without the prior written consent of the copyright holder, nor be otherwise circulated in any form of binding or cover other than that in which it is published and without a similar condition being imposed on the subsequent purchaser.

A CIP catalogue record for this title is available from the British Library.

Contents

Varangian i
Chapter 1 2
Chapter 2 14
Chapter 3 25
Chapter 4 36
Chapter 5 47
Chapter 6 60
Chapter 7 73
Chapter 8 85
Chapter 9 96
Chapter 10 107
Chapter 11 118
Chapter 12 131
Chapter 13 142
Chapter 14 154
Chapter 15 166
Chapter 16 178
Epilogue 193
Characters and places in the novel 195
Historical note 197
Other books by Griff Hosker 199
Prologue 206

Varangian

Chapter 1

The Captain of the ship looked at Ridley and me with suspicion. There were not many Saxon lords left now and certainly none here in Scotland at the port of Leith. I could see that he suspected that we had allies and ulterior motives. "Why do two lords such as you wish to visit Denmark? I hear that their king ravaged your land."

In that he was correct and I had reason to hate Sweyn, King of the Danes, who had broken his word but he was a lesser enemy than King William, the Bastard, who pursued us. We were the last two Saxon rebels and, unless we could escape from this island, we would be killed. King Sweyn owed us a debt and I would claim it.

"Let us just say that this purse of silver allows us to travel with you and we will keep our motives to ourselves."

He weighed the purse in his hand and nodded appreciatively. "This is sufficient to pay for your passage but understand me, lord, I trade frequently with the Danes and I cannot afford to transport enemies to them." He spread his hands as he returned the purse to me. "You understand?"

I nodded. "I give you my word that the King of the Danes will welcome us and I wish him no harm." I could feel Ridley, my companion bristling at the man's suspicion and the captain still looked dubious. "I never knew a Scot yet who did not want to make a little money. I am Aelfraed of Topcliffe and I give you my word that I will not cause you to lose trade."

He suddenly paled and bowed, "My lord. I did not know it was you. Forgive me. I will take you but," he looked urgently over my shoulder, "we should hurry to catch the tide and to avoid a certain Thegn who, we hear is not well disposed towards you."

I grinned, no, the Thegn of Fife, the man who had stolen my wife, Gytha, would remember me for he now had a scarred face as a reminder of our last encounter. The Captain hurriedly grabbed the purse and helped us aboard with our bags. As we stood by the stern we saw the ferry bringing the Thegn of Fife's men to apprehend us, fortunately too late. We saw them wave their fists at the waddling cog on which we stood. Ridley gave a cheeky wave back and then turned to me. "Do you think we shall ever return?"

I looked in the sky as though seeking inspiration. "I do not know old, friend, I truly do not know. We are in the hands of *wyrd* now. Remember Sweyn speaking of the Norns and the webs that they weave?" He nodded. "Well, I feel that even more strongly now. Aethelward told me that we could travel east as did Reuben and the fact that this is the only ship we could board in Leith makes me believe that we have been sent to the east, but for what I know not."

The last time we had been aboard ships was when Harold Godwinson, my father, took us to invade Wales. There we had hugged the coast; now we headed into the stormy, blackened seas and skies of the German Sea. The Captain had told us that the journey could last up to a week if the weather was against us for our destination was Hedeby on the northern coast. Again, our destiny was being shaped for that was where Sweyn held his court. Some mysterious hand was directing my life and I just accepted that.

We fell into a routine aboard the ship; the first day we oiled and stored our mail and weapons for they would not be needed aboard the ship and the salt air would rust them. Then we set to repairing the pieces of equipment and clothes which had been damaged. The ship's sailmaker, a wizened little man helped us, for a few coins, of course, to repair the larger items. We knew not when we would be able to buy new clothes and we had been forced to leave our homeland that we had not had the opportunity to acquire new ones. Both of us had brought coin from home and we had promissory notes for Constantinople. So long as we were careful the money would eke out. The rest of the time we exercised. It amused the captain when we asked if we could aid his crew when they hoisted and lowered the sails. He did not know that it was not us doing him the favour but the other way around. Ridley was still recovering from the wounds he had received when capturing Jorvik from the Normans and I had never truly recovered my strength after the wounds I suffered at Stamford Bridge. We both enjoyed working with the sailors who soon got over their amusement at two Housecarls working as seamen. They were good company and we enjoyed singing their songs with them. We also spent some time with Cnut who was a Dane serving on the ship for he taught us a few words as we toiled across the grey and black sea. He was a good teacher and we quickly learned the words we needed. I knew that we would have a long journey down to Constantinople.

One night, after a supper of dried meat and week-old bread, washed down with the weakest beer I have ever drunk we asked Cnut about the route to Byzantium. He shook his head, "I have only ever done that once masters and I swore never to do it again. You sail through the land of the Rus across lakes and rivers. The people who live there are savages and the boats have to sail in numbers for protection. Then there are the portages."

"Portages? Is that a Danish word?"

He laughed, "I know not where the word comes from but it is a cursed word in any case. It means you empty the boat and carry it and your belongings overland until you find the next piece of water. The savages and barbarians who live in the land know that the merchants have to do this and they attack each time you do that."

Ridley could not comprehend such a journey. "Why do the ships do that then? Why not sail around the coast?"

"A much longer journey and there are many pirates and storms. No, the merchants take the risk because the prizes are so rich. Byzantium pays much for the wood and furs from Rus and the merchants can buy spices quite cheaply to sell at home. Oft times the ships sail in little groups for protection." He looked shrewdly at the two of us. "If I were you two I would hire myself out as guards to a merchant and you will be paid to travel on the ships."

"Thank you, Cnut, that makes sense for we would have the same hardship whether we were paid or we were passengers."

"Are the ships like this one?"

I knew what Ridley was thinking; these ships were so big that it was inconceivable that they could be carried. Cnut laughed. "No, they are like the dragon boats; you mainly row them unless you are lucky enough to catch the wind. They are quite light and they are low to the water for there are no high waves on the rivers and the lakes."

We were five days from Leith and, according to our new friend Cnut, about to begin to turn east to our destination, when we saw the pirates. There were three small dragon boats and they were approaching from the northwest. "Look like Orkney Vikings, nasty buggers they are." He looked at us as we hauled on the ropes to get the maximum sail. "They were the ones who you lot beat at Stamford Bridge. That is where they went."

We could see them gaining on us. Ridley shook his head. "These Norns that the Danes have, spinning webs, they are cunning, aren't they?"

"They are that, and if they catch us and find out who we are, then I am afraid we would not have a glorious end." I wondered as we pulled and tugged on the thick rope if the captain might not offer us in exchange for his freedom; our fame had spread before us and we were known, amongst the Danes at least. I glanced up at the captain who seemed oblivious both to the danger and to us. I took heart from the fact that he was not concerned. He kept glancing up at the masthead pennant and nodding. I saw why as the bow turned slightly south and the wind was on our quarter; I had learned such terms from the sailors. We suddenly leapt forwards. Although the wind helped the dragon boats too, they did not have the spread of canvas available to the captain and the merchant ship began to pull inexorably away. The low freeboard of the dragon ship also slowed them for the wind made the waves a little choppier and, as we later found out, the faster you go in rough water, the more you take on board.

He wandered down to us. "I think someone must be watching over you Saxon, for that wind came from nowhere. I had thought that we had lost the cargo and you two until the change in the air." We had come close to capture. I thanked Nanna and Aethelward although there were so many of those close to me who had gone beyond this world that I knew not who to thank.

Hedeby was an old town nestling on the northeastern side of Denmark. My military eye saw that its wooden walls would not stand up to an assault by a modern army but as the only enemies in this part of the world were other Norse warriors then Sweyn would not have a problem. It also showed why he had been so ill-equipped to take Jorvik. Perhaps if I hadn't helped him then the people of the north would not have been slaughtered? The complex threads of my life threatened to strangle me.

We had become quite close to Cnut and we tried to persuade him to accompany us as a translator and guide. He shook his head, "I like you two and I think it will be an adventure but I would not undertake that river voyage again for all the gold in Araby but if you will take my advice then you will hire someone as a servant for you will need one." He looked askance at the bags we had, "and I would make it someone big because they are not small bags are they?"

As we stepped from the gangplank onto the stone jetty, we felt unsteady on our feet, having been on the ship for six days, it felt as though the land was moving, not the ship. However, I felt a lot more comfortable and at home for there was no sign of the Norman influence and it was like Jorvik when I was growing up. We stopped at the edge of the streets, partly to regain our balance and partly to decide where we ought to go. At least we had a smattering of Danish but I knew if the speaker spoke rapidly then I would understand nothing.

"Well Aelfraed, what are we waiting for? We know where we have to go; the court of King Sweyn."

He was right of course but now that we were here, I wondered about the wisdom of that for we could, just as easily, get a boat and sail off to Constantinople but at the back of my mind was Sweyn's promise to give us aid should we ever need it. Much as I wanted to take his head off with the Dane axe, Death Bringer, I knew that would not happen and yet I wanted him to pay, in some way for the deaths he had caused in my homeland. "You are right. Let us beard the bear in his den!"

We could see the huge hall whose roof dominated the town and we headed up that way. Death Bringer was slung across the back of my shield and I saw many interested looks as we made our way through the crowded streets. King Sweyn had told me that it belonged to a famous Viking and it obviously intrigued many Danes. There were two guards at the door and they recognised us at once. One held up his hand to halt us while the other went inside. I wondered what sort of reception we would receive. There was no reason to think that Sweyn would not make us welcome but I suspected that he knew of both my animosity and my words. The meeting, if it happened, would be an interesting one. The guard came back and beckoned us in. We dropped our gear and weapons at the door. There was little point appearing to be tooled up for war when we only intended to speak and it would make him think we feared him, which we did not. The dimly lit hall reminded me of the warrior hall at Winchester but this was had a higher roof. There was a raised dais at one end, just beyond the blazing fire. Sweyn was sat on a huge chair. I noticed that he had put on weight and he looked a little greyer but he still had his distinctive plaited beard with just the one strand unlike his famous ancestor Sweyn Forkbeard. There were five men who stood near him. I recognised one as his son Harald but the rest I did not. Sweyn was famous for his large number of illegitimate sons. I should feel in good company then for I was one of Harold Godwinson's bastards.

As we neared the dais he stood and came down, grinning like a drunken bear. "Aelfraed! I wondered how long it would take for you to come. Have you come to kill me then boy?"

Those around him stiffened and their hands went to their daggers. Sweyn just held up his hand. "I suppose I should but if I had wanted you dead then I would not have left Death Bringer at the door."

He suddenly laughed and then wrapped his arms around me. "By the Gods but it is good to have a man here again." He turned to the others. "Do you see my sons this is a warrior? He fears neither me nor death. You would do well to be like him." He pointed at them. "Harald you know, the surly one with the sneer is Canute named for his grandfather. The fat bear is Ole and the weedy pale one is Eric." He leaned in to speak into my ear, "We gave him a warrior name but he is more of a poet and singer than a warrior. And where is the archer, Branton, the king killer? Do not tell me the Bastard managed to kill him too?"

I too laughed, "No he still lives although he has found out that crossbow bolts hurt as much as arrows. He stayed in England with his brother to annoy the Normans."

"Good. Your men were good. And the others?"

"All dead! We are the last of the Hooded Men."

"Come sit and drink." We sat at the huge table and were served drinking horns with foamy ale. "Here's a toast to the band of men who made William's life so hard." He looked at his sons. "If you want to make money quickly then take these two back to England for William will pay a Prince's ransom."

I did not know if he was joking or if he meant it. You never knew with Sweyn. I just laughed it off. "I am not sure the tight bastard would have paid." I looked Sweyn in the eyes, "It seems to me he paid quite a lot to get rid of you, your majesty."

There was a sudden silence and I could see the anger on the faces of Canute and Harold, the one called Eric just smiled. "Aye well, I did charge him a mighty price to be rid of me." He suddenly looked serious, "Now, enough of these barbed blades Aelfraed or I shall become angry. Tell me why you came here, apart from the fact that England is too hot for you at the moment."

All the while we had been talking Ridley had kept his hand on his dagger. I leaned over to pat his hand and he relaxed. "We wish to go to Constantinople, the place you call Miklagård, and I remembered you said once that you were in our debt, for Jorvik. I come to claim that debt."

I think I saw him relax a little. He must have thought that our price would be higher. "It is a long and dangerous road to Byzantium but I am a man of my word and I will do all I can to aid you. Tomorrow I will get my people to make the arrangements but tonight we feast. "

The feast passed in a blur of too much food and too much beer. The other warriors were keen to hear my stories of my combats with the Normans and the Welsh. Many had heard of Ridley's heroics at Jorvik and he was forced to show his scars off. None could believe that he had survived such wounds. Eric, sat closely listening to the stories. He had a quick mind for he composed a song about Ridley at the battle of Jorvik which moved Ridley to tears. That was the last conscious thing I heard for I passed out soon after. When I awoke it was with a mouth which felt as though I had been chewing sawdust. I staggered to my feet in the huge hall filled with sweating foetid bodies and made my way to the doors. It was daylight and the shock of the cold and the sun soon sobered me up. I went to the water butt and poured a bucket of it over my head. The town was busily going about its business and I stood for a while watching something I had not seen in England for years, peace, with ordinary people able to go about their business freely. Would England ever enjoy such peace again?

It was mid-morning before the hall was totally awake and I felt better for having eaten something. Sweyn was as good as his word and, by the time Ridley had once more joined the land of the living he had managed to make arrangements for us. "There is a ship leaving for Uppsala at the end of the week. You will then take a ship from there. There is a merchant, Bjorn of Gotland with whom I have had dealings. For a small fee, he will take you to Miklagård."

He smiled as though he had done us the biggest favour in the world when, in reality, he had just given us one short voyage on a ship and provided an introduction to a merchant. "Thank you, King Sweyn, for your help. I wonder however if I could press you to find us a servant who can speak languages for we will be travelling through strange lands."

He frowned, "Men with languages do not come cheap my English friend but I shall look for one. Hopefully, I can find one before you sail."

Suddenly a Danish voice piped up. "I will go with them, father."

The waiflike Eric stepped forwards. He was hardly the sort of servant I had expected. He was the son of a king and looked to have no strength. How could he possibly help us? I looked at Ridley and saw that he shared my views. The King, however, looked delighted, as though the solution had been sent by Thor himself. "Excellent suggestion, my son. Does he meet with your approval Lord Aelfraed?"

The sardonic smile playing on his lips told me that this was deliberate; he had put me between a rock and hard place. If I said no then I would be insulting the royal family. "Of course, it does your majesty but it would then require me to ask if you had a servant we could employ for we have much gear and I do not think that the son of a king should have to carry our bags." I gave Sweyn back the smile he had given me and the slight nod of his head showed me that he understood my ploy.

"Of course, we have many such men and he could act as bodyguard for my son." He waved over his steward and said something. "And now I will leave you two to become acquainted with Eric while we conduct the business of the court."

With that, we were dismissed. Ridley looked as disenchanted as I did; I knew I was prejudging the boy but I could not see how he would be of use to us. Had we been staying in Danish waters then his royal connection might have been of some use but we were going much further east. I put on my 'new man' smile as Osbert used to call it. "Well, Eric. Are you sure you want to do this? I suspect the road will be hard."

He had an eager, keen face and was always an open boy. His smile lit up his face, "Oh yes Lord Aelfraed. I have always wanted to travel and…" he glanced nervously over to his father.

I saw the look. "Come, let us take the air for it is stuffy in here and I would walk."

It was a relief and something else I saw on the boy's face. Ridley grumbled. "I'll bet it is cold out there."

"Tell me, Eric, what you know of the lands to the east and the peoples there."

He became animated, "I have never been there but I have heard many stories. The first peoples are like us but are Rus. Later we pass through the Khazar Khanate where the Mongols live."

Ridley looked interested, "The Mongols?"

"They are a group of fierce tribes who ride fast ponies and use bows which can shoot great distances. They have no king, as we do but they fight under chiefs and great warriors. And then we reach Byzantium."

"How old are you Eric?"

"I have seen sixteen summers, my lord."

"I think that we can dispense with the '*my lord*', as I have lost my land and I am an outlaw. Besides aren't you a Prince?"

He shook his head happily, "No, I am a bastard."

He said it so cheerfully that I laughed aloud. "Well, you are in good company then for so am I. Tell me, Eric, why is your father so keen to send you off with us." I held my hand up. "What you should know about me is that I prefer plain words and the truth. We will survive this journey a little happier if you remember that. I saw something in your father's eyes which told me that he wanted you away from the court."

"That is true. He wants me away for I embarrass him. I am not a warrior. I never have been. I do not like the fighting and the violence."

I shook my head, "So you would travel with two strangers through, by your own admission, extremely hostile lands to serve two warriors who will fight for an Eastern Emperor. How does that sound to you, Ridley?"

"It does not sound right Aelfraed. Perhaps he is a spy?"

Eric's face filled with colour and he shook his head violently. I could see his eyes were filled with terror; was it the terror of being left behind?

"You are right and there will be danger but I have heard that Byzantium is a magical place with many books and many other cultures. True I serve two warriors but when we reach our journey's end I will be safe within Byzantium's walls and, when you are away fighting then I will order your house and be able to study. The journey is the risky part but I am willing to endure that to escape my prison and reach heaven."

He sounded honest but I knew that there was something else he was not telling me. However, he was being as open as he could be bearing in mind he had just met us. I suspected this was *wyrd* again. We had needed a translator, Cnut had told us that. The fact that he did not fit the picture we had of him was our fault, not his. "Well, Eric son of Sweyn, welcome to our little group. I just hope that your father picks us a strong servant for our bags are heavy and, from what we have heard, we need to carry our boats across parts of the journey."

He eagerly nodded, "Aye my lord, the portages."

"I would ask your father but can you tell us what we would need for the journey?"

He shook his head, "I do not yet know. But I will find out for you."

"Good. Had you lied to me and pretended that you knew I should have been unhappy. Always speak the truth and be honest and we will get on."

We wandered around the town with Eric chattering away and telling us many stories about the people and the buildings. We discovered that his mother had been a slave from the far south which explained his slight frame and his slightly darker appearance. He was the only of Eric's sons who had black hair and that, it emerged, had caused him to be beaten and bullied by his siblings. When he told us that Ridley and I exchanged a glance for we both knew that was my story. The boy was very gentle. His voice was soft and it did not seem to suit the harsh words of the Danish language. He told us that he had escaped the warrior training by hiding in the local church where the priest, who had been a Saxon captured by the Danes, there taught him to read and to speak other languages. The more he spoke the more we understood why Sweyn had taken the chance to be rid of this illegitimate child who would never stand in a shield wall and would never fight for his inheritance. I did not think this to be a bad act from Sweyn rather the opposite, for he was doing the best he could for his son, as I had when I had left my son with the Earl of Fife.

By the time we returned to the warrior hall, it was late afternoon and the King's business had been settled. His steward, Bjorn, greeted us at the door. "His Majesty has found a servant for you. Come with me."

He led us to the thrall quarters. Outside the wooden hall were some warriors who were lounging and throwing knives into the empty wooden water butt. To one side sat a huge man. His broad back was to us but I could see that he was powerful. Bjorn was heading towards him and I began to assess this servant the king had provided. It seemed in direct contrast to Eric who seemed more like an aelfe than a man.

Bjorn shouted over, "Ragnar!"

When he turned around I saw that he had suffered in some battle or other. His scarred face looked as though someone had tried to hack it from his body. Where his right eye should have been was a patch but the deep gouge above and below showed where the blow had been struck. There was a piece of his nose missing and a savage looking scar running across his throat. He favoured his right leg slightly and I saw that he had two fingers missing from his left hand.

Eric translated Bjorn's words as he spoke. "Ragnar, the king has ordered you to serve his son and these Saxons as their servant. Is that good?"

Ragnarlooked suspiciously at the three of us and then wandered closely. He stared at me and then his face lit into a grin which showed black holes where many of his teeth should have been. He nodded vigorously.

"Get your gear from the thrall hall and return here." Bjorn turned to us. "Ragnar was a great warrior and served the King's son in law Gottschalk. He received these wounds over ten years ago defending the banner." He looked sad. "He was left here when the Prince returned to his homeland and Ragnar has lived here in the hall of the thralls with nought to do. He lost the ability to speak and his world is now a silent one." His eyes pleaded with me as he spoke. "Lord Aelfraed, you are a warrior and the king believes that Ragnar can still have honour in his life. He cannot stand in a shield wall but what else is there for a warrior?"

I glanced at Ridley for confirmation of the decision I had already made. Ridley nodded. This was *wyrd* again. This was a reminder of all the men who had died for me. I would take Ragnar with me if only to haunt me with the face of those who had fallen for me, Tadgh, Aedgart, Edward and hundreds of others. He was the opportunity to thank those who had sacrificed themselves for me. "Aye, he will do. He makes the last of our company."

I stood looking at the three expectant faces. Ragnar, who towered over both Ridley and me, little Eric who looked as though Ragnar could hide him under his arms and Ridley, open honest Ridley, who would follow me to the ends of the earth and beyond. I realised that I did not want us to have to spend a night in the warrior hall again for I needed to get to know my two new companions. Our journey would be long and if there was one thing I had learned about leadership it was to get to know the men on whom you depend. "Eric, we will find a tavern and stay there. Do you know of any that would suit?"

"It will not be cheap my lord."

I ignored his deference. "Do not worry about money."

"But you will need money to buy passage."

"I said do not worry, Ridley and I have coin but we will not be paying money for our passage believe me. Now a tavern?"

He shrugged. "There is the Hawk. It is the best tavern in Hedeby and has many rooms."

"We only need one."

Eric looked shocked while Ragnar just smiled, and I wondered if was simple as well as wounded. "In one room! But you are a lord!"

"And you are a prince and Ragnar is a warrior. Why waste time giving us our titles? We know who we are."

Ridley grinned for he knew me well. "Aye Eric we are the company of the red horse."

Eric looked puzzled. "Fetch our gear from the hall and it will become clear. Tell your father that we need to be together to plan our voyage and I mean no disrespect to him." Eric nodded and Ragnar started to run after him, "Eric tell Ragnar to leave his gear here. We will watch it for him." The grinning giant dropped his bag and loped off after the speedy Eric.

"Well, old friend they are not the men I thought we would take with us. They are not Branton and Osbert."

"I know but it is something to do with you Aelfraed. I was lonely until you befriended me. Remember Wolf? And Branton and Osbert were seeking a leader when we found them. No, this is *wyrd*. We were meant to take these with us and, who knows, they may have qualities which we need on this long voyage into the unknown."

Ridley rarely made long speeches and this was one of his longest. "You are right and there is something in both of them which spoke to me. When I met Ragnar, I was reminded of all the men of war who do not die but have to eke out a living amongst the whole. Aethelward was lucky for he was a lord and rich but those who fought with us like Aedgart and Osbert. Had they been too wounded to fight what then?"

He shook his head. "You have a short memory Aelfraed. You looked after those too. Remember the men who guarded and looked after our camps?"

I nodded. I had forgotten the six men who had been too wounded to fight in the shield wall but had still served me, bravely, until they were killed in the last assault by the Normans. "You are right but Ragnar is a walking reminder of the debt we owe our comrades."

When they returned Ragnar had managed to carry all of our equipment. I took from him my shield. "Do you see Eric? The Company of the Red Horse." Now lead on." I started to take my axe and shield from Ragnar but he gripped it and shook his head. I turned to Eric. "Tell him that there is too much for him to carry and that Ridley and I are warriors. We carry our own weapons." Eric translated and understanding lit up Ragnar's face. He grinned and allowed us to take our weapons and picked his own bag up.

The tavern was comfortable and, after paying high prices in Jorvik, seemed more than reasonable. The four of us ate in the main room and I could see that Ragnar had not had the company of others for some time. It was hard having Eric translate all of our words to him and I wanted to speak with him. I knew he could not speak in reply but he had the most wonderfully animated hands and we found it easy to understand him. "Eric, you must teach us your language."

Eric looked crestfallen. "Why, my lord, would you be rid of me?"

I laughed, "No you foolish young man. I would speak with Ragnar and others in their own language. It is only right. You will be needed do not worry. Ridley and I have learned over the years that your Norns weave fantastic webs and threads. Who knows what skills you have that we know not yet?"

"I am glad that you came to my father's court for there they believe that a man is born with one purpose, normally to fight, and they understand no other."

"Without meaning disrespect to your people Eric, that is wrong. I have seen peaceful men like my old Steward, Thomas, fight as ferociously as a warrior for what they believe and I have seen tough warriors being gentle. We are complex creatures who make their own choices and decisions."

Ragnar made the gesture for Eric to translate his words and when he had finished the giant nodded eagerly to show he agreed and he took my right hand in his, shook it and then kissed it. The gesture should have been embarrassing but it was not and I nodded, "Thank you, Ragnar."

That night the Company of the Red Horse was forged and its links were stronger than steel.

Chapter 2

When we sailed from Hedeby it felt exciting. I was now further east than I had ever been and soon I would be in unimagined lands. We had spent the last few days before embarkation buying the equipment, we thought we might need; furs, knives and short swords for Eric and Ragnar; a couple of bows, flints, water skins, the list was endless for we knew not what we might encounter. We found a Jew in the back streets of Hedeby who knew Reuben and had heard of us. We sought his advice about the journey for he was a merchant and understood such things.

"You will need trade goods my lord, not large things but small precious things which might be used to barter rather than fight."

"But if they are precious how could we afford them?"

The wise old Jew shook his head. "No, my lord, you mistake my words. I meant precious to them, not to you. Well-made daggers are much sought after as are pieces of jet."

I mentally cursed myself for back in England there had been many jet mines close to where we lived and I could have brought much of it with us. We thanked the merchant and he directed us to where we could buy such things. Thus equipped, with a new helmet for Ragnar we stood at the quayside. Ragnar was more pleased by the helmet than anything apart from the sword for they marked him once again as a warrior. I noticed him casting envious glances at our shields, replete with the red horse and I knew that he coveted them.

Sweyn had come to the quay to see us off. As we waited while the cargo was offloaded he took me to one side. "Rather than this paying off a debt, I fear it has put me once more in yours for much as my other sons dislike him I have a soft spot for Eric. He is like his mother who was a soft skinned beauty from the east, more used to pleasure than work. It is wyrd that my son should return to the place of his mother's birth. The Norns must love you to spin such a web for your life." He became serious, "Look after Eric, he is not like other men and I have chosen Ragnar to accompany you for he was the finest warrior I ever knew until I met you and Lord Ridley. Should you return I will reward you more than I did this time," He was almost apologetic. Sadly, the old rogue died before he could redeem his pledge but I am glad that we parted on good terms for when I meet him in the afterlife I would have him tell me tales of going a-Viking.

Varangian

The captain was a roguish sea dog who looked so ancient that he could have been sailing with the Romans. His ship was old and decrepit but sailed quite well and was comfortable. He was known as Thor. I never knew his real name but I found out why he was called Thor the first time he struck one of his sailors who had been slow to reef the sail- he did not have hands he had hams! One blow could almost fell a man. He must have owed Sweyn a favour or two for he gladly took the four of us and we found there was an added bonus. After Uppsala, he was sailing to Lake Ladoga and offloading some goods to a riverboat. It gave us two opportunities to find a berth on a boat heading south.

Thor proved to have a mine of information. For some reason he took to Eric; perhaps he thought he was ingratiating himself into Sweyn's favour but I do not think so. It was something else. Whatever the reason, we benefited. He confirmed Cnut's view that we were warriors and merchants would pay us to row the waterways and protect the cargo. The fact that three of the four of us would be able to do so was an advantage.

Eric had looked downcast at that; no man likes to be thought of as cargo, all men want to feel valued. Thor had shaken his head wisely. We had learned enough of the language to be able to pick up most of the words Thor spoke. "Eric you can read and the merchants value that for they need a record of their goods as they travel down the river. Even if you were not with such warriors as these you would travel for nothing."

Thus reassured we spent the next week as we toiled up the Baltic, learning as many words as we could. We discovered that even though the Rus came from a different region many of their words were the same and there appeared to be a common spine of words that could be used. Ragnar enjoyed our stories of the wars once we had mastered the basic vocabulary and, with the song maker helping us we told the tales of the battles in which we had fought. I suspect that when Eric translated some of the words he was not as modest as Ridley and myself who tended to praise others like Harold, Aethelward, Osbert, Aedgart and Branton but they enlivened a few nights of the voyage. Ragnar's eyes lit up when we spoke of the death of Hadrada. Eric explained that Ragnar had been with the fleet which Hadrada had defeated and many of his comrades had drowned. He was pleased to meet the killers of his enemies. The voyage finally sealed us as a tightly knit company. We would still have to learn the important things about each other such as how we all reacted to danger and to hardship but I was confident that we would only see good and we would not be disappointed in each other.

Uppsala was a huge port. It looked to be the hub of the Baltic with many different kinds of ships. As we sailed towards it we were amazed by the sheer number of vessels, it seemed impossible that they did not collide. Thor nudged his ship into a berth that looked too small to fit but he managed it with much creaking and grinding of wood. The four of us went ashore to meet the merchant whose goods were to be taken by Thor. As we walked he tapped his nose and explained, through Eric, about the merchant.

"This may be your opportunity for this merchant, Folke the Fat, does not like to journey down the river. He normally hires warriors to do his bidding. Unless he has already chosen a man we might be able to persuade him to take you all on."

I looked at him suspiciously. "You are being very generous with your information and help. Without meaning disrespect what is it in it for you?"

"I understand your suspicion but I am an old man now and I have been married to the sea. You three seem like brothers and I would like to think that had I sons they would have turned out like you, leaders, warriors," he nodded to Eric, "singers and poets. I have enjoyed your company and I would like to voyage to Ladoga with you."

Satisfied I nodded, "Then thank you, Thor, for your kindness and I apologise for my rudeness."

"No Aelfraed Godwinson, even here in the Baltic we heard of your fight and how you were betrayed by so many. I understand your suspicious nature and it will stand you in good stead for the land of Miklagård is a treacherous place. I will go in first and introduce the idea."

Folke the Fat was well named for he was the fattest man I had ever seen. Unlike other fat men I had seen, however, he was not jolly and appeared to have no sense of humour. However, he had an acute business sense which had made him one of the richest men in Uppsala.

"Thor here tells me you wish to be hired on as guards and bookkeeper for the voyage?"

Eric spoke for us all. He translated what Folke said and then answered for us. That day I was glad that we had agreed to take Eric on for he spoke with confidence which had not been visible in Hereby. "We would; we have three strong men and two acclaimed warriors and I have the ability to read and to write."

"You are the son of Sweyn are you not?"

"One of many, yes."

He looked us all up and down as though appraising us. "I usually use my own men. None of you has the experience of the river, do you?" We

Varangian

all shook our heads. "This makes you not as valuable as others who might wish to serve me."

Something about his words did not ring true. I tried out my few words. "Why not use your own men then?"

Eric and Thor shot me a look that suggested that I had lost my mind. Folke coughed and reddened a little. "Well, the truth of it is the last men I used took my cargo and did not return."

Eric's smile and look told me much about his thoughts. He began to speak, "So you need men you can trust?"

"How do I know you can trust you?"

Eric spread his hands, "I could say that Lord Aelfraed and Lord Ridley have names which tell the world of their honesty and for mine own part I do not believe I have ever been found to be lying."

Folke pointed a finger at Ragnar. "What of the dummy? The one who speaks not?"

At first, I knew not what he had said but when Ragnar reddened and Eric looked shocked so I asked for a translation. When it came I exploded. "Then find your own guards. It seems to me that you have piss poor judgement in men if you decide we are not to be trusted despite our reputations and yet the men you do trust rob you. This man may not be able to speak but he has more honour than you will ever have, Folke the Fathead! Come we will seek another merchant."

Surprisingly for a fat man, Folke jumped to his feet and stopped us from leaving. "Apologies Lord Aelfraed. You are right." He looked at Ragnar. "I am sorry to have offended you."

I suddenly realised that he could speak English. "So we are hired?"

Sitting down he mopped his reddened face with a cloth. "Yes, you are hired."

"And what is the pay to be?"

"My men normally take a piece of the profits, one part in ten."

I nodded, "Clever, it makes them look after your goods. And how do you get the money?"

"There is a Jew in Miklagård who deals with my affairs. Isaac, he is called."

"I have dealt with the Jews myself in Jorvik, Leith and Hedeby. We will do it for one part in ten and Eric here will be the bookkeeper. Agreed?"

"Agreed." Folke seemed relieved.

"And have you hired other guards?"

"No, not yet, my man normally does that."

"Your man who now lives in Miklagård with your money?" He nodded. "And you pay them how?"

"With coin." He threw over a purse.

I turned to Thor. "Captain, would you say we would get better men here or at Ladoga?"

"Ladoga, for they will have experience of the river and the men there will be looking for new berths."

"Then Folke you have your guards." I leaned over. "And when I give you my word that your goods will reach Byzantium or we will die protecting them then you know we speak the truth?" He nodded his face a mixture of relief and fear. I think my outburst had terrified him but when you have faced charging Norman horse then a fat man full of his own self-importance does not worry you.

When we were outside Thor smacked me on the back with one of his hams. "I will use you again my lord. I thought he would throw us out at one point." He pointed down the quayside. "There is a fine tavern there. We will sail on the evening tide when we have loaded our goods."

The ale was good and Ragnar's appreciation of my defence could be clearly seen in his face. I had always hated bullies and that was what Folke was, a fat bully who used his power to get his way. Ridley toasted me, "Here's to Aelfraed and the one thing we can say is that he is not mellowing!"

The cargo was one of rich furs. Thor grinned as we edged away from the quayside with the sun setting to the west. "A bit easier for you to carry than the iron ore we sometimes carry."

"Do you know the captain of the ship we will be using?"

"Probably, there aren't that many and we captains are a close-knit bunch. Why do you ask?"

"I assume that he takes all the decisions about the boat and I am just responsible for protecting the cargo?"

"Aye, that is about it and don't forget you will have to provide food."

"And row?" Thor nodded. "It seems to me that the captains have the best of it."

"Sometimes the guards decide just to run away when there are too many trying to steal the cargo and then, the captain loses, not only his ship and livelihood but his life as well."

The Baltic Sea appeared slightly calmer than the German sea we had crossed to reach Denmark. It was certainly a busier sea. I had worried about pirates, remembering the ones who had pursued us near Leith but Thor assured me that the Baltic was safer. "England is seen as a milk cow and pirates know they can prey on the unwary. Here the kings have fleets of ships and any pirate can expect quick and ruthless justice."

I looked westwards. England had had such a navy until the Confessor, a pious man, had disbanded it along with his elite warriors, the Thingmen. Sometimes peaceful men did things that caused more pain and suffering than war.

As the land approached the Captain shortened sail a little but not as much as I had expected. We seemed to be heading for the land at a brisk pace. He seemed calmness personified and then I saw why; there was a large gap between two headlands where a mighty river flowed out. He was heading for the river which would take us to Lake Ladoga and the next part of our journey. We steered towards the right bank and I saw that the ships coming the other way took the opposite side of the river. There was understanding and compromise amongst these disparate peoples. They had found a way to work together for the good of all.

Thor came over to me. "I will find the ship we are seeking and berth next to it and then it will be up to you and young Eric to give Captain Folke's instructions."

I nodded and went forrard to speak with Eric. "You have made a copy of the merchant's instructions?"

The eager youth showed me the two documents which looked identical. Fortunately, Folke's ring mark was an easy one to copy. My own, which was a rearing horse was a complex one and difficult to fabricate. I had paid much for it and now I saw the benefit. "Good. Give the original to Ridley for safe keeping." Giving something to Ridley was like locking it in a steel box; no one could have it unless Ridley allowed it!

We found a berth between two low riverboats. They were longer than we were and slightly narrower. I would get to know them well soon enough. After we had tied up Thor stepped ashore and Eric and I accompanied him. We left the other two to assemble our gear. The ship he took us to was called The Maiden. I took that to be a good sign for it was *wyrd*; my home at Topcliffe had been Maiden Bower. We stood on the quayside. "Captain! Ho!"

Jarl Gunnersson came to the rail. He was a younger man than I had expected for the other two men were much older. He had the lean look of a warrior and I knew, from his title, that he was like me, a lord. His looked every inch a Viking warrior with the clear blue eyes which bored into you. "Are you Thor, from Folke?"

"I am that."

"Stay there and I will come down to speak with you."

As he began to descend Thor said, quietly to me. "I have heard of this one but I do not know him. It is said he was a warrior who chose the sea; A fearless captain."

"Honest?" He shrugged.

Varangian

He was as tall as me and I watched him appraising me as he stepped down the gangplank. He put his arm out for Thor. "What do you have for me from our fat friend then?"

"Furs, Jarl Gunnersson."

He rubbed his hands, "Good that means a speedy voyage. Do you have the documents from Folke?"

Thor gestured to me and I nodded to Eric who handed over the copy he had made. He glanced at me and then read them. Seemingly satisfied he addressed me. "So you two are the representatives of Folke?"

"We are, I am Aelfraed Godwinson and this is Eric Sweynson."

He gave me a quick look, obviously recognising the name, but said nothing. He reread the papers. "He must trust you, especially after his last man betrayed him."

"Were you the captain of the boat?"

His eyes narrowed and flashed anger for a brief moment. "No, but it was a friend of mine who was the captain and, if I ever catch the whoreson who robbed him, I will cut his black and treacherous heart out." I nodded, understanding the feelings. "How many men do you bring?"

"There are two more."

"How many would you say we needed Jarl Gunnersson for this is my first voyage to Miklagård?"

"I have some rowers, tough men but the Pechengs were a little lively the last time we passed through their lands. Their chief Kurya is seeking to enlarge his wealth at our expense."

Thor looked surprised. "I thought the Pechengs were allies of the Emperor."

"They were until the Emperor and all his guards were slaughtered at Manzikert." My face showed my surprise. "You did not know?" I shook my head. "Emperor Romanos was defeated by the Turk and all of his guards were slaughtered. There is a new Emperor Michael." He gave me a shrewd look. "Do you still wish to travel?"

"As I am going to enlist in the Varangian I would think that I will be even more welcome now that the Emperor has no warriors left."

He smiled for the first time. "A man who is not afraid of the Norns; I like it. To answer your question, if you are as good as your reputation then another six warriors would suffice." He tapped his nose. "And it would save you money eh Saxon?"

I shrugged. "Money is not an issue. Would you come with me to choose the men? You may know them and you will have a better idea of the type of fellow we need."

"Aye." He turned to Thor. "Have your men put the cargo here by the side of the ship and we will load it when I return." He turned to Eric and me. "Come we will peruse the sweepings of Ladoga to find some likely men."

There was a roughly built hut outside which men were lounging. From the steaming cauldrons at the back and the heady smell of barley and hops, I deduced that it was an alehouse. We wandered along the groups of men who were standing there, some were drinking some were asleep and some watched us carefully. Gunnersson drew us to one side. "I know some of these and others I do not. I will point out the ones I believe I can trust but the decision to hire is yours. But I ask you to remember this, Aelfraed Godwinson; the men you choose must be able to fight from a ship or on land and be able to carry large weights. Many warriors deign to do such manual labour." His tone suggested that I might be one.

I laughed, "Do not worry about my men and me; we have toiled long and hard with our hands and we can fight anywhere."

He seemed satisfied, "Good." We wandered back to view the men. None of them had mail; most had leather jerkins and trousers, most had a shield or buckler and all carried an axe or a sword. I suppose it made sense that they would not need a spear and I wondered if I would get to use Boar Splitter again. He looked down the line and he pointed at a huge man who was drinking with a man half his size. "Those two are reliable and old friends. The big one is called Hammer for that is his chosen weapon and the smaller one is Stig. They served a lord who went a-Viking and they were the only two to return. You may like them for they hate the Normans."

I gave a smile, I liked them already. "The smaller one, he can row?"

"He is small but powerfully built. He can row."

"Then let us hire them."

We walked over to them and I nodded to Eric. He was the negotiator. He coughed for he was nervous and shuffled a little. When he spoke, his voice seemed a little reedy and thin. "We are seeking men to guard a cargo and to row down to Miklagård. Are you interested?"

The smaller one, Stig, wiped his mouth. "Pay or a share?"

I spoke, "Which would you prefer Stig?"

"Pay."

I nodded. "I will give you half now and half when we reach Miklagård."

"How much?"

Eric and I had put money in various purses and I took out the second smallest one and threw it to him. "For two." He opened it and, without looking at the Hammer, nodded. So he made all the decisions. "Get your gear on board, it is the Maiden."

They grinned, "Aye we know Captain Gunnersson but we don't know you yet."

"I am Aelfraed Godwinson, from England." The look they exchanged told me they had heard of my name. They hoisted their bags, finished their ale and sauntered down the quayside. The other four all chose a share of the profits but they seemed sound men. There was Ulf who was nothing like my old master in the Housecarls, this one was a surly unpleasant man but the Captain assured me that he was a fierce man in a fight and a hard worker. We were going to work not to party so I took him. Then there was Harald, a young Norwegian who had served Hadrada. I did not know if he had been at Stamford but that was in the past anyway. Olaf was the opposite of Ulf and had a perpetual grin on his face. He too was, apparently a good warrior but his background was vague and he told us he had sailed around for some years and finally there was Pig. He had a proper name but we never discovered it for he looked like a pig, even down to the squat nose and he was fat. He did not seem to mind the name but he did like his food. His other skill, which emerged later, was that he was a good cook.

By the time we had returned to the Maiden the cargo was ready for loading. Jarl Gunnersson took over. "You men stack your gear over there; we will load that when the cargo is in." He then proceeded to have all the bales of furs placed precisely in the right place. There was a hold beneath the rowing deck into which he had the precious cargo placed. It was hard work and even Eric was used for he was small enough to fit into the tight hold. I would not have liked to endure it for it was dark and felt like a grave to me. Eventually, the Captain was satisfied and I saw that he had left just enough space on the top for our gear. He grinned at me. "When you and your men need your weapons, they will have to be handy. Now get some food for we will be sailing when the tide returns." Although Ladoga was some way inland it still enjoyed the effects of the sea.

The men began to drift back down to the alehouse but I halted them. I spoke and Eric translated. "Before we take food, I would like to let you know with whom you fight and to give you the chance to leave." They all halted and watched me intrigued, my original companions stood behind me and I noticed Jarl Gunnersson taking an interest in the proceedings. "Firstly, I am Aelfraed Godwinson, son of Harold Godwinson, Thegn of Topcliffe and outlaw with a fine price upon my head." They grinned at that and I could see that some of them had understood my English. "You have taken money or promises of money but we are warriors first and I have never fought with men who are not oath bound. If you travel with me you will be oath-bound and be men of the Red Horse." They looked at each other and Gunnersson leaned over the side of the boat with a smile playing along with his lips. "If you do not wish to be oath-bound then I will pay you for your time and seek others." I paused to allow them to make the decision.

Stig stepped forwards, "You being an outlaw and having a price does not worry me for we have a price on ours but why the oath, my lord?"

"Good question Stig. I have fought many times, against the Welsh, the Normans, aye and the Norwegians." I saw the smile appear on Harald's face. In all those battles none of my men ever ran and I lost many good comrades in the shield wall but other lords who had no oathsworn ran as did their men. You need to know that I will not run when the Pecheng attack us and I will be at the fore. All that I need to know is that my oath sworn will be behind me."

There was a silence and then Stig ran his dagger across his palm. "I am oathsworn."

I took out the richly made dagger given to me by Malcolm Canmore, did the same and held my palm against Stig's. He then joined my comrades behind me. Hammer followed suit, as did Ulf, Harald and Olaf. There just remained Pig, who scratched his head. "We still get our share of the profits?"

I smiled and held out my hand, "Aye and plenty of food too."

I pointed at Ridley. "That is Ridley who was a Housecarl with me against the Welsh and the Normans."

Stig grinned, "Not Ridley the mad berserker of Jorvik?" Ridley looked a little shamefaced while Ragnar and Eric looked confused,

"He is that although he has promised me, he will not go berserk again."

"I will enjoy hearing about that battle master Ridley for the Danes were full of the tale."

I gestured to Eric. "This is Eric Sweynson, who will keep a record of our journey and act as translator."

Pig nodded, "I served your father King Sweyn and your brothers." There appeared to be no slight intended and Eric nodded.

"Finally, this is Ragnar who King Sweyn has given to me as a servant. He is a valiant warrior who cannot speak because of the wounds he suffered. That is our company."

There was a slightly embarrassed silence and I nodded to Ridley who said loudly. "And I will buy us all one last ale before we voyage." With a roar, they followed him.

Eric and Ragnar remained with me and Jarl Gunnersson nodded his approval before he went aft. "You did not ask us to be oathsworn Lord Aelfraed."

"No, for you volunteered to come and you are not a warrior. Ragnar is a servant."

"I wish to be oathsworn." He took out his dagger and cut into his palm.

Unlike the others, he winced and I suppressed a smile. "You know what this means Eric?"

He held out his hand, "I do." I clapped his hand to mine.

Ragnar walked forwards and held his own, bleeding palm, out.

"You do not need to do this Ragnar. I know of the sacrifices you have made." He shook his head vehemently and held his hand out. I took it. "Then I am honoured to have you as an oathsworn brother."

Chapter 3

By the time Ridley and the rest of my men had arrived back at the boat, we were ready to sail. They had had a good drink and, although not drunk, they all had the cheery glow of men who are comfortable. Ridley winked at me as they boarded. I had wanted my oldest friend to become a friend of the men we led. The relationship I had had with Osbert and Branton was unique and I could not replicate it with mercenaries but I was pleased with the men who seemed to have a healthy attitude.

The captain summoned me over. "You are fortunate Aelfraed that the wind is with us across the lake. You will not need to row until we meet the Volkhov." I started to move away but he restrained me. "Stay here for I would talk with you. We too should get to know one another before we embark on this long and dangerous voyage."

The crew scurried about the decks hoisting the sail and loosing the ropes which held us to the land. Gunnersson leaned on the tiller and we began to edge inexorably away from the shore. Slowly at first, we headed east and then the wind caught us and we began to move swiftly. Gunnersson seemed happy with the way the ship was handling and he signalled for his first mate to take over. He took me to the side. "That was well done back there but risky. Tell me why you took such a chance?"

"Your friend's crew betrayed him and the merchant. You and I both know that an oath sworn by a warrior is more binding than money."

"You are interesting Aelfraed son of Harold. I had heard of you before I met you for I had friends who served King Sweyn and that is how I know his son. You are said to be fearless and intensely loyal." He gestured with his arm at my handful of men. "It does not seem to have done you any good."

"That depends upon how you measure good. Most of my men fell in battle defending our country against an invader. Surely that is good?"

He laughed, "You are right. I am from Orkney myself and, like you, dispossessed. This time by a Norwegian. One of the ones you defeated at Stamford Bridge. So you see that I owe my present state to you."

"*Wyrd.*"

"You are right, truly *wyrd*. And some of the men you have taken on have connections too, like your Harald who also fought at Stamford." He looked up at the sky. "The gods are watching you."

I shook my head. "There are spirits watching over me but they are the spirits of my ancestors and they care for me."

He nodded and gestured towards Eric who was busily translating for Ridley. "He is interesting. He is what you English call the runt of the litter and he is, well he is different. Did his father force him upon you? Was he glad to be rid of him?"

"No, I was happy to take him. Not every man is chosen to be a warrior and I had the feeling that Eric would make the difference at some time during this voyage but his father was, I believe, a little sad to see him leave."

"He is nothing like his brothers."

I laughed, "No, you are right there, it was as though a bear had sired many young bears and a lamb."

"Aptly put." He became business-like again, "When we begin rowing, I will assign you your positions." I gave him a questioning look. "It is all a matter of balance, having the right weight distributed on each side. Your bookkeeper can row for he is the same size as Stig and they will balance each other."

"He is lighter."

"True but I can move heavier men to counteract that. You have never rowed before so take a word of advice, wrap a cloth around your hands."

I watched the shoreline recede into the distance. "Do you anticipate trouble?"

"Always and yet the last two voyages have been trouble free so who knows. The first part is hard for we travel upstream. After the first portage, we have an easier stretch for them we will be going downstream. When we are going downstream, we do not need to stop at night but your men will have to take turns as guards when we anchor midstream."

I wandered back to my men; I had been given a number of problems to solve and I decided to use Eric's mind to help me. "Come, Eric, let Ridley try out the words he has learned so far."

Ridley shrugged and I was pleased that, Ulf apart, they all appeared to like being with Ridley. That was important. "Now then Eric we have to stand watches and that needs organisation. What do you suggest?"

I already had my ideas for I had stood watches before but I was interested to see if this poet and singer could put his mind to that problem too. "Using all of us?"

"All of us Eric, that means you and me as well."

He suddenly smiled. There are ten of us which means five pairs. Some are obvious like Stig and Hammer, me and Ragnar."

Varangian

I held my hand up. "I like the pairs but not you and Ragnar."

He looked crestfallen. "Am I not to be trusted?"

"The first thing you need to understand Eric is that there is never anything personal in this. We do things because they work. Ridley and I have stood sentry before you and Ragnar have not. You will be with me and Ridley with Ragnar. Now go on."

He grinned with relief. "It seems to me that if we all do the same duty at night that is unfair so we have four watches each night so that one pair gets a night off. Then each watch moves on one."

I nodded. It was well thought out and, more important, fair. "Well done. Divide the men up, put Ulf with Harald, it might lighten him up and then tell the men."

The river we would be travelling down was the Volkhov and fortunately, it was wide for there were boats under sail coming in the opposite direction. We anchored while Jarl Gunnersson fussed amongst us, arranging us. Ridley and I were in the middle, opposite each other with another of the crew next to each of us. Once he was happy, he pulled up the anchor himself. "Up oars!" I could see the wisdom of putting the newer rowers with experienced men. I never knew the name of the man next to me for he spoke neither English nor any of the other words I had learned but, as he kept grinning at me with a furtive grin, I called him Weasel. He soon answered to weasel although I doubt, he knew what it meant. "Stroke!"

Ridley and I just held onto the oar and pulled when Weasel and his companion did so. As soon as the blade struck the water you could feel the resistance and the boat barely seemed to move. "Stroke!"

The next one was just as hard and it was another ten strokes before I could discern any movement. My son Harold would be a warrior before we reached Miklagård at this rate. I pulled hard and Weasel rewarded me with another inane grin and I saw that we had now picked up speed. We soon fell into a happy rhythm but it was a relentless pace. The Jarl soon stopped shouting stroke when we reached the speed he was happy with. I wondered why no one was at the bow watching for danger but the captain seemed happy enough. Soon my arms began to burn with repetition and I risked a glance at Ridley who appeared to be unfazed by the pain. I took comfort in the knowledge that Eric would be struggling more than I. As night began to draw in Jarl Gunnersson perversely upped the rate and we were flying along but I felt certain that I would collapse before he slowed down.

Suddenly he shouted, "Up oars!" As he did so he prepared the anchor; he waited until we were much slower then dropped it over the side and I saw that we were in the middle of the river. I could barely breathe, let alone speak and so I grinned at Weasel and Ridley. The oars were passed in and stored in the middle as a lighted torch was hung from our stern. We had learned that one of the duties of the night watch was to replace the torches so as to avoid a collision with a downstream boat.

I was still lying on the thwarts when Jarl Gunnersson came along. "Well, Housecarl how did you find that?"

"Give me a shield wall any day. That was brutal!"

"When you get to Miklagård seek out the apothecaries for they have oils and potions to ease the pain."

I shook my head, "No Captain, once I leave this boat I will never row again."

I heard a roar of laughter from behind and my Red Horse company, even Ulf were all laughing at me. I looked at Eric. "How did you manage?"

"I might not be a warrior Lord Aelfraed but I learned to row as a child. You will soon get used to it."

I shook my head ruefully, "I doubt it."

I had chosen the middle watch for Eric and me. I regretted it as Stig woke me but I had to take the worst duty for myself. As I rose I felt the stiffness in my limbs. In another few hours, I would be up again and having to row once more. And this was but day one! Eric changed the torch and we sat at the bow watching for any ships coming downstream and any ripples in the water which should not be there.

"Do not look at the light Eric or it will spoil your night vision. Look to the dark."

"Thank you."

There was silence for all the creatures of the night were either far away or too quiet to be heard. "Do you regret coming, Eric?"

"Oh no! It is even better than I thought it would be. And the stories the men tell! They will make wonderful songs."

It had surprised me how well this Prince of the Danes had taken to the life but then I thought back to my childhood at Medelai and the bullying of my brothers. After that anything was preferable so I suppose Eric was just pleased to be away from his prison. I looked at my hands; the cloth had helped a little but it was now in tatters. I resolved to use my gauntlets the next time and hope that the leather protected me more.

By the time we pulled in to the town of Velikiy Novgorod my hands had toughened up and my muscles felt toned. I no longer felt the burn and the Weasel and I grinned and nodded to each other all day. Jarl Gunnersson had confided in me that there were two or three towns at which we could stop on our way south but this was the safest. When I

Varangian

saw it I wondered what the others were like for it looked like nowhere I had ever seen before. The buildings were all made of wood but their design was radically different from those in Denmark and England. They had long sloping roofs and looked, somehow, like small churches. The people too were different. Many of them had a sallow, almost yellow skin and eyes which appeared narrower than ours. Their clothes were mainly furs and those who had footwear had wooden shoes rather than leather ones.

Gunnersson called me over. "I need three of your men to escort me and my men to get some supplies, the rest should stay here on guard. This is the safest town we pass but I still would not trust them an inch."

I wanted to see the town but I needed experience too. "Ridley, keep the rest of the men on board and make sure nothing is stolen and the men don't leave. Stig, Hammer, come with me we are escorting the captain."

Stig and Hammer looked delighted but the others, Ridley included, cast me dark looks. Uncle Aethelward had told me that every decision a leader made would upset someone, even one as trivial as this. I took my sword rather than Death Bringer, it was easier to wield in a confined space and I strapped my shield to my back. There were four men with us and I went next to the Jarl with the other two warriors bringing up the rear. We ploughed our way through the throngs. People soon learned to avoid the mail shirt which was wrapped around my huge frame.

We did not have to travel far for there was a shop which sold the food we would need to eke out our rations to Miklagård. The Captain gave his order. "Leave your men here we will have to get our travel documents."

We left the shabby little shop and entered the half stone half wood building next door. There were four guards but they recognised the Jarl and let him in. Inside there were three small figures who were reading lists. Clerks. I had seen many such in Winchester although there they were priests and holy men. These looked like shifty little thieves. I did not understand a word which was spoken but I did recognise the bribe which the Jarl paid to ensure that we could leave quickly. I waited at the door for the captain to finish and I saw one of the furtive little ferrets go out of the back door. I noticed him because he had a split nose, normally a punishment for some transgression, but it made him look as though he had two noses. I should have ignored it but something about the way he looked at us and then left made me suspicious. All the way back to the boat I kept my eyes peeled for the little man but they were all little men. The Jarl and I stood a head taller than any of them. The goods from the shop next door were still being assembled and I waited in the street with the Jarl.

"That is why we stop at few places. It costs money and all comes from our profits." I knew from Folke and Thor that the captain and the merchant shared the profits once the guards cut had been taken.

"Will we need to stop again?"

"At a town? No. But we will need food. From here on we forage, fish, hunt animals; there should be berries at this time of the year. But I warn you Aelfraed, the hardest is yet to come. We have another lake and then portage. And we must slip through two towns at night to avoid the taxes. Soon you will earn your passage."

It was coming on to dusk when we reached the boat and I could see that something had happened. Ridley looked red and angry while Eric looked worried. Ulf was dabbing at a bleeding nose. Gunnersson glanced at them and then at me. I shrugged. It would have to wait until later. We rowed until dark and anchored in the middle of the river. The men had eaten aboard the ship in the town and I waited for the Weasel and the others to leave before speaking with Ridley.

"Well?"

"Well, what?" He almost pouted and I was tempted to laugh.

"Well, tell me what happened when I was in the town?"

"How do you know something happened?"

"From your face, Eric's face and Ulf's bloody nose."

He sighed. "I was not paying attention; I was talking with Pig and Harald when Eric came to tell me that Ulf was not aboard. The two of us went ashore and found him down a side street. He was talking with someone but I could not see who. Eric asked him who he was talking to and Ulf went for him." He paused. "I hit him first."

I put my hand on his shoulder. "You did right and now we will go and see this Ulf and find out what is amiss."

My men were sat at the stern under a small awning. Ulf was off to one side and the others all looked at him when we approached. I was pleased to see Ragnar and Hammer on either side of Eric protecting him. Ragnar was sending filthy looks towards Ulf.

I had learned enough of the language now to be able to speak without the translation skills of Eric. "Ulf come here."

He slouched over and I noticed that he had his hand on his dagger. Not a good sign. "Why did you leave the ship? You were ordered to guard it." He said nothing but stared malevolently at Ridley. "I asked you a question. Now answer me."

"You did not order me. He did." The finger stabbed out accusingly at Ridley.

"What Thegn Ridley says, I say. You disobeyed me and you tried to hit Eric."

He leered at me. "I could blow him over!"

I walked closer to him. "Ulf you disobeyed me. I cannot have that. Tomorrow I will put you ashore and pay you off. I must have men I can trust."

His hand moved as quickly as a snake striking and he stabbed at me with his dagger. He had forgotten that I wore my mail shirt beneath my tunic and the point merely broke two or three links and cut me slightly. Thwarted he pushed me back with one hand and then leapt overboard into the black waters of the night. Ridley roared out and raced to the stern but he had disappeared. "The rat! I should have really damaged him."

Eric rushed to me. "Are you hurt my lord?"

I shook my head. "I have hurt myself more when I fell over drunk."

The Jarl came to see what had happened and we told him. He turned to Eric. "What did the man look like that Ulf was talking to?"

"One of the locals my lord, a little man with a cut down his nose."

"I saw him in the port office! He left before we did."

The Jarl nodded and looked at the masthead. "Well, I am sorry I recommended him. He was obviously up to no good. Not only does it leave you shorthanded but it also means we are likely to be attacked." He waved over his first mate. "We leave at moon rise. We row through the night and put some distance between us and Ulf's friends."

By the time dawn broke, we were exhausted. We had rearranged the rowers to accommodate the lack of Ulf and it meant that Eric could stand lookout forrard. I looked aft to Jarl Gunnersson but he showed no sign of wishing to stop. It was hard to see how long we could keep going but then, I reminded myself I had found it hard to row for a few hours when we had first started the voyage.

The jarl saw my looks and shouted down, "I am heading for Lake Ilmen. It will be safer there and is not far away."

I nodded, for I needed all my breath for the rowing. I wondered how Ulf had been recruited. Had it been pure luck that I had chosen him and, any boat he served on would have been a target? It was hard to say. I was pleased that the others had not been happy about the traitor and then I thought that was what a traitor would do to allay suspicion. I shook my head to clear it of the confusion. The only ones I could really trust were Ragnar, Eric and, of course, Ridley. It would take combat for me to truly assess the worth of my remaining five warriors; only then would I know the value of their oath.

Varangian

When we finally stopped in the middle of the lake and the Captain dropped the anchor, I almost collapsed with exhaustion. The others just slept at their oars but Jarl Gunnersson beckoned me forward. "I have set Eric to getting some food ready and you and I must stand guard for we are still not safe."

I remembered something Cnut had said as we sailed from Leith. "Perhaps if we wait for other ships travelling the route we might have more safety with the larger numbers."

He shook his head, "That is an excellent plan but the last two ships sailed the day before we left. We were waiting for Thor's ship."

And that was it, the Norns again. The ship had delayed sailing from Hedeby to accommodate me and my party and that had meant we had missed the other ships. We would be safer in their company. I hoped that the Norns planned a grander end for me than being killed by river pirates on the Lovat River which was our next waterway.

It felt like I had been asleep for moments when Ridley woke me but he assured me I had had hours of sleep. Certainly, the sun was lower in the sky. "To oars. We row." The jarl hoisted the sail and caught the little breeze that was available and we found it easier to row, despite our tiredness. There was little current on the lake but, once we struck the Lovat then it would be hard going. The Jarl kept watching the pennant for a change in the wind's direction for if it swung too much we would have to lower the sail and it would be hard work again. While we had been standing watch, the Captain had told me of his plan. "We will sail into the darkness and when we anchor I will not light a torch, we will rely on the eyes of your men."

The resourceful Eric had changed the duties so that one man had a night off watches and we watched with a different partner each night. Now that we had all experienced watches it made sense and it allowed me to get to know the others of my company. So far I had not detected any other with traitorous intent.

I wondered how much further we would sail, as dusk descended when the Jarl suddenly shouted, "Back oars!" We had rarely had to do that manoeuvre; it was used to stop the boat quickly. "Up oars! Saxon get your warriors there are men in the reeds!"

We quickly sprang into action. The hatch was below the Weasel's feet and he jumped away to allow Ridley to open it. I grabbed my shield and sword and strode to the side, knowing the rest would follow when they could. The riverside was covered in thick reeds, the perfect place for the nesting birds who lived there. Suddenly one of them, a heron, fluttered noisily into the sky. It made me jump but, at the same time focused me on the place it had left. I too could see a face. "Ridley, get your bow. There is someone out there."

"Hold fast Aelfraed. Let me give them a chance. Ho! You in the river. Show yourselves or be prepared to die."

By now my men lined the sides and even Eric stood there with his sword and buckler. I had never seen the boy fight but I doubted that he would be much use. Still, it showed that he did not lack courage.

A voice sounded from the reeds. "Is that Jarl Gunnar Gunnersson?"

Warily our captain replied, "Aye it is."

"It is Siggi Rosmusson and what remains of two crews."

The Jarl said quietly to me, "They may be friends but watch them and listen for my command." I nodded to show I had understood. "Come ahead then, we will watch for you."

Slowly eighteen men limped, crawled and staggered from the reeds. I could see that some had been wounded and others carried injuries. When they reached the side, I looked up at Gunnar, who nodded. "Come on lads; let's help the poor buggers aboard."

As they scrambled aboard we began to see to their hurts. Some had broken limbs and others bore sword cuts and arrow wounds. Eric and I took the stoic warrior who had an arrow sticking from his back. Despite that he still clutched his sword and shield; this was a warrior. "Eric, fetch some clean water." Much to the amusement of the crew, I had had Eric boil water when we could and fill water skins with it. The murky brown water of the river did not look healthy and I needed to dress the wound with good water. "I am Thegn Aelfraed and what is your name?"

"Snorri Bjornson. Thank you for stopping." More to keep his mind off what I was doing with my dagger than anything I asked him what had happened. "We stopped for the night. We put out the torches and set the guards."

"Were you the two ships who left the day before we did?"

He shrugged, "We were two ships. They swam to the other ship and slit the throats of the guards. They would have done the same for us but Benni, our leader saw them. He died giving us the warning. There were too many of them and, when we saw the bodies being thrown from the other ship then we knew we were lost. The captain led us into the reeds and they left with the vessels."

"This is the part which will hurt." I gave him his dagger. "Bite on the handle. Eric, hold his arms." I put my knife, which I had heated in the torch, into the wound to loosen the arrow. He barely flinched, even though I knew that it must have been excruciating agony for him. The strength from rowing enabled me to pull the arrow from the wound with a satisfying plop and I was pleased to see that the blood which erupted was healthy. "Eric, hold a cloth to the wound while I heat up the knife." A glance at Eric told me that he was close to breaking, the sight of the blood and the operation had been too much. "Just hang on Eric. Snorri has survived. Just help him."

As I heated the blade, I heard the warrior talking to Eric. "First time you have seen a wound?"

"Yes. How did you stand the pain?"

I heard a deep laugh, "The pain would be there whether I wanted it or not. What good would it have done me to cry out? I knew that it would pass, or I would die."

I returned smiling, Snorri was like every warrior who had stood beside me in the shield wall. "Hold his arms again Eric." The hiss of the blade and the smell of burning hairs and flesh were too much for Eric who passed out at Snorri's feet. In spite of his pain, the gentle Snorri lowered the boy to the ground. "It is his first voyage."

"He did well and he is a kind boy. Did you say that you were Aelfraed the Saxon." I nodded as I bandaged his shoulder. "Harald Godwinson's bastard?"

"Aye for my sins."

"I have heard of you. They say you defeated a Welsh champion, a Scots' champion and killed Hadrada."

"My men killed Hadrada and the rest is true."

"If you would have me, my lord, I would serve you for I believe the Norns intended me to be here."

"How so?"

"When they were hiring, I had a bad feeling about the ships and a voice in my head told me to wait but I ignored it."

"How does that relate to me?"

"Benni told how he fought at Jorvik for King Sweyn and there were two mighty warriors who saved many Danish lives, Benni was one, and how he wished to go to England one day and serve you."

"Aah, well the other warrior, the berserker? Is over there, Thegn Ridley. I will gladly have you in my company for it is wyrd. One of my men deserted, he was a traitor."

"Thank you, lord." He clasped my arm.

"There is one thing; my men swear a blood oath."

He grinned, "Then it is *wyrd*; for that is my wish also."

While a recovered Eric and the rest of the crew found clothes for the wet men I joined the two captains at the bow. "Siggi this is Thegn Aelfraed, the captain of the guards."

"I am pleased that you have warriors, Gunnar. Only one of mine survived, Snorri."

"And he has asked to join my company. Is that a problem?"

Siggi smiled, "No for I would not have been able to pay him anyway." He looked serious. "There were many of them Gunnar and I fear that they will attack at the portage."

"Will you be staying aboard captain?"

I asked the question because I liked the idea of extra men. "We will have to, with Gunnar's permission of course. Once at Miklagård then I can get the funds to get another ship."

"You are welcome Siggi for I could not leave fellow sailors here but we can only feed you."

He shrugged, "As the alternative is death, that seems a good bargain."

"Gunnar, if we had more weapons then we could defend ourselves a little better."

"Once past the portage then we pass a settlement on the Toropa river where we could buy them. But the money?"

"I will buy them and try to sell them in Miklagård."

"You will not get as much."

I laughed, "Aye but if that means we actually get to Miklagård then it is money well spent is it not. And Captain, it will not come out of your share."

The jarl gave me a shrewd look. "You are a strange one Englishmen. Are all Englishmen like you?"

"The ones who did not die at Senlac and Stamford are."

I left him with that enigmatic thought and went back to my men. We were now ten again and I liked the roundness of the number. The Norns were weaving again and the traitor had been replaced by a hero, it seemed a good bargain to me.

Chapter 4

The next few days were tense as we had a very crowded boat, half of whom were nervous about the prospect of being attacked again. We did have a full complement of warriors to watch again and, with two captains, the navigation proved easier. When we reached the portage, I was intrigued for the Weasel and the other rowers had told me what it entailed and I thought that they were joking for they said that you had to pull the boat up the side of a hill and down the other. Once we were at the portage, I saw that they were speaking true. At the side of the river, we could see many logs, some of them showing the signs of damage. As soon as we landed Gunnar sent me and my warriors, with our axes to cut down another ten straight logs whilst he and the others began to offload the cargo.

I had never chopped down trees with Death Bringer and I was loath to do so. Harald laughed and offered us his. "I care not what my blade cleaves so long as I am paid."

After a few hours' work we had the ten logs trimmed and cut and we trudged back with them. By the time we had returned the cargo was offloaded and the bow of the ship was lying on six logs. The others were spread before them. Gunnar placed our new logs in the right place and we hauled the ship out of the water and onto the logs.

"I will stay here with most of my crew and we will repair the hull while it is out of the water. Siggi will take his men and lead you over the hill to the other side of the portage."

As the men picked up the cargo Gunnar gestured for me to join him. "Leave Eric, Stig and the wounded warrior to guard the cargo and then you and the rest can return here to help pull this beast over the hill."

Carrying the bales of furs was not hard but they were awkward to grip and after a good three hours' climb and descent, we reached the river. Siggi was all for just dropping the bales. "No captain. I want the bales made into walls and then Stig, Eric and Snorri will have some defence should they be attacked."

Siggi and the rest of his men were incredulous. "But that will take time!"

"I don't care. These men may be here all night and the bales will provide shelter and protection. Don't argue, do it!"

The Hammer and my men grinned at the interchange but eventually, the bales were stacked as I wanted them. We left an entrance so that they could get in and out. "Stig you are in charge. If anyone should try to take the bales then we have made it difficult."

Stig laughed, "And bloody cosy, my lord!"

I was just leaving when the first arrow flew to embed itself in the back of one of Siggi's men. Rivers were new to me but I knew ambushes. "Shields! Get inside the bales!"

My men swiftly picked up their shields, as I did and we heard the pock, pock as they were peppered with missiles. Once everyone was inside, I joined them. "Hold your shields up to make a roof. They will soon realise that the bales can absorb the damage."

Sure enough, the barbarians began to fire up in the air but the small space of the interior of my improvised fort was easily protected by our eight shields. Siggi looked worried. "The fort is a good idea my lord but when it becomes dark, they can close with us and slaughter us."

I looked at Ridley and grinned, he nodded. "If we are here at night time. Stig, you take charge. Ridley and I will deal with these."

Even Stig looked amazed. "But you have no idea how many men are out there!"

"True but tell me this; are they armoured?" Siggi shook his head. "Do they have arrows which can pierce mail?"

"No, no one does."

Ridley grinned, "Not quite true but it matters not. Ready?"

"Aye but follow me this time!"

I burst out of the door with my sword held before me and my body protected by my shield. I knew that Ridley was to my left and would follow me wherever I went. I saw the barbarians who were pulling back on their bows having left the safety of the forest. We took them by surprise and they watched in horror as these two giants leapt, roaring at them. I killed two before they had time to run and then they shot their arrows at us. The shields took most of the damage but I heard them ping off my helmet and felt them tug at my tunic as they became embedded in the mail. They had thought to kill us quickly but we reached them unharmed and then it was a slaughter for they had no protection against the sharpened blades of two Housecarls. The survivors ran. Ridley and I pursued them for a good eight hundred paces and even caught a couple whom we despatched. Exhausted we halted to catch our breath.

"If all the barbarians at Miklagård are like that we will have an easy posting."

"I somehow doubt it. Pick up the quivers and break the bows as we return." By the time we reached the bales, we had ten quivers and two bows. The rest had been destroyed. "Stig you can come out now. It is safe."

The incredulous survivors came out and inspected us. Siggi shook his head. "But you are not dead."

"I should think not. They were only armed with bows and we wore mail."

Harald laughed, "Now I understand the story of Ridley the Berserker. All Englishman must be mad!"

"No, but we have a short temper. Harald, you had better stay here, they may be back and here are two bows. I hope you can use them."

Jarl Gunnersson was worried at our late return but when Siggi told him of our exploits he smiled. "The Norns, Thegn Aethelward, they like you."

The boat was now on a line of logs with long ropes attached. We were split into four groups and given a rope. Four men were left to move the logs. They had the hardest task. We began to pull. The ground was flat and we moved quite quickly at first. The four men raced from the stern to bring the logs we had rolled over and put them at the front. Then, as we went up the incline it became harder and only two men ran with the spare log, the others jammed a log to prevent the boat from slipping back down the hill. There was a technique to it which we quickly mastered and we found the going much easier. Once we reached the top we halted to catch our breath and to move more logs in front of the ship.

Gunnar was pleased, "Now we stop pulling and we stop the ship from travelling too quickly." The boat was balanced at the top of the hill. Gunnar, Siggi and the First Mate went to the stern and tipped it up. The momentum moved the bow forwards and the ship started to slip down the slope. It was hard to stop it crashing through the trees and being destroyed; we had to dig our heels in to make it move at a reasonable speed. The log men were soaked with sweat as they raced around us to replace the log rollers. By the time the sun was setting we could see the river and, soon, the boat was once again, in its natural home, the water.

Stig and the others had had no further problems and, as the furs and cargo were packed again the talk was of the two mad Englishmen and their charge. "Why are you not dead my lord?"

"Simple Olaf. There is only one kind of arrow that can pierce this mail and my old friend Branton is the only archer to use them. Unless you are unlucky and an arrow strikes bare flesh you should be safe and, besides, it is hard to concentrate when two giants such as we charge you screaming and waving our swords. We learned that at Stamford Bridge when the three naked berserkers held off a whole army. Most men, even soldiers, fear death and some who seem reckless make them think twice."

They all examined the armour for signs of damage but what we did gain from that wild charge was the respect of our men who had seen us put ourselves in harm's way to protect them. They knew that we would never back down from a fight and, in the next few weeks, that was the difference between survival and death.

Partly because we now had more men and partly because Jarl Gunnersson was worried about another attack we were excused rowing duties. "You are the warriors. The men we rescued are sailors and rowers. No offence Aelfraed but each man to his own skill."

I was not offended and I took the opportunity of finding out how good my men were as archers. As well as the two bows we had collected in the woods we had found four others including a strange looking bow that had horn and wood combined. Stig held it to show us. "Now had this archer fired at you then you would have been dead for this is the bow of the men of the steppes and it is a fearsome weapon."

When Ridley tried it out he found out that, despite its relatively small size, it could hurl an arrow to embed itself into a mighty tree. Someone had been watching over us. "So the Pechengs will have bows like this?"

"Aye my lord."

"Then we need to improve the shields we use." Ridley and I were the only ones with the large round shields studded with iron plates and we set about manufacturing shields for all of our men. The wood was plentiful along the river and we cut down a couple of trees and began to make them. Each day without an attack became a bonus. Although the wood was not seasoned it would afford some protection. The problem was finding the metal and we scoured the ship for mails and small pieces of discarded metal. We did not find many but each shield had some and it was better than nothing. The archery of the men was adequate and a bonus was that it was a skill which Eric had. He might not be able to stand and fight with a sword but, if we came to grips with barbarians, he could annoy them with a bow. Snorri had taken to the boy for Eric had tended the wounded warrior's wounds and they soon became inseparable. Snorri was a sound warrior who was very quiet but, when we had a practice with our swords, I saw that he was more than competent and increasingly reminded me of Osbert.

I was still worried about Ulf. I hoped that he had drowned but I suspected that he had survived; he had had that sort of look about him. The attack on the other boats had happened too soon for him to be involved which meant he was still out there with the confederates from Velikiy. As we were not rowing the night duties were not as tiring which was fortunate for two days after the portage, when we were anchored on the Dvina River the attack came. Olaf was one of the sentries and he came to shake me. "My lord, I have heard noises by the river."

I had drilled into them that they should wake me for anything which seemed strange. I would rather lose a night's sleep than men's lives. "Wake Ridley and the others."

"It may be nothing."

I smiled in the dark. "True Olaf, in which case, I will apologise for the loss of sleep."

I went to Pig, who was the other sentry. Silently he pointed to the low trees which overhung the river. I could see nothing clearly but the shape of the trees seemed wrong and there was total silence along the river bank. That in itself was unusual for there were many animals that lived along the river and you would normally hear a duck or a waterfowl at night. It all pointed to men being on the bank. When Ridley arrived with the other men, all armed, I left them to wake the captain.

He had the nearest thing we had to a cabin; chests surrounded a sleeping matt and an awning gave him protection. As soon as I touched him, he awoke. "It may be nothing but we think there are men on the bank. My warriors are ready." He nodded and I returned to my men. We were downstream and it would be simple enough to raise the anchor and float down the river but travel at night was dangerous. My men had told me of the rapids we would have to navigate and we did not want to try those at night time. When I returned to the side of the ship, I could see that there were men at the riverside and they were slipping into the water. A horrible thought entered my mind. What about the other side? "Ridley, stay here, Snorri, Hammer, Stig. Come with me."

I took them to the other side and sure enough, I could see the slick bodies of the barbarians pushing reed mats through the water. There was nothing to be gained now from silence and I roared. "To arms! To arms!" The crew were instantly awake for the attack on the other boats had served as a warning. Each man grabbed whatever weapons he could and they ran to the two sides. I slung the bow I had with me as did Eric and we began to fire at the bodies coming towards us. From the screams and shouts on the other side, I knew that Ridley was doing the same. The night was dark and it was hard to aim accurately but I am sure that we struck four or five before they reached the side and began to clamber up. They were wiry half-naked men, each one with a topknot and ponytail. They carried wicked sharp curved blades and they were numerous. I dropped the bow and took up Death Bringer. We were spread out along the length of the boat so that there were warriors and crew intermingled.

"Watch my blade!" The crew had seen me practise and they gave me room. The singing blade soon began to strike every warrior who dared to board within eight paces of me. My long arms and the long handle meant that I could swing with impunity. Stig and Snorri also had axes whilst the Hammer was also causing casualties. Eric had retreated to the stern and was firing at any we missed. Soon there was no one left to attack but the deck had eight bodies littered along its length. The first rays of the red sun peeped from our left and I saw the horde retreating. Had Olaf not woken me we would have all perished for they were numerous. It was then that I saw Ulf on the river bank sitting astride a pony with, what looked like a couple of chiefs. He had survived! He still had his scowl; Eric chanced an arrow which plunged just before him and the party retreated. We had halted them, but they would be back.

As the anchor was raised and the rowers began to take us south I checked our casualties. My warriors had emerged unscathed but some of the crew had suffered wounds. At least we now had some extra weapons from the bodies left littering the deck. We also took the metal bracelets and torcs. They would all make useful additions to the protection for the men's shields.

The warband followed us down the river. They had ponies and, whilst we moved swiftly with the current, they could cut out the loops in the river and get ahead of us. It was a warning that we could not be distracted for an instant and, when we reached the next portage, we would have a battle on our hands. As we chewed on our breakfast of dried meat Snorri came to look at my axe. The others had all the opportunity of examining the blade but Snorri was new. "It is a fine Danish blade, my lord. May I hold it?"

"Of course."

He swung it easily. "It has a fine balance and feels like a smaller axe. It is a good weapon. How did you get such a weapon?" I told him the story of my first battle in the woods of Mara and he nodded, "*Wyrd*. I can see that I was meant to serve with you, my lord."

"Why is that Snorri?"

"The other warriors I fought with were mercenaries. They fought for the coin."

"I am now a mercenary. I now fight for coin."

He shook his head, "No my lord, Eric has told me that you seek to fight with the Varangians and I know why."

Varangian

No one, not even Ridley knew the real reason I had headed south to Byzantium. How had this man who barely knew me divined the reason? "And why is that? Do you not see me as a sword for hire?"

He laughed, "No my lord for Eric has also told me that you have coin, no, the real reason is that the Byzantines are the only ones who can defeat the Normans. You hope to go to Italy and fight them there."

"As the Emperor is now a prisoner of the Turks and the Varangians lie with bleached bones it does not seem to matter."

"There will be a new Emperor and there will be more Varangians but you, my lord, you are a strategos."

I was going to ask how he knew that but I worked it out myself, "Eric again?"

He smiled, "Yes my lord. The boy sees you as some sort of hero who has taken him away from the hell that was his home. He told me that he has never been happier than on this voyage."

"He is a fine boy; he did not deserve to suffer in Hedeby."

"No my lord, but a mercenary would have demanded money to take the boy and then been rid of him as quickly as possible." He was right but it unnerved me that he had seen all of this through his words with Eric.

"I hope that he will find all he seeks in Miklagård."

"He will, my lord, I will see to that for he has shown kindness to me and that is a rare thing in our world of war."

Late in the afternoon, I was summoned to the tiller where the two captains were in conference. "That was well done last night Aelfraed and we are safe for a while. I intend to sail through the night. I will rest this afternoon. I would like you to have half your men on watch for the rowers will be tired."

"As you wish Jarl Gunnersson."

"We have another portage coming up and that makes us vulnerable to attack. I would make the quickest passage possible."

"The problem is that Ulf knows our route, you told me that. He is a cunning man and he will anticipate our vulnerability and be at the portage waiting for us. I now know how perilous that journey can be."

He shrugged, "There is little else we can do."

I smiled for I had an idea that had been fermenting since our last attack. "Do you have a map of the river?"

"Aye, we have a chart." He brought it out.

"Where is the portage?"

He pointed to it on the chart. I saw what I had hoped to see. "Here the river takes a loop, just before the portage. How far is it by land between the two loops?"

"Three or four miles, it is low lying and I have known other captains use that as a portage when the river is iced. Why?"

"If you stop there then I can take my men across land to ambush the barbarians."

The two of them looked at me. "But there are only ten of you!"

"True but do you think they will be expecting to be attacked? Or do you think they will be watching the river for the moment when we start to climb over the hills with our bales?"

"Even so ten against that number!"

"If the ship can make a speedy passage around that loop then we will have a refuge and we will be no worse off than we are now."

"But you may have lost men."

"We are here to guard the ship. It is like having a guard dog and keeping him in the house for fear of the wolf. We are not afraid of this wolf and remember I have seen these people fight. They are brave and they are tough but they deign to wear armour and they will not stand against my men."

"Even Eric?"

He was right Eric was our weak link. "Aye, even Eric."

"If you think you can pull this off then so be it."

"I will need one of your sailors as a guide and a messenger if anything goes wrong."

"If anything goes wrong Aelfraed, then we are all dead, not just you and your warriors."

Surprisingly my men were all happy about the idea. Even Eric looked excited. "Ragnar you will watch Eric. It is his bow which will help us."

"I can fight with a sword."

"I am the leader Eric and I say that you will use your bow for we will be outnumbered but you can make the difference. While we fight them you can thin them out. Our advantage is our armour and our weapons; that and the fact that we are all better warriors!" They roared their approval and we prepared for war.

Bjorn was chosen to accompany us. He had been the First Mate on one of the ships which were captured and his brother had been killed in the attack. He was not only knowledgeable, but he was also keen to get revenge and he came armed with us. It gave us eleven men as opposed to ten. The Jarl pulled in as close as he could to the bank and threw out a plank to save us from getting too wet. I was grateful for the brief respite we had. The land we traversed was marshy and covered in high reeds; although it gave us cover it also made movement slower than I hoped. Within a hundred paces we had lost sight of the mast of The Maiden and we were in Bjorn's hands. He navigated by looking up at the sky and sniffing. I did not ask why as I assumed he knew what he was doing. I followed him with Ridley bringing up the rear. Our small numbers meant that we would be hard to see, or at least I hoped we would.

Bjorn turned to me. "The river is close."

How he knew it I had no idea but I trusted him. I halted the men and spread them out in a line abreast with Eric and his bow at the rear. Bjorn scurried on ahead and we waited for his return. His gleaming smile told me that he had spotted them long before he opened his mouth. "They are in the woods overlooking the bend of the river and I saw the mast of The Maiden, she is working slowly down the river."

At least this part of the plan had worked; the attention of the barbarians should be on the river and we would be able to strike them from behind. I could see why some captains had made a longer portage for the ground was flat and then we saw the hill leading to the next valley as it rose slowly with a wide swathe in the trees showing where the ships were dragged. It was obvious to me that the barbarians would be on both sides and that also gave us an advantage. We stealthily made our way through the undergrowth and I, for one, was glad to be free from the cloying mud through which we had trudged. The greatest relief, however, was from the biting insects which had plagued us and we all sported red blotches where the insidious insects had bitten us. We laboured up the hill with Bjorn a little way ahead. Suddenly he raised his hand and we all dropped to our knees. He gestured to me to join him and I slithered along the ground like a serpent.

Bjorn had done well and found a spot about fifty paces above the ambush site. I could see the lighter part of the forest where the portage lay and I could see the twenty to thirty warriors who waited there. The number did not worry me, I had anticipated more than that. There would be more on the other side but, in my experience, a surprised warrior always sees two enemies where there is only one. We slithered back to the rest and I gathered them around me. "We can take ten out quietly, sneak behind them and slit their throats. When they are dead, draw your weapons and charge. Our aim is to make them run but listen for my command and when you hear it run down the hill to the boat. It should have reached the portage by then. Eric, you shoot the warriors the furthest away from us and keep moving. Make them think there are ten of you." I saw Snorri pat him on the back and his face beamed like a torch in the night.

I waved them forward and we slipped through the trees. The barbarian's slick sweaty bodies stood out against the brown of the wood and they were intently watching The Maiden as Jarl Gunnersson edged her slowly around the bend. The caution was deliberate for he wanted their attention on him alone. My axe and shield were slung for we would not need them at first but I had my dagger ready. Bjorn eagerly sliced through the windpipe of the rearmost warrior and slowly lowered the body to the ground. My warrior was oblivious to everything as I wrapped my powerful left hand around his mouth and ripped across his throat with my dagger. He was small and he was light; I laid him at my feet. Ridley's mark began to turn but Ridley held his hand over the man's mouth and stabbed directly into his throat. I do not know how many died silently but, inevitably, one cried out and the others turned. Even as I was yelling I saw the arrow embed itself in the chest of the warrior at the edge of the trees. We roared forwards. I had slipped Death Bringer around and hacked at the first warrior who foolishly stood in my way. The blade cut his torso in two. I had to be careful with my swing because of the trees and I smashed the head into the face of the next warrior and, as he fell, stamped down onto his face, crushing his skull. They ran.

"After them!" We burst through the edge of the trees and there I could swing unimpeded. A few brave souls tried to charge me but, as I swung the axe around my head and struck three of them, the rest fled. Suddenly I caught sight of Ulf. He was racing to attack Ridley from behind. "Ridley, down!"

My old friend just dropped to his knees and the blow intended for his back struck his opponent in the chest. I swung my axe at Ulf who tried to bring his sword round to deflect it but it was caught in the dead barbarian's rib cage. By the time it met the axe head the blade was sliding down the sword and slicing into Ulf's arm. I saw the blood spurt and terror appear in his eyes. He started to turn to run but I raised Death Bringer, and, true to its name, it sliced down the length of Ulf's back, splitting him in two. When I looked up there were no living barbarians left. I quickly looked up and down the portage way and saw that, although some of my men were wounded, they were all standing. Ridley began banging his shield and the others took it up, "Aelfraed! Aelfraed!"

"Eric, go down to the ship and tell the Jarl that the portage way is secured. The rest of you, well done. Salvage any weapons and armour which may be useful and then keep watch for their return."

Stig wandered up to Ulf who was lying in two ugly pieces. "Now that would have been a nice piece of armour if some dozy bugger hadn't sliced him in two."

"I am sorry Stig, next time I will just take the head."

"Much better my lord, and a lot less messy."

The Jarl decided not to use us to pull the boat as long as the barbarians were still around. His sailors carried the bales, carefully avoiding the gruesome bodies which lined the portage way. I sent Stig, Olaf, Pig and the Hammer to guard the bales along with Eric whilst the rest of us watched the woods. I did not think they would return for there were too many bodies in the woods; it was uneconomic and I suspect we had taken their leaders for three of them had many battle bracelets and torcs. It did not pay to be complacent and a little extra watching was no hardship. As they started to pull the ship up we joined in to help them. Our extra strength gave impetus over the last steep section. As they lowered the boat down the other side we stood guard at the top of the ridge until Eric came to tell us The Maiden was afloat again. It was dark by the time we made our weary way down and the Jarl had decided to make a camp by the river and cook up some hot food. Eric had managed to shoot a young deer on his way up to us and we ate our first hot meal in weeks. We washed it down with a barrel of ale the Jarl had been saving and it was a happy group who sat around the campfire sharing stories of the day and its battle; battle is probably a little grand for the skirmish that it was and my dead comrades from Fulford and Stamford would have laughed at us but we felt as though we had won a battle for the odds were against us and none of us had died. Probably the most pleasing part was that Ulf had been killed.

Harald summed it up, "Those who break oaths die, and it is as simple as that. A man cannot lie to himself and if you take an oath and do not mean it you are lying. I served with Ulf and thought he was a friend now I know that I was deceived. My lord, I am your oathsworn until you release me." The others echoed his sentiment and they raised their drinking horns. I noticed the Jarl raising his too. That was a good night.

Chapter 5

The next couple of weeks were not as tough as the previous ones as we rowed downstream towards the Dnieper. We had only been sailing for a day when I was summoned to the tiller. "You did well back there Aelfraed. I did not think that you would succeed but I am coming to believe your promises now." I gave him a sharp look. "I meant no offence but I have often heard warriors make promises and then they fail. You seemed so sure of yourself that I did not believe you."

I smiled for I had not been upset. "I was taught well Jarl Gunnersson and told that a man had to live up to his words. That is all I try to do."

He waved at the men who were happily chatting and laughing. "You have achieved something rare Aelfraed, you have bonded your men behind you and in all my voyages with warriors, this is the first time I have seen that."

"It has always been my way; when you fight alongside a man, you must respect him and more importantly trust him."

"Good, you have done so but we now have a new problem. After we pass Boatyard we have to pass a number of rapids. There we will be close to the Pechengs. Travelling south is not as bad as north as we will be pulling the boat downhill. We will not unload it for the furs are not heavy but your men will have to be to the west in a screen to warn us of attack."

"How many rapids are there?"

"Seven and they stretch for over fifty miles. I am telling you this because that is where we will be most likely to be attacked."

"How long before we get there?"

He looked up at the sky. "At this speed, it will take about three days."

"Good, then that gives me time to prepare my men."

I went to the bow, which was largely empty for the river was wide and the rowing easy. "Ridley, gather the men around."

They squatted around me in a half circle. "We did well the other day and our next challenge will be the rapids. "

Olaf spat over the side. "They are a bastard and that is where the horsemen will attack."

I nodded. "And it will take us days to get through them so we will need to be prepared. Make sure you all have a shield that has as much iron on it as you can manage. Repair any mail you have and those of you who have bows check them. We will be forming a thin screen to warn the ship of their attacks. If you can hit the horses for, as Ridley and I learned, a horseman without his horse is like a one-legged man in an arse kicking contest!" They all laughed and I paused for the Jarl had left unsaid what I now had to say. "If you fall then it is unlikely that we will able to come for you. We are not going to be in a shield wall but a long line a hundred paces in length. I tell you this because I do not want you to lie out there, wounded thinking someone will come for you. Even if I fall the rest will carry on."

There was a silence until Stig said, "You really need to work on how to motivate your men, my lord!"

Everyone burst out laughing and I could see that they understood, they were warriors. I looked at Eric, unlike the rest, for him this was new and I would need to speak with him. Ragnar had blossomed and bloomed as the voyage had gone on. It was as though his wounds and injuries were forgotten and he was a warrior once more. None of my men treated him differently and I treated him not, as he was intended to be, a servant but as a fellow warrior.

"Eric."

"Yes, my lord?"

"You do not need to be with us as the skirmish line. You can stay with the boat."

He looked downcast, "Have I displeased you, my lord?"

"Of course not."

"Did I not swear the blood oath?"

"Yes."

"Then I will stand with my bow and fight with my oath brothers." I looked at him and saw that he had changed. He was still the gentle poet and singer but he now had steel and a backbone. He had come through battle and survived; that is powerful for a man learns that the worst thing to fear is fear itself.

"Your father would be proud of you."

He smiled at the compliment. "The question is Thegn Aelfraed, are you proud of me?"

I grasped his shoulders, "Of course I am! Without you, we would not have got as far as we have."

"Then I am happy." He grinned. "I wonder what my brothers would make of me now."

"What indeed!"

We slipped past the Boatyard at night so that none could see us. Gunnar had been worried that they might have had a chain across the river but they did not which made him think that they had been involved, in some way, in Ulf's plot and perhaps did not expect any ships to reach this far south. Certainly, we all breathed a sigh of relief as

Varangian

dawn broke and we were clear of the last town which could halt us. Now it was just the rapids and the horsemen of the Pechengs who could stand in our way. Miklagård was almost within touching distance.

We pulled to the west bank of the river and I could see the logs awaiting our use. When I took my men west I could see the rapids which looked like a boiling cauldron. I could see why they need to carry the boat and I felt sorry for any boat coming upstream for it would be a hard slog. The crew of The Maiden had the slope on their side. We formed a line a hundred paces long. I was at the northern end and Ridley anchored the southern end. Eric, Ragnar and Snorri were the middle three and the rest split between us. Ridley had his bow and I carried Boar Splitter. If there were horsemen then I would deter them. The first two rapids were trouble free and it was when we were feeling comfortable and relatively safe, on the third day when the Pechengs struck.

They appeared halfway through the portage. They were small wiry riders on small ponies. They galloped hard and low and I hoped my men remembered to go for the horses. To my horror, I saw that they aimed for the middle of the line, Eric! I began to jog south and noticed Ridley heading north but the Pecheng line would reach our middle before we did. I saw Eric's bow send his first arrow and felt relief as the other four men armed with bows did the same. I was relieved to see Ragnar and Snorri cover Eric with their shields so that he could continue to fire. Their shields were soon peppered with arrows but I saw at least six ponies and riders had fallen. Stig and Olaf reached the small group, followed by Hammer, Harald and Pig. The archers were protected by the shields of the others and there was just Ridley and me who were not protected. *Wyrd* determined that they would direct their attacks at Ridley and avoid me. I watched him continue to shoot even though I saw arrows strike him. "Back to the ship!" I continued to run towards Ridley who I saw had taken an arrow to his right arm and was now protecting himself with his shield. Out of the corner of my eye, I was aware of the rest edging back and then I saw the horseman veer towards me. I did not slow my pace but I held Boar Splitter before me and kept my eye on the warrior who was pulling back his bow. I sensed, rather than saw when he loosed and whipped my shield before my face. The arrowhead actually pierced the wood but by then I was close enough to stab Boar Splitter into the horse's neck. It reared suddenly and plunged to the ground. I withdrew the spear and, leaping the horse stabbed the surprised warrior in the neck. Ridley was fighting off two warriors who were trying to capture him. His weakened right hand held his sword but they were attacking from two sides. They must have assumed that I would have been killed by the horsemen for they ignored me. It cost one his life as I rammed the head of Boar Splitter through his bareback. Ridley grinned as he sliced his sword through the other's neck.

"Can you walk?"

"Don't be daft, it is my arm, not my leg. 'Course I can run."

Putting our shields on our backs we ran as hard as we could through the darkening dusk towards the others whom we saw clambering aboard the refloated ship. I felt the arrows thudding into my shield and pinging from my helmet but none struck me and we were dragged aboard. I fell laughing to the deck and looked up at the face of Jarl Gunnersson. "We survived that one then."

The silence that greeted me told me that all was not well. I rose to my feet and looked around at my men. There was no Ragnar. "Where is Ragnar?"

Eric looked tearful. "He must have fallen but we heard no shout."

I looked out and saw, to the west, the departing Pechengs and to the north the bodies which littered the rocks. "I will meet you at the next rapids."

The Jarl stepped forwards. "That is madness. You told your men you would not go back for them."

"No, I said they should not go back for anyone. Ragnar is my man. I will go."

"And I will come." My men all spoke at once.

"No! Ridley is to command until I return. I command you all to stay and I will return; I am not destined to die a lonely death in the land of the Rus." I looked at their crestfallen faces and pointed to the skies. "The Norns are spinning again." I clambered over and dropped to the water. It was now dark and I struggled to make the bank. Once ashore I was amazed to see that the ship was now invisible and I was alone in the land of the Pechengs.

I was not worried about the Pechengs finding me; I suspected that they would be back at their camp licking their wounds; I was worried that I would not find Ragnar for he could not cry out. I came across the first Pecheng body and then knew that I was in the right area. There was no moon but the bodies could be seen as softer shapes than the rocks around them. I found myself counting Pechengs. When I reached double figures I felt incredibly proud of my men. I was also beginning to fear that I would not find Ragnar or if I did then he would be dead. I suddenly caught sight of a movement and I held my spear before me and approached the shape. When Ragnar's face looked up me with the resigned look of one who thinks he is about to die I was so relieved I almost shouted. I quickly went to him. "Where are you wounded?" He pointed at his leg. He had taken an arrow to his knee and I could see the bones of his shin peering up at me. The arrow had missed the kneecap but broken the leg. "I will be gone briefly."

I went back to the last group of Pechengs I had seen. One of them had had a spear. I found it and took it back. I snapped it in two and, taking some leather cords from the dead Pecheng who lay beside Ragnar I straightened the leg and tied the two halves of the spear. It must have hurt but he showed no signs of it. The arrow had come through the leg and I could see the head. I snapped off the feathered end and gave him my dagger. "Bite on this!" I dried as much blood off the arrowhead as I could and then I pulled for all I was worth. It slipped out with a sickly plop and Ragnar fell back, mercifully unconscious. While he was out I tied a bandage tightly around the leg to stop the bleeding and then hoisted him upon my back. I hauled him across my shoulders so that he rested against my shield and axe. I then held Boar Splitter beneath him and across my shoulders to take the strain on my arms. It meant he would not fall off and I could concentrate on walking. He was a big man but the rowing had given me a strength I had not had before and I gritted my teeth as I headed south. Even though it was dark I could hear the river and I headed in that direction.

After a thousand paces I thought I could not go on but I knew I had to. I played a game with myself. I would walk a hundred paces and then stop. After a hundred paces I did not feel so bad and I repeated it. A silly game I know but it helped me to get along. Then I found myself talking to Aethelward and Nanna. *'You never thought I would travel to this forsaken land, did you? You never saw me fighting barbarians who wear human teeth around their necks. I thank you both for watching over me.'* Then I began to think of my wife Gytha and wonder how my son Harold was growing. I realised that it was highly likely I would never see him again. As I looked up at the moon rising over the desolate land I suddenly thought that, perhaps, I would never even see Ridley again.

The ground soon became uneven and that helped me because I had to concentrate so much on placing my feet in the correct place that I had no chance to think about the pain in my back and the weight on my shoulders. By the time the land had levelled out, I could see the first thin line of the false dawn. I wondered if I ought to lie Ragnar down and have a rest but I knew that if I did so I would never be able to lift him again and I trudged on. What I should have done was to see if his wound was bleeding, or that he was still alive but I did none of those things and I kept going. At one point I was so tired that I closed my eyes and it felt blissful. I quickly opened them again but I was sorely tempted to shut them again, just for a moment. When I did so it was almost a disaster as my toe struck a rock and I stumbled; how I retained my balance I do not know but I did and I stood breathing heavily peering ahead to see if I could see the mast of The Maiden. Sometimes the captain had struck the mast when he felt we would not need it as it hid us from our enemies and we had used it since before the portage. I now prayed that Gunnar would step it if only to let me know how close I was to the ship and safety. Of course, that was grossly unfair because the mast would be like a beacon for the Pechengs to tell them where we were.

The sun had now, finally shown itself above the distant horizon and its first rays peeped out, lighting the land before me. The land was flat for I was not near the next rapid and that meant I was still some distance from safety and the ship. I shook myself. I was insane! How could I think that Ragnar and I would survive? The ship was miles away and we were surrounded by hostile Pechengs. I would have thrown away Boar Splitter if it were not for the fact that I thought that throwing it away would be throwing away my life and I was not ready to do that; not yet. The noise from the river began to grow and I wondered why. I glanced to my left and it still flowed serenely on; I was well away from the edge and I wondered why it was so loud and then the thought drifted into my befuddled head. I was close to the rapids. I peered ahead through the mist and the spray and then I saw them, they had their mouths open but they were silent. It was Eric and the others of my Red Horse Men. I sank to my knees and closed my eyes, thanking those who had protected me and seen me through my ordeal and then there was blackness.

I heard voices which seemed from afar off and I wondered where I was. I recognised Ridley's voice and that of Jarl Gunnersson. "He has always been loyal to those who served him. When his people were killed at Topcliffe he went into their stronghold to wreak revenge. He believes that he has a responsibility to his men."

"But he pays them does he not? They will share in the profits? Why risk his life for them?"

"He has always been that way and I cannot see him changing."

"It has brought him to death's door and for what? A lame servant who cannot speak and will be of little use for the rest of the voyage."

Ridley was right of course I did make gestures I need not. I had forgotten about Thomas and Sarah but I knew that I would do it again. It was comfortable lying there in the dark but I knew that I had to make an effort and I opened my weary eyes and tried to pull myself up.

"Ah, the sleeping beauty awakes! We thought we had lost you old friend."

I took Ridley's proffered arm. "How long did I sleep?"

"A day and a half and you have awoken at the right time for we have another portage."

"And the Pechengs?"

"They have left us alone."

I nodded, that was what I had hoped as I had lain dreaming the strange dreams of near death. "And Ragnar?"

"His leg is healing but he will be of little use hauling the boat." I sensed the anger in Gunnar's voice.

"And yet, Captain, had Ragnar not fought off the Pechengs you might have had no boat to haul."

He had no argument against that. "Well, this is the last portage and our last area of concern until we reach the Ford of Var."

"The Ford of Var?"

"It is quite close to St George Island where we become a sailing ship again, the Pecheng like to attack there for they can close with the boat and the narrow channel makes us move slower than we would like."

"How far?"

"Two days."

"Then Ridley and I have two days to think of a way to beat these Pechengs."

Ridley put a protective arm around me and said, quietly in my ear, "We thought we had lost you. You were exhausted and were barely breathing. Do not do that to me again old friend."

"He was heavier than I thought." I attempted to lift my arms up but I could not move them beyond my shoulders. I would not be wielding an axe for a while! They had erected a shelter for me and as I emerged into the thin sunlight there was a huge cheer from my men and the crew as they saw me. Ragnar was sat by the rail and tried to get up. I hurried over to him. "No, stay there you have a wound."

He grabbed my hand and kissed it. He mouthed the words, 'Thank you.' And placed his hand over his heart and then at me.

Eric rose and came to me. "Thank you, my lord. I have never heard of a lord risking his life for a servant before."

I shook my head. "We are one company. If one is hurt then I am hurt. Enough of me and my troubles. We will have to fend off the Pechengs again in two days' time and this time they will be much closer and I knew from bitter experience that their arrows are dangerous. We need to make oblong shields, the size of a man. They need not be polished and finished but they should be thick enough to absorb the arrows."

Stig nodded and asked, "That is your plan my lord, to hide behind the shields until we are beyond them?"

"No Stig for we must also stop them closing with the ship and boarding. The shields are to protect us while we shoot arrows at them and throw spears."

"We have few spears, my lord."

"I know Olaf but we can cut saplings at the next portage and use the daggers we took from the Pechengs. We need to kill, not the Pechengs but their mounts and even a badly made spear thrown by a poor shot can still hit a large target like a man and a pony."

They looked satisfied and I saw nods from the experienced river men like Pig and Harold. Ragnar slapped the deck and when I looked at him pointed at himself, miming shooting a bow. "Yes Ragnar, you can have your revenge and you can sit at the bow and kill our enemies!"

Ragnar had to stay aboard as we dragged the boat over the last portage close to the rapids. We kept Snorri and Eric as scouts to watch for the Pechengs but I agreed with the captain, they had learned their lesson and would wait until we wallowed like a whale at the fords where they could surround us and bring their numbers to bear. While the ship was prepared for the voyage I took the men to cut down trees and saplings to fashion the shields and the spears. We split the logs into rough lengths by the river and then hammered them into shape on the ship. They were crudely made but each one was three fingers thick. We laid them next to the rail, out of sight. They would be raised when the Pechengs were in confident archer range. We found five daggers which we fixed to the saplings and then Eric had the idea of tying arrows to the other ten. They were crude spears but needs must when danger threatens.

The rowers all pulled even harder as we made our way down the last part of the river for once we reached St George Island their rowing days would be numbered and the sooner we got there the sooner we would be free of the threat of the Pechengs.

I had worked on recovering my mobility for I would need to be able to use my shoulders to fight the Pechengs. I worried at first that I had irrevocably damaged my shoulders but Eric displayed a skill hitherto unknown to us. His mother had taught him how to massage and he used some oil we discovered on board to soothe the pain in my shoulders. Within a day I could raise my arms and within two I felt that I was back to normal.

"That is a skill, Eric. Why did you not tell us of it?"

He looked shamefaced. "My brothers mocked me, telling me that I was a girl going a girl's job."

Varangian

Stig summed it up, "I have never met them, but your brothers sound like dick heads to me." He was probably right but two of Eric's brothers became Kings in Denmark- the fact that their rule was short-lived and perhaps reflected their narrow minds. The men laughed and Snorri wrapped a protective arm around his shoulders. The desertion by Ulf and Snorri's arrival had made us a much more tightly knit company and I felt now, as I had in England, when fighting with my men of the Red Horse Company.

The Fords of Var came after a very wide section of the river. It was shallow but our ship had no problem then the cliffs rose and the river narrowed but still remained shallow. It split into a number of different courses most of which were shallow enough for horses. As we made our way south we saw them gathering like the vultures we had seen on the plain, gathering to devour the dying beasts. They looked like a swarm of deadly flies and they watched, from both banks, to see which channel we took. The channels were so narrow that even the deeper ones could be swum by the powerful Pecheng ponies.

Jarl Gunnersson pointed to them. "There is your enemy Thegn and we are in your hands now."

We had armed as many of the spare crew as we could but we knew it would come down to the ten of us, five on each side. Ridley had four on the eastern side of the boat and I had the rest to the west. We had been armed and ready since dawn and we now waited for the moment I would order the shields raised. The closer we came to the fords the more certain our enemies were of our selected channel and they began to gather. I estimated that there were almost a hundred on my side and perhaps sixty on the other. They meant business. They were spread out in a semi-circle, obviously intending to attack us from all sides. I hoped that the shields would protect the rowers but, if they fire directly in the air then the plunging arrows could cause devastation. "Be ready to pass your shields to the rowers if they target them." I walked to the stern and handed my shield to Gunnar. "You may need this captain; I suspect they will try to harm you."

I noticed, for the first time that he had put on a mail shirt and wore his sword. He grinned, "It is not the first time I have faced arrows and an enemy who wished to end my life. Look to yourself Aelfraed."

I wondered as I returned to my post, how he had come to be a river captain for he looked to me like a warrior and he spoke knowledgeably of weapons and warriors. I had no time for speculation for we were now close to the Pechengs and they launched their attacks, riding hard and low towards our side. I had to judge the moment for too soon and they would withdraw. I needed them committed to the charge so that we could begin to whittle them down. With only ten men the most that we could hope to take was eight or nine and we could afford no casualties. When they were forty paces from the side I saw the leading riders pull back their bows. "Shields!"

We all grabbed a shield and jammed it into position. The ones at the end had two shields to erect and we heard the thud as the arrows hit the defences. We had no time to congratulate ourselves on our defence for we needed to kill and kill quickly. I was not the greatest archer but at thirty paces even I could not miss a pony and I shot arrow after arrow at the mass of men who hurled themselves at the ship. Despite the rower's efforts we were moving slowly as Gunnar and Siggi, who were standing at the prow, negotiated the twisting waters. The squealing of the dying ponies and the screams of wounded warriors filled the air. I saw a hand appear towards the stern and I dropped my bow and grabbed my axe. I sliced down and the fingers spurted blood as they were severed. The screaming warrior fell to the water but his place was taken by others who had closed with the ship. "Eric, Ragnar, keep loosing arrows. The rest of you! Swords!"

With only three of us to defend the side, it was inevitable that they would make the deck. I was just glad that they had not tried plunging arrows for that would have been disastrous. I hacked at another arm which grabbed the rail and then saw a Pecheng racing aft to Gunnar. I ran behind him and Death Bringer split his skull like a ripe plum. Gunnar nodded and said, "Behind you!"

I swung my axe in a circle and decapitated a surprised Pecheng who had thought to strike me in the back with a wicked looking curved sword. An arrow flew over my shoulder and I turned to see another Pecheng fall overboard with one of Ragnar's arrows in his throat. Two approached me with their blades ready but Death Bringer and my long arms meant that I had a longer reach and they stumbled backwards away from the scythe of death. One fell and I hacked into his chest. The other tried to stab me but I grabbed his blade in my mailed hand, pulled him towards me and head-butted him over the side. I suddenly sensed that we were moving quicker and there were fewer Pechengs. I glanced aft and Gunnar waved to me but there were two dead bodies close to him, one without a head and the other with an arrow in his back. I looked over the side and saw two Pechengs, their feet on the oars as they tried to climb aboard. I swung Death Bringer one-handed and took one warrior full in the face. That was too much for his companion who threw himself in the waters and then we were through. The decks were a river of blood but they had not stopped us and, as the river widened I looked in our wake to see the remains of the warband waving their weapons in the air. The Maiden remained intact; the Pechengs had not soiled her.

I looked down the side and saw Snorri, Eric and Ragnar's smiling faces but Olaf lay between Snorri and me. I ran to him. He had three arrows in his back but his head had been severed so that it hung only by his coif. Around him lay five dead Pechengs; his sword, bright with blood still in his hand. He would go to Valhalla and join his old comrades. I looked to the other side and saw Ridley. He grinned at me. There was blood on him but, knowing Ridley, that would be Pecheng blood. Stig and Hammer were busy pitching bodies over the side while Harald was binding a wound. Pig lay in an ungainly heap, again, as with Olaf, surrounded by his foes but dead nonetheless. The rowers had not emerged unscathed and four of them lay dead with arrows in their necks as was Siggi who, like Gunnar had been the target of attacks at the vulnerable prow of the ship. We had won but it had been an expensive victory. A third of my men lay dead.

We hove to at St. George Island. There we were safe and we could see to our wounds and our dead. St. George Island is a bare place but there was enough wood to provide kindling and we made biers from the huge shields which had served their purpose. We laid the warriors together, with their weapons atop a bier and, after we had sent Siggi and the rowers to the next world we said goodbye to our friends. They had fulfilled their oath and died well. Gunnar told me that Olaf had died protecting my back; an action which cost him his own life. After the flames had consumed them and there was just Gunnar and my men left I asked, "Did the Pig and Olaf have a family?"

"I do not think so Aelfraed. Why do you ask?"

"I would send their share of the profits to their families."

Gunnar and my men looked at me as though I had spoken Chinese. "When a man dies it just means more profit for the leader. You have the profit Aelfraed."

I shook my head and looked at Eric. "When we reach Miklagård and the accounts are done then share the money due Pig and Olaf between the rest of you. Ridley and I came here not for profit but to fight the Normans."

Eric looked stunned. "But your profit my lord, what of that?"

"I told you, I take no profit from this voyage. You will all share what was due to me."

Ridley nodded and we clasped arms. What did we need with coin we both had enough waiting with the Jews of Miklagård. These warriors had shown me loyalty which I would reward.

Varangian

With the mast stepped and the oars shipped we sailed swiftly down the Dnieper towards the Black Sea. We saw many Pechengs but they were always in the distance, watching for us to make a mistake or fall foul of the river but Jarl Gunnersson was too wily a sailor for that. I spent some time with him in the weeks which followed the battle for I was intrigued. "You were a warrior, Gunnar."

He nodded, "Aye." He looked at me shrewdly. "I fought alongside my father until the day I was wounded." He rolled up his sleeve to show me a savage scar on his right arm. "I did not sail with him when he went to his last battle." He paused to gauge my reaction, "At Stamford Bridge."

"Ah, I see now, the Norns."

"As you say. When I first met you I knew that you had fought at my father's last fight."

"I do not remember him."

"I do not think you fought him for I knew that you fought against Hadrada and the survivors of my father's band told me that they were not near Harold."

"I am sorry."

He shrugged, "He was a warrior and he died a warrior's death but you, Aelfraed the Housecarl, you interested me for my father's men spoke of you and your deeds and I expected a boastful warrior full of fight, or as my father would have said, piss and vinegar and I was ready to despise you but the more I saw of you the more intrigued I became and you have surprised me the whole way south."

"You did not fight because of your father then?"

"All of my friends died with him. The warriors, who returned, like Siggi, chose a more peaceful life for the best of the warriors died with Harold that day. You, my friend, are the exception. You and Ridley are the last warriors."

The voyage around the Black Sea seemed like an anti-climax after the trials and tribulations of the river. Ragnar began to walk aided by a pair of sticks fashioned by Snorri who showed great skills with wood. My talk with the captain had set me thinking. I had had no idea of his feelings and wondered how many other times I had taken things for granted. At night, after we had eaten we sat and spoke of the battles along the river and thought of Pig and Olaf for that is what warriors do; they remember their comrades by talking of their deaths knowing that, when they die they too will be remembered in a tale. Eric composed a song of the two men and he showed a real skill for he put in Pig's humour and his appetite, which had been as much a part of him as his courage as a warrior.

Varangian

Sometime Jarl Gunnersson joined us. He turned to me one night when the songs had ended and we looked up at the stars. "Would you not consider making this your life? You are a fine leader of men, Aelfraed, and I am sure that other ships would join us. We would have a greater chance of survival with you at our head."

I could see that my men were keen for me to continue to lead them. I shook my head, "I have enjoyed the journey and enjoyed leading you but my destiny lies in Miklagård. Events have happened which lead me here. What of the rest of you? I know that Ridley here will join me but what of all of you?"

Stig spoke first, "We have spoken and although we hoped you would join us we can see now that the Norns have plotted a different life for you. I will go to Fat Folke and offer to lead warriors, Harald and Hammer will join me for I have learned much from you Thegn and I thank you."

"And you Snorri, what of you? Do you not wish to serve on the river?"

"No my lord, I have had enough; I have lost too many friends. I will stay a while in Miklagård. As you have been kind enough to offer me Ulf's share of the profits, I have no need to return to the river and I can plan my life."

"Eric, will you and Ragnar return to Hedeby?"

They both shook their heads and Eric said, "No, Thegn, I told you when I volunteered that I had always wished to visit the land of my mother and Ragnar is happy enough to serve me."

I was pleased that they all had their plans and that our lives were settled and sorted but I would be sad to see them depart for I had grown to like the men with whom I had fought. I wondered if my life would be ever thus; making friends and then leaving them to move on. Would the grass always be greener elsewhere?

Chapter 6

Constantinople 1073

Constantinople was the modern wonder of the world. It was the largest city and, it was said, dwarfed its mother, Rome. We knew where the city was long before we even got close for the number of ships and boats we saw increased dramatically. There were far more people travelling along the roads which led to the mighty city and I began to wonder just how big it was. Even though we could see the entrance to the harbour at noon, so many ships were attempting to enter that it took us until almost dark to navigate into the safety of the Golden Horn. It was dark by the time we had tied up. The crew were sent ashore to return the following day and receive their pay. It was now the turn of Eric to earn his money. Gunnar and I accompanied him to Isaac the Jew. I had thought it might be late but the Jarl laughed. "Where business is concerned it is never too late for the Jew. He will see us."

We reached the Jewish quarter which was considerably better apportioned than the one in Jorvik. It seemed to me that Jews were held in higher esteem here in the east. He recognised the jarl but when I was introduced, he bowed. "And I have heard of you Thegn Aelfraed of Topcliffe, protector of Jews. You are most welcome."

As we entered the Jarl said quietly to me, "You are a man with many layers. I have never heard Isaac speak so highly of another. When we return to the ship you must tell me the tale."

My connection with Reuben made the meeting pleasant and speedy. Like Reuben, he insisted upon feting us with wine and eastern delicacies. When we eventually made to leave he said, "I hope that you will use me for your business while you are here Thegn Aelfraed, your promissory note is good in my house."

"Thank you, Isaac, that is kind but, at the moment I need no coin."

"As you wish, I will bring coin tomorrow when I inspect the cargo."

As we walked back I told them both of my dealings with Reuben in Jorvik."

"It is as they said Aelfraed, there is a thread which connects us all. If we break the thread then it is our disaster but you bind the threads with more threads. I am tempted to stay here with you just to see how your life progresses."

The next day, true to his word and with armed men guarding him, Isaac returned. He was a little amused at the arrows in the bales. "I am not certain that Folke would have approved."

The Jarl shrugged. "They saved our lives."

"They will not affect the value." He already had Eric's figures which he checked. He turned to Eric. "Your writing is excellent and I can find no fault with your figures. Will you be on the ship in the future?"

"No, I intend to make this city my home."

"Just so? Well, I hope that I can be of use to you for it is good to deal with an honest man."

"Meaning that the others were not honest?"

"Meaning this is the first time that the figures have tallied with the goods. Many times goods have fallen overboard."

The Jarl became indignant. "Not from my ship!"

"Apologies captain, no slur intended. Let us just say that the captains of Folke's ships thought that they were bringing all of the goods sent by the merchant but the guards had changed the figures. Folke will be pleased." He counted out the money and put it in a box he had brought. "My men will move the bales to my warehouse and I will send the letter to Folke with you captain apprising him of the value of his trade."

"I will be here for a week loading my next cargo."

"Farewell Aelfraed and Ridley. Please come to see me at my home when we can talk a little easier."

We went aboard where I gave the Jarl his share for he had to pay his men. He was more than pleased as he normally received less. "I can see the wisdom of hiring honest guards."

"Then use Stig. We both know that he is honest."

"He has become so but I will do as you suggest for I think he has been changed."

I summoned the men and divided the money between the six of them. They tried to give the money back to me but both Ridley and I refused. "No. We do not need it and we are not greedy men. You have earned it and, I fear, you will need it. Take it as payment with my thanks for it has been an honour to serve with you. I now release you from your oath."

They all looked at me and Stig spoke. "I speak for all of us my lord, including Ragnar who wishes he could speak. If you ever need us then we will come. That is our oath."

"Thank you that means a great deal and Stig I have suggested to Isaac and to the Jarl that he uses you and your men as guards. If you will take my advice you will choose guards carefully."

"I will my lord."

The three of them left for they knew the city well and had a tavern in mind. Snorri, Ragnar and Eric remained. "What of you? Where will you go?"

Varangian

"I also have lived here and I will take these two and find us somewhere to rent. It will be cheaper than a tavern and our money will last longer."

I was pleased that they would be together for all had been damaged or wounded in some way and it seemed fitting that they should be together. "Leave word with Isaac where you are and we will meet with you when the time allows."

We embraced as they left for we had shared life, death and near death. I thought that Ragnar would never leave go of me and, when he left, I saw tears not only in his eyes but Eric's.

Ridley and I made our way through the busy streets carrying our war gear. We had emerged from the journey without further wounds but we had learned a great deal about ourselves. Ridley was far more confident and had thrown off the shackles which had weighed him down when he was a lord. He enjoyed the company of soldiers and their banter. Even though we were alone once more he had a calmness about him I had not seen since the time before Coxold. For myself, I had learned my limits and I had learned to think more. Inside I was smiling as I thought that Aethelward would have approved. My poor decisions had been due to poor information from others and that was a valuable lesson. I would take advice from more than one person in the future.

We were not considered outlandish here in the home of the Varangian Guards. Many men dressed such as we lived in the metropolis. I wondered how we would join. Ridley left that decision to me; it was his way. "We will head for the gates of the palace. I am sure the guards there will know where we should go." I noticed that the road gradually inclined upwards to the huge palace which dominated the skyline.

I had, of course, let my translator, Eric go, but, having mastered the languages along the river so that I could now converse well with the rivermen I was confident that I would soon master the language of the Byzantine. The huge gates were guarded by four warriors. I slowed up as we approached them for I wished to look at their armour. They had a helmet such as I wore but without a nasal. The shield was a rounded version of the kite shield and in their hands, they held a spear. It was their armour that intrigued me the most for the mail shirt only came to their knees but their shoulders and upper body were protected by metal plates such as Ridley and I wore. Like us, they had metal greaves on their legs. They were obviously not Varangians but they looked like soldiers who could fight.

As we approached I saw them tense and their spears crossed to bar our way. We halted and I spoke in English, which they did not understand. I tried them in the language of the river. "We wish to seek employment as warriors."

One of them understood and said, "Wait here." He went through the open gate and we were left to be examined by the remaining three guards. I could see that they were interested in Death Bringer for the finely made blade always attracted attention. They were well-trained men and I could see that although they looked keenly at the weapon they were constantly watching the street behind us. Eventually, the guard returned with a small neatly dressed clerk. "I am John and I understand from the guard that you wish to enlist."

I was astounded with his English which was perfect. "I am Aelfraed Godwinson and this is Ridley of Coxold."

"I see from your weapons that you were Housecarls."

"We were."

He paused as though he expected us to add more information and when we did not he shrugged. "What made you travel here?"

"We heard that the Emperor valued the axes of our comrades and we would like to serve him."

He gave a wry smile, "And yet I would hazard that you do not know his name?"

I blushed and shook my head, "No, I heard that the last Emperor died at Manzikert but I do not know who has succeeded him."

"Ah, I do so love Anglo-Saxons for they are naïve in politics. You have much to learn but Aelfraed Godwinson your name and your reputation will gain you entry into the palace but as for employment, that will depend upon the commander of the guard. Come with me."

The guards parted and we followed the tiny man into the palace. He might have been small but he walked as though he was a giant. He strode with the confidence of power. It was my first lesson in the ways of Byzantium. I remembered my uncle's words and determined to speak little but hear all. The people we met were either officials or soldiers there was no sign of either women or servants. I suspected there would be both but the fact that they were not outside was of interest to me.

The warrior hall of the Varangians was only recognisable as such when you entered. On the outside, it was the same pale colour of stone as all the other buildings. Inside Ridley and I recognised it immediately. The guards who were there were dressed much as we and, as we entered, there was a dip in the conversation. John was unperturbed by the attention and led us to a small antechamber at the back of the hall. He gestured for us to enter. "I will await you outside for a while in case…" Enigmatically smiling he left us.

Varangian

A huge warrior suddenly filled the doorway. "You two wish to join the Varangians?"

He was a Norwegian but thanks to Harald I could understand and speak the language. "Yes, we are from England."

"I know who you are, Aelfraed Godwinson, you are the bastard of Harold and you killed my king Hadrada at Stamford Bridge for I, Olef the Bold, also fought there."

The Norns again and our past had now come to haunt us. I felt Ridley stiffen and I put my hand on his arm. "I fought against Hadrada at Stamford and I defended my land. What has that to do with joining the Varangians?"

"It has everything to do with that for I am commander and I determine who serves the Emperor and I would sooner shovel shit in hell for eternity than allow a glory hunter such as you in the guard. Now fuck off and the next time I see you have weapons ready for that will be your last on this earth for there are many men here who remember you from Stamford and Fulford and would have their revenge."

I smiled, "Many men have made that promise and yet I am still standing. You say I killed your king but had you been closer to this man you hold so dear you would have known that one of my archers killed him but I slew many brave Norwegians that day. Where were you?"

His face filled with rage and I wondered had I pushed him too far. "Go you have used up all the time I will allow you."

We walked into the warrior hall to total silence for they had all been listening. Ridley said as we walked to the door where I hoped John would be waiting. "Well, I see we have managed to piss off the Varangians too."

"*Wyrd* old friend, *wyrd*."

A smiling official awaited us. "I see your reputation is not exaggerated, Thegn Aelfraed."

"You knew what his reaction would be."

He cocked his head to the side. "Olef has only been the leader of the Varangians for less than a year. He is trying to fill its ranks with fellow Norse. The other Saxons who came were also shown the door but none of them had the temerity to stand up to him. Now would you still like to serve the Empire?"

"Of course it is why we came here but I thought that my services would only be needed by the Varangians."

"Come with me." He led us off at a brisk pace, chattering all the while. "The Varangians serve Michael the joint Emperor of the poor Romanos who was captured. There are other Strategoi who enjoy employing Saxons. I will take you to meet one such and, who knows, perhaps he may employ you."

I halted and the man turned to face me. "You are being very helpful to two men whom you do not know; why?"

He laughed and clapped his hands together, his voice suddenly high pitched, "Excellent, you are suspicious and do not take things at face value. You are learning the politics of the East. To answer you as honestly as I can I will say that I serve the Empire in all things and I see in you and your companion two men who may be useful to its continuation. I have heard of your exploits fighting the Normans and I know that you do not give in easily. I suspect you came down on the ship which docked yesterday for the port is filled with the story of how the Pechengs suffered defeat at the hands of a handful of Norse led by a Saxon." He looked at me his blue eyes twinkling, "You, I believe." I cocked my head to one side and nodded. "Just so, just so. It confirms my opinion. Do not worry Aelfraed I care not for you but I care for my Empire and it needs men like you. Men who can die for the Emperor."

We walked on. "Reassuringly blunt."

He did not turn around but I saw his shoulders shrug. "That is as close to honest as you will get from me and believe me that is far more honest than you will see anywhere else in this city."

We went through a warren of passageways and he suddenly halted at a large door. He opened it and we were in an antechamber with a table and two chairs. "Put your war gear over there and sit, this may take some time. I will send in refreshments for you."

As we sat down Ridley looked troubled. "I am not sure we have done the right thing Aelfraed. This is not what I was expecting."

"Me neither. I hoped to strike back at the Normans but it seems the Norns have other plans for us." I was not overly worried by the turn of events but, like Ridley, this was not what I had expected. I had thought we would have been welcomed with open arms; we would have joined the Varangians and had a glorious career. That was not meant to be. A servant girl, the first female we had seen, glided in with a tray and put a jug and two metal chalices on the table. She left bowls of fruit and, nodding to us, left. I wondered if the drink and the food was poisoned but then dismissed the idea, John could have just taken us out of the palace if he wished to be rid of us. Olef and the Varangians would have seen to the rest. I poured us some of the rich red wine and sipped it. It had a slightly bitter, although not unpleasant taste. The fruits I did not recognise but I had heard them described and I thought they were figs and olives. I tried them both and found them to be quite pleasant.

Varangian

Ridley watched me and my reaction and then tried his. He pulled a face when he tasted the wine. "I would rather have ale." I laughed, you could take the Saxon out of England but you could not take the English out of the Saxon. He seemed to like the figs but not the olives. We spent some years in the east and Ridley never quite came to terms with the food, he always yearned for the food and drink of Northumbria.

I do not know how long we waited but the room itself was pleasant and cool. We still wore our mail beneath our tunics as it had become a habit and we were sweltering in the heat of the city. Fortunately, there was a slight breeze from the Sea of Marmara which made the room bearable, evening armour. It was not even summer yet and I envisaged a time when we would actually melt like spring ice. "Events have not turned out as we had hoped eh, Aelfraed?"

"We plan Ridley but our lives are shaped by others. We are here for a purpose. I had thought that it was to be a Varangian Guard and to fight the Normans but it seems we are destined for other things."

"Very philosophical of you Saxon and more perceptive than most of your colleagues." I jumped at the quiet voice which appeared from behind me. Alexios Comnenus and John had not used the door which we were watching but had emerged from behind a tapestry. We both stood. The strategos was not a big man but he looked as though he had been used to a warrior's life at some time. He looked to be about the same age as me and I later found out that we had been born within a year of each other. "I am Alexios Comnenus and John here tells me that you wish to serve the Empire."

"We do. You are the only people fighting the Normans and I would fight the enemy of my people."

He flicked a quick glance at John and nodded. "Leave your war gear here. John will make arrangements and we can go to my chambers which are more private and will allow us a more intimate conversation." We were led through the labyrinthine corridors which were behind the tapestry. His rooms were modestly furnished but had the most magnificent view of the Golden Horn. He lounged on a couch as did John but Ridley and I sat on the hard chairs; it was easier wearing mail. The strategos smiled at us. "You will soon learn to dress for the climate."

"We are warriors and have been so for many years. We are accustomed to wearing mail."

"John has told me who you are and, indeed, we have heard of you. Do not take offence at my next words but I do not see every Saxon who wishes to fight for the Empire but you are different. All the reports I have had of you have told me that you, like me, are a strategos." I now understood the delay; it had not been a mark of disrespect but rather a briefing from John who lay smiling beatifically at us. "I command an army and I am leaving later this day for an expedition and I would have you join me."

I looked over at Ridley who nodded in that confused way he had when he did not understand events. "Just like that, my lord? You would take us on my reputation?"

"As I said, I had heard of you before but your success on the river confirmed you as someone whom I could use. Let me speak plainly." I saw the smirk briefly appear on John's face and thought back to his words earlier. Should I trust this man or not? "When we lost the battle of Manzikert, I say we although I was not present, one reason was the lack of support from some of our mercenaries, the Normans and the Franks." I sat up my eyes wide with interest. "Ah, I see I have your attention now. Their leader Roussel de Bailleul was forgiven and led an army to retake Galatia. In that he was successful but we should have known better for he has set himself up as a prince leading his Norman cavalry to control the land." My face betrayed my thoughts and Alexios laughed. "John is right you are intelligent and see my purpose for I know that you have fought successfully against the Norman horse as well as the Pechengs. So will you serve with me and help me to capture and defeat this rebel?"

"As soon as I knew it was a Norman knight I decided to join you. But I am still a little confused. What is my role?"

"It is good to ask questions and to clarify now for later will be too late. You will command the small group of warriors who I have taken on. They are the ones Olef did not want for the guard." He gave a wry smile, "I think he only wishes for Norse warriors and seems to hate you and your kind of warrior. You will also advise me on the tactics I would use. You would command a Droungos of five hundred warriors. You would be the Droungarios in command and receive the appropriate pay."

"And Ridley?"

"Ah, the one who says nothing? It is true what they say of you, Aelfraed, you do think of others. I will ask bluntly and, as he is present, rudely, what is he like as a soldier and an officer?"

"He has commanded large numbers in England he is resolute and sound. Give Ridley a command and it is done. Ask him to hold a position and none will take it while he lives."

Nodding he said, "I knew this already but it is good to have it confirmed. He is a Komes and in command of two hundred of your men."

"Then I accept."

"Good. I believe that you were sent here for you are the last piece of the puzzle. You may have the answer to defeating these horsemen. John will take you to your men. You will have to become acquainted on the road for we leave this night."

"And our war gear?"

He waved the question away airily, "Oh John had it sent to the barracks. It is waiting for you there."

As we were led through the main corridors following the sprightly John I said, "He was confident I would accept."

Without turning he said, "Of course we were confident. Your hatred of the Normans means you would have accepted the post of an ordinary soldier. We all knew that."

I saw Ridley grinning at me and nodding. Was I so transparent? I had not expected things to move so quickly and I would need to get a message to Eric and the others. I just hoped that we would have time.

The barracks were the smartest looking warrior halls I had ever seen from the outside. The fine white stone was unblemished. Once inside however it was the same as any warrior hall save that it had more light and less smoke! Warriors are, by nature, messy creatures with everything but their arms and armour.

John entered and, taking a sword which was lying on a table began to bang with the pommel on the wood. The men inside stood silently watching with curiosity this little man who smiled benignly at them all. His piping voice reached those within thirty paces but I could see from the blank looks that those beyond heard not a word. "Men of the Saxon Droungarios I would like to introduce your two officers, the Droungos, Aelfraed Godwinson and the Komes, Ridley of Coxold." He turned to me. "They are now your commander. I will be along shortly to see if there is anything you require." With that, he almost skipped out. I wondered at his age, he could have been anything from fifty to seventy but he had a young heart that was obvious.

I knew they had not all heard John and so I stood on the table and spoke loudly. "I am your new commander. Some of you may have heard of the two of us. I served in Harold Godwinson's Housecarls with Ridley here and then I led my own men at Fulford and Stamford Bridge. I do not know you yet and we have little time to become acquainted for we leave this evening for war." There was a healthy murmur of approval and I held up my hand for silence. "Get your war gear together. If there are any shortages I need to know now! When your gear is ready, I will try to talk to as many of you as I can but know this first and foremost. We fight for the Emperor and the Strategos Alexios

Comnenus but I will expect the same standards and discipline as though we were fighting for our lord in a shield wall!" I was reassured by the banging of swords on shields. They were with me so far. I turned to Ridley, "Are you ready?"

He gave me a weak, lopsided smile, "As ready as I can be. I just don't know what is expected of me."

"That is simple, be a leader."

Ten men made their way towards me clamouring all at once for equipment. I realised that I had no way of noting it and I held my hands up. "Wait here and I will be back." I needed to find John. I had just left the building when he came scurrying along with two clerks. "Ah we heard the noise and my fellows here were worried that you were being murdered. I told them that it was the way of the Saxons to be noisy. I take it you need to make a note of what they require?" He was the most efficient man I had ever met.

"Thank you, John, that will help."

Once inside the numbers requiring our attention had grown but John was in his element. He put the two clerks on each side of the table and turned to me. "Separate them for me and put them in two lines."

"Ridley!"

The two of us pushed, shoved and cajoled the men into their lines and in a remarkably short space of time, there was just a gentle hum of conversation. John inclined his head and happily peered over the heads of the clerks. Ridley and I walked down the lines. Occasionally warriors would speak to us.

"I served alongside you at Stamford my lord, we whipped those bastards that day!"

"I fought behind you in Wales my lord when you killed their champion. That was a glorious day."

Others had not fought with me but they reached out to touch my arm, "I have heard of your fame my lord and it has always been my wish to fight alongside such a hero."

I was grateful for the praise but even more grateful for the English voices. It would make command much easier. The afternoon flew by as the list grew. John came over at one point. "Normally the Imperial Treasury would fit all of your men out in our armour and uniforms but we have not the time. The missing equipment will be regulation but when you return it will all be regulation. "

"Does that include weapons?"

He smiled, "You Saxons and your weapons. Are they all magic blades eh? To answer you they can use their own weapons but each man must have a sword and a spear as well as his shield. But you and your

Komes are to be kitted out with the new armour. The strategos does not want you to look like barbarians. Come we will get you kitted out."

I bridled a little at the insult, barbarians! But I suppose to the Byzantines, we were barbarians, uncouth and ill-disciplined. "Come on Ridley, the clerks can handle this now. Time for a change in armour."

As we followed John, Ridley whispered, "But I like my armour. I have had it since I became a warrior."

"Then it is time for you to change it then is it not?"

He was not convinced but when we reached the armoury he changed his mind. There was a thin mail shirt that was lined with cotton and leather over the shoulders. It felt much lighter than the one we wore. Above it was a corselet made of armour plates sewn onto leather. It was one stage further advanced from our own crude plates. The helmet covered the neck and the mail coif covered all but the eyes. The gauntlets were more metal than leather. When we donned it we were amazed at how light it was and finally, we were each given a tunic of white which we wore over it all. I looked dubiously at the tunic and John wagged his finger. "Before you complain, my lord, this will keep you cool when you got to war."

At the time I was sceptical but, as with all things, John was right. By the time we returned the men had all been equipped and they were lined up outside the barracks. When they saw us so finely dressed and armoured they took to banging their shields again. John shook his head, "I can see I will have to apologise to the ladies of the court. They are not used to such unseemly shouting." Before I could reply he wagged his finger again. "Come, my lord, it is time for you to embark. One of my clerks will take you to the boat."

"Are you not accompanying us, John?"

He looked appalled. "Me, leave the palace? Go amongst the barbarians and the heat? Dear me no. I will see you when you return and we will have armour such as yours for all your men," then he added darkly, "those who survive of course!" With that, he scampered off.

"Right Saxons. Two lines. Pick up your gear and try to keep together. I would hate to lose you before I know your name." We strode to the end of the line where the clerk waited with the rest of our gear. It was then I saw the two burly servants who stood with our bags and equipment over their shoulders. Officers were obviously treated differently here. We marched out of the gates and into the thronging city. The sudden noise after the quiet of the palace seemed to assault my ears. This time however we did not have to force our way through the throng for five hundred heavily armed and armoured barbarians have a way of parting crowds before they reach them. Soon we were like a

Varangian

parade as we tramped through the streets. We were not cheered but rather observed as something of an oddity, a freak show.

It was not long before I could smell the sea and knew that we were close to the port. As we turned along the quayside, I saw The Maiden being loaded and I shouted, "Saxons halt!" The clerk leading us looked less than pleased but one look at my face made him stand there mute. "Captain Gunnersson."

The Jarl's face appeared. "By Heavens is that Aelfraed looking so resplendent?"

"It is and I am leaving, I am going…" I suddenly realised I did not yet know where I was going, "It matters not. Could you get a message to Isaac that Ridley and I will be away for some time and we will see him and the others when we return?"

"I will. I see that you have fallen on your feet but not yet a Varangian?"

"This is better, these are Saxons."

My men heard the word Saxon and roared out, "Saxons!"

Stig and the others appeared at the rail and waved at the noise and I could see a wistful look in their eye which meant they wished they were with us. I heard a discreet cough from the clerk and I sighed. "We will have to go. Good luck on your journey."

They waved back and I heard Stig shout in broken English, "Look after Aelfraed, he is a prince!"

In answer, my men banged their shields again and I heard the clerk sigh his displeasure. He would be glad to be rid of us that was for sure. He had his wish granted soon enough when we reached the two ships which would transport us. "These are your ships Droungarios." With that, he left.

I looked at Ridley. "It would make sense for half the men to be on one ship and half on the other."

"That makes sense."

"You divide the men into two and I will see the captain."

I chose the largest boat and made for the gangplank. I dreaded having to speak for I knew not their language but the sentry recognised my uniform and stood aside for me to climb aboard. The captain was waiting for me and he saluted. I had never saluted before and did not know the protocol so I just saluted back. I was grateful that he spoke passable Norse which I could understand and speak. "This is the ship for you and half your men Droungarios. Your Komes will be aboard the other."

"Thank you, captain, I will tell them."

I returned to the quayside. "Take half the men on the other ship, I am to be on this one." I turned to order the men aboard, "Get aboard as quickly as you can."

As they tramped up the gangplank Ridley's panicked face loomed close to me. "What if they want to speak with me I can't speak Greek!"

"Don't worry, they understand Norse besides you can just talk to the men eh? As long as they feed you…"

We clasped arms and I boarded after the last of my men. At the top, I waved to Ridley as the servant returned to nod to me. As his arms were empty, I assumed that he had put them somewhere. I just hoped that I would find them. The captain came over to me. "The Strategos will be along shortly and he has asked the officers to meet him in his quarters. One of my men will show you."

"Could I just see my men first?"

He smiled, "Of course."

After I was certain that they were comfortable I was taken to the sumptuously apportioned quarters where there were many platters of food and jugs of wine. As I was the first to arrive, I chose a seat that allowed me to see all who entered and I waited, anxiously for my first meeting with my fellow commanders. I was going to war again.

Chapter 7

I was soon joined by the other officers who would be joining us. I had thought my armour and uniform to be magnificent but when they stepped into the cabin I could see that mine was as a grouse next to a splendid pheasant. I nodded to them as they entered but I dared not risk speech for fear of making a fool of myself.

The strategos followed soon after the last man had strode into the cabin. He had with him another of the ubiquitous clerks and officials I had met. He nodded to me and the clerk came next to me. "Aelfraed, I have brought this servant to translate for you and to help you to learn our language. I hope you are a quick learner." I gave a weak smile.

The strategos spoke and they all began to eat. The clerk began, "The strategos says to enjoy the food."

I gave a wry smile and said, "I got that. What is your name?"

"Aidan, my lord."

"And where did you learn to speak English?"

"I am English, my lord. From Holy Island."

I was intrigued, "How did you end up here at the Imperial court?"

"I was a priest and the Vikings captured me and sold me as a slave. I escaped and came down the rivers working as a rower on the boats. "

"That must have been hard after a life as a priest?"

"I was young and besides the life of a priest is not easy. Once I reached Constantinople my ability to read and write was recognised and I now work for the Emperor."

"Well, I hope you can teach me quickly Aidan and then you can return to the safer world of the court."

He smiled, "I think I shall enjoy the travel and, I assume you will not require me to fight?"

"No, I think my warriors will do that."

"Good, then the journey should be illuminating."

"Do you know where we are going?"

"I believe it is Galatia which is close to the land of the Seljuk Turk."

Alexios clapped his hands and all talk ceased. Aidan sat close to me and spoke quietly in my ear. It was then I noticed that he smelled of perfume. I had never known a man who smelled so but then I remembered that John also had a pleasant odour. The thought went through my mind that they must find my smell offensive. I resolved to ask Aidan about that when the meeting was over.

Varangian

"I am pleased that we are all together and that we can go some way to avenging the tragedy of Manzikert. Many of you know my feelings about this Norman traitor. Had he supported our Emperor then we would not have lost and now for him to set himself up as a prince in his own right goes beyond the pale. You will see a new commander amongst us. This is Aelfraed Godwinson who fought at Stamford Bridge. He will command the five hundred men of the Saxon Droungos. But our new leader also has experience of fighting the Norman horse whom he defeated a number of times. He will now tell us how he managed that feat."

He held his arm out for me to begin speaking. I was unprepared and I looked pleadingly at Aidan. "Do your best my lord and speak honestly." He gave a sardonic smile, "They will not expect that."

"You have mighty horsemen yourselves, the Cataphracts, but the Norman can ride more quickly than your heavy horse. We found that we had to defend our front with obstacles and force them into our axes. Their horses are not like yours, they do not wear armour and our axes found the horses easy to kill." One or two of the officers turned their nose up at this while others smiled. I think I had worked out who the cavalrymen were. "We also found we could use our mailed gloves to grip their lance as they struck and pull them from their horses. Once on the ground, they were easy to kill. But our best weapon was this." Branton had left me one knight killer as a souvenir and I brought it out. "We called this a knight killer for it can penetrate mail better than an arrow with a barb." I passed it around and they all looked at it with interest. "We had no horse to face the Normans but you do. I would imagine that your Cataphractoi would make short work of the Norman."

Alexios held the arrowhead in his hand. "Sadly that is not true. It is as you say the Norman horse is swifter and can evade us, but if our soldiers had these arrows it might make a difference. Thank you Aelfraed you have given me food for thought."

A tall soldier came up to us and spoke with Aidan. "I am Nicephorus and I command the Cataphractoi, although we only have five Kontoubernia. Not enough but all that we can take. I like these arrows; may I keep it to have more made."

"Of course for we serve the same man do we not?" He gave me a strange smile as though trying to read my words. Aidan said something to him and he shrugged and left.

"What did you say to him?"

"I told him that Saxon warriors always speak from their hearts and speak the truth."

"But we do!"

Varangian

"Aye my lord but you are now in Byzantium."

We reached our destination in two days and there was a mighty camp set up there already. It seems that Alexios had planned on taking the Saxons anyway and my arrival had been propitious as it gave them a commander and a focus. Although they did not have wyrd in their language Aidan told me that they called it fate and believed that it marked me as a lucky emblem. I could see the relief on Ridley's face when we met again. He had enjoyed getting to know his men, a pleasure I did not enjoy for I had to meet with the other senior officers but it did at least help me to understand their character traits. The cataphracts looked magnificent as they led their mounts down the reinforced gangplank. Covered from head to toe in armour as were their mounts I could not see how they could be defeated. Nicephorus had told me that they had a few weaknesses; they were so heavy that one charge winded them and they could not pursue and their enemies had taken to sowing caltrops, small pieces of metal with wicked points which always had a sharpened barb for a hoof no matter how it landed. I decided to get some just to protect us against the Normans.

Aidan was a resourceful man, as demonstrated by his ability to escape slavery, and he discovered where we were to be quartered. The Byzantines had learned much from Rome, from whom it was descended. The camp had a ditch and wooden wall surrounding it and the tents within were laid out in neat rows. The tents each accommodated eight men and there was one for the three of us. We left the men to sort themselves out and Aidan to arrange our tent and I took Ridley with me to meet Alexios for the conference he was holding. This was a much larger affair than the one on board the ship. I wanted to arrive early, partly to get a good position but more importantly to speak with the strategos alone.

The bodyguard recognised me and frowned at Ridley. I had picked up a little Greek by then, however crude it sounded, "With me!" He let us in and Alexios was at his desk poring over a map.

He glanced up at me, "You are early, commander. Trying to impress me?"

"No my lord but I thought that as my Komes had been on the other ship I might be able to let him know of your plans."

He nodded, "Sensible. Welcome, Ridley." He leaned over the map. "You will not know that this Norman has sacked Chrysopolis which is a town across the water from the city. It is the reason we are here. He has retreated to Ankara where he awaits us. He has at least three thousand cavalry and they outnumber us. As for his other troops we estimate that there are ten thousand soldiers under his command." He looked up from the map and his eyes bored directly into mine. "You should know Aelfraed that I intend to send you along with my light cavalry archers to watch his city for the army will have to move slowly as we are taking siege engines."

I studied the map even more intently. "Would I be able to have a copy of this?"

"Of course, send Aidan to me and he can make a copy."

"How many cavalry?"

"Four Droungoi."

"Not a large force then, strategos?"

"No, for you are not there to fight but to watch. The light cavalry are swift and can see much but if the Normans attack they will need to hide behind your wall of shields."

I smiled, "Shield wall."

"Yes, that is it. Do you know the ancient Romans had just such a device? They called it the testudo."

"Yes, my uncle told me of it."

"So you will build and defend the camp and watch the road to Ankara. In that way, we can arrive safely and without ambush and we will know what this Roussel intends."

"Thank you for that sir."

Just then the other officers began to drift in and Ridley and I made our way to the side so that I could observe them and their reaction to the briefing. Nicephorus nodded to me as he came in and gave me a half-smile. I had learned that a smile from a Byzantine can sometimes be the prelude to a knife in the back but Nicephorus seemed as honest as most men. I could not get over the magnificent armour which was paraded. The Byzantines might not have a huge army but the one they did have was well protected. Aidan scurried in and stood next to us, just before Alexios began. We already knew our role and all heads turned in my direction when our names were mentioned. The cavalry commander was Andronikos who nodded at me when his name was spoken. We discovered that we were taking a Thema of infantry from the region along with the cataphracts of Nicephorus and the engineers who would service the siege engines. I looked at Ridley when the numbers were read out. "We will be seriously outnumbered."

Ridley nodded but the grander plans were not Ridley's strong point. He could understand the men he could see but larger numbers meant nothing to him. I could see that Alexios was relying on the ability of both myself and the light cavalry to secure himself a base and I wished that we had had time to train the men and practise shield wall and wedge formations. Much would need to be done on the road.

Andronikos and I were asked to stay. "Your role is vital. You are both Droungarios and I expect you to work together." He gave an apologetic smile to Aidan, "It means, priest, that you will have to accompany Aelfraed into danger."

Aidan bowed, "It is my honour to serve." Aidan had learned the politic reply well in his time in this place of intrigue.

"You will leave tomorrow morning and remember you must secure a camp close enough to spy on the enemy stronghold and yet defensible. You must control the road."

Once outside, Andronikos shared his knowledge with us. "My men are from this region Droungarios and we know the area well. There is a round hill just to the west of the town which would be perfect."

"Excellent. How are your men armed?"

"We have bows and swords."

"Armour?" I looked at his own magnificent breastplate and mail.

"No, they wear a helmet only." He looked at us. "You will not be moving quickly."

"Faster than you think. An English army dressed as we are once marched over two hundred miles in four days and won a battle against the Vikings."

He looked impressed. "We may be quicker for we have wagons which will carry our tents." He held out his hand. "I look forward to this expedition and to fighting alongside men who carry such fearsome weapons."

I like Andronikos and he was not a man of politics. He was a young noble who was passionate about Byzantium and his one regret was that he had not been at Manzikert where his father had fallen. In all the time I knew him he never played me false and was a true friend; would that I could have said that about all my fellow commanders. He had told me that we would be marching for almost three hundred miles. The strategos had arranged for the few ships the Byzantine fleet had to accompany us along the coast which would be twenty miles to the north of us. In the old days, we would have all been transported closer to our destination but the fleet had been neglected. It meant that, if we were in danger, we could retreat and be evacuated by sea. I hoped it would not come to that. I decided that we would try to march at least sixty miles a day. That would be tough going but it would help to harden up the men and give me an idea of their ability. Ridley and I had discussed the men and realised that if they had taken the trouble to make their way to Constantinople then they already had a toughness about them on top of their natural ability. If they were not the elite yet they soon would be.

We left before dawn had broken for I wanted to use the cool of the morning. I took a risk that first day and told the men to put their mail in the wagons along with their axes. It meant we could be faster on the first day and Andronikos assured me that the people of this region were not aggressive. Once we neared the capital of the rebel homeland then we would need to be aware of enemy attacks.

By the end of the first day, we had covered seventy-five miles but we were too exhausted to build a camp and Andronikos offered to use his men as sentries. He had been impressed by the efforts of my men. "We could not have travelled much further today and we were mounted." He looked up at Ridley and me. "Are all your warriors as big as you two?"

We stood a head taller than the Byzantine and his men. I laughed. "No, but the Housecarls," I waved a hand at my sleeping men, "are always big men for their wear heavy armour and wield heavy weapons." I pointed to their ponies. "It is the difference between your swift ponies and the horses of the cataphracts."

"Ah, now I see. You have to stand and fight but we can evade and harry." He shook his head. "It must take bravery and courage to stand and know you cannot retreat."

"If we retreat, we die so we stand and we fight. That is what a Housecarl does." Aidan had fun explaining the word Housecarl. I had been impressed by the priest for he had not complained once but taken a great interest in the land around us. The next day as we once again made an early start, I spoke to him of his dreams.

"My dreams, my lord?"

"Yes, Aidan. What do you wish? Where would you like to be?"

"Jerusalem, my lord, in the land of the Turks. I would like to see the place where Christ was born."

I had not thought of that but we were as close to that holy place as any and I wondered what it would be like to see such a famous place. Such thoughts filled my head as we trudged eastwards through the heat, and the dust and the flies. The journey was uneventful until the end of the fourth day. One of Andronikos' riders galloped to a halt before us.

"My lord, the Droungarios begs to report Norman horsemen ahead, a large patrol."

I looked around and saw, about a mile ahead, a small hill topped by a wood. "Tell your commander I will take my men to that hill and form a defence." I was glad now that, for the past two days we had worn armour. The men had complained but it meant that we were now in a position to fight. I turned to them. "There are Normans ahead; I want us to run to that hill and form a shield wall." It says much for their past life that they all fell into the same rhythm of a steady run and all kept perfect time. The shield wall does that to a man; if you lose step in a wedge then you all die! I glanced at Aidan, although he was not dressed in armour I knew that we were far beyond what could have been expected of an aesthete, a priest. "Can you manage it, Aidan?"

"Yes my lord. I am discovering parts of my body I did not know existed before."

By the time we reached the hill, I could see the whirling horsemen of the Droungos as they retreated to our position. They were firing behind them as they came. Branton would have been impressed. "We have not formed a shield wall before. Thegn Ridley will be to my right. I want three lines forming. We will organise this better when we reach our destination." It could have been a disaster; five hundred men jockeying for position but, although they had not fought together before, they had fought in a shield wall and they naturally found friends and men of similar heights to stand next to and soon we had three lines with shields to the fore and spears in hand. I was impressed. I had placed us so that the wood was slightly to the west of us and protected that flank. With only three ranks there was plenty of room behind us.

Andronikos grinned as he rode up. "Well done my lord. You look like the hedgehog with a wall of spines. The patrol was made up of scouts and it is a column. There are less now than there were."

"Any foot?"

"No, purely horse."

"I would suggest your men on the left and to the rear of us. The hill will slow them up and your men can harass them with their bows. If you put a screen in front of us we might just give them a surprise." I was diplomatic and I gave the young noble the chance to choose his own dispositions but he nodded and gave his orders.

The Normans came on eagerly anticipating slaughtering lightly armed horsemen. As they came and I saw their pennants I saw that they were a mixture of Franks and Normans. The former were distinguished by the lack of a nasal on their helmets. There looked to be about four conroi and they were all heavy cavalry with no archers. They were in for a shock. My view was soon obscured by the hundred horsemen who screened us. I hoped that Andronikos would judge his moment well. "When the archers move stand firm. The second ranks will bolster the front rank. Those who have never faced a Norman charge fear not. Their horses die easily and a Norman on foot is like a one-legged man in an arse kicking contest." It was a familiar joke but they all laughed and it gave them confidence.

I could just make out the Norman line as it steadied for its charge. They were confident that they could brush aside the archers and then chase them. They placed a high value on their shields protecting them. I saw the archers loose three quick volleys and then I heard the command which made them all ride to the left. He had timed it well for they were but forty paces from us when the screen moved. "Stand by!"

The arrows flew from behind us to smack into the shields and ping off the helmets of the charging Franks and Normans. A couple of the horses went down but the armoured warriors still came on. I could see the surprise in the eyes of the lead warrior as he saw the shield wall before him. I had confidence that my men would know what to do and would not require any unnecessary orders and I concentrated on the lead rider. He was leaning forward with his lance ahead of his horse. I deflected it easily with my shield and then plunged Boar Splitter into his mount's throat. Even as it was dying it tried to move away from the pain and it reared up smashing into the warrior next to the leader. The Norman fell at my feet. The horse's death throes had disengaged the spearhead and I stabbed it down through the knight's open mouth. Ridley had killed his opponent and now the archers behind and to the side were having more success as the short-range enabled their arrows to find the chinks in the mail. I sensed them wavering and I took a chance. There was no one before me and I swung my shield behind me and stabbed Boar Splitter into the ground. I grabbed Death Bringer and yelled, "Front rank! Wedge!"

I knew that Ridley would know what to do and I hoped the rest would. I felt the men around me tighten up and I shouted, "Forwards!" The run to the hill had shown me that they were well trained and as the enormous one hundred man wedge began to move down the hill towards the milling Normans and Franks. They were taken by surprise and as our axes whirled before us, they tried to get out of the way but their path was blocked by riders trying to reach us. I cared not who I struck for I was intent upon causing terror. Death Bringer struck one horse in the flank almost severing its leg and on the backswing took a warrior's leg off. I could see blood on Ridley's axe as it sliced through the knights to my right. Andronikos took advantage of the mayhem and his warriors closed with the enemy loosing not only arrows but drawing their wickedly curved swords to hack at unprotected horsemen. It proved too much and I heard a Norman command I had heard before, "Retreat!"

Decapitating a dismounted and disorientated knight I yelled. "Halt!"

My men stopped and Andronikos led his whooping men to chase the Normans off our hill. My men began banging shields and cheering. We had won and the field was ours. "Despatch the wounded, Komes."

Ridley did not answer for I had used his title. "Ridley, that is you, you are Komes now!"

"Sorry, Aelfraed."

"See to our wounded, Aidan!"

Aidan scurried up so quickly he can only have been a few paces behind me. "Yes, Droungarios?"

"Help Ridley with the wounded." I held his arm. "Were you close to the battle?"

He shrugged, "I thought you might need me, my lord."

I shook my head as he ran to help Ridley. I could see Normans and Franks still falling as the eager horse cavalry pursued them. I turned to see my men behind me all grinning. "That felt good my lord! Your father would have been proud of the way you led us into their ranks!"

There were other such fulsome praise from my men but I just nodded. It was easy to lead if you knew you would be followed. We had butchered the dead horses and were cooking them by the time Andronikos arrived back. He jumped from his horse and embraced me, kissing me on both cheeks. "Magnificent. I had wondered what use you would be so heavy and slow but I have never seen Norman cavalry so put out unless by cataphracts. I can see why the strategos sent you."

"Thank you, Droungarios. Did you lose many men?"

"Twenty but that is a small price for over a hundred of their warriors lie dead and others will carry wounds but the biggest injury will be to their pride and their confidence. They rode here to flick us away like bothersome flies but instead they have a bloody nose. If we can make it to the town in the next day then I think we will have achieved all that could have been expected of us. And you? Many losses?"

"Eight dead and three wounded but they are grievous losses for they cannot be replaced. The Saxon Housecarl is no more. When we die we are the last."

He looked crestfallen. "I did not know." He watched as they began making the pyre for the dead. "They do not look sad."

"No, they are not for their comrades had died in a shield wall with a sword in their hand fulfilling their oath to the strategos. When they are burned their spirits will rise to join all the other Housecarls who fell before them."

The camp was made defensible and we all ate a meal which was hot and which was enlivened by each man's tale of their own part in the skirmish. Eric could have made many songs up. I sat with Ridley and Aidan while Andronikos went round his men and horses to see how many would be fit for the last part of the journey. "They did well today."

"Aye Aelfraed, especially as we had not had time to allocate the places."

"I do not understand my lord. Why does it matter where a man stands? Surely any place is good enough for a man to die?"

"Explain Ridley."

"You see Aidan, I stand to the right of Aelfraed because my shield can defend his right side, prevent others from attacking that side. The man to Aelfraed's left does not need to be as skilled for Aelfraed will protect him. The best warriors stand where we stood but the next in skill stand on the far right. There you need your most dependable men, men who will not panic; for, if the right falls, then the line folds up and we all die."

"Ah. And it is normal for infantry to charge cavalry?"

I laughed, "Good point and the answer is no but if the horses are tired and you have a slope then yes, you can charge. You choose your moment well. But we will not be so lucky the next time for they will bring archers and foot. The combination of all three means we have to stand and take our punishment. When we do that your skills will be more in demand."

Aidan had shown great skill as a healer. The main army boasted doctors but we were just a detachment and did not merit one. Still, the few wounds we had sustained would soon heal. Andronikos joined us. "The men are in good spirits. The Normans are a force that, before today, my men feared. They have now seen they can be beaten."

"I have said many times that a cavalryman without a horse is easy prey. Your men should shoot the horses."

"I know but it goes against the grain for a horseman to deliberately kill a horse."

I held up the piece of meat I was chewing. "I don't know why this tastes good!"

Andronikos shook his head, "I am learning much on this journey, Englishman."

We rose early knowing that we were within half a day of our destination. The cavalrymen were spread out in a thin screen well ahead of us for we pushed on hard the men buoyed by their success. Andronikos himself brought us the news that we were less than a mile from the hill which lay to the south of the main road into Ankara. He had placed scouts there and he told us we would be there within the hour. I was relieved as I had dreaded another encounter. Had I been Roussel I would have sent out a stronger force to deal with us but it seems he had been too busy or deemed us too insignificant for him to bother with. I wondered what the survivors had reported? I suspected we were a dilemma and he delayed; whatever the reason I would not look this gift horse in the mouth.

We still had plenty of fresh horsemeat and cooked horsemeat so I put the men to dig a ditch while others cut down small trees to make a rampart to surround us. I made it big enough for all one thousand of us and horses. Alexios was following us but he would not do the journey in four days. I suspected we would have at least five days to hold until they arrived. Aidan found a small spring which we used to fill the water skins and we had the three things vital to our survival: drink, food and protection.

Andronikos rode up to us. "I will keep half of my men on patrol and I have sent a Kontoubernion to the walls of the city to spy out the land."

By the time night fell we had a ditch, albeit shallow yet and we had the ramparts up. Andronikos had returned with his men. They had suffered eight losses when they went too close to the walls and archers sortied after them but they were able to report many banners on the walls and the ramparts filled with men. Our presence had alerted them; so Roussel had assumed that we were the vanguard of a larger army. What he did not know was that we were an isolated group and he could have swatted us away easily had he not been cautious. It was a good sign and bode well for the coming campaign.

The next day the cavalry continued to act as a screen with half of them resting ready for night sentry duty. Ridley and I organised the shield wall and wedge. Aidan had been standing at the rear during the battle and had seen which warriors took charge; he identified them and I gathered the five of them around me.

"You all distinguished yourselves the other day and I will reward you. You are all Kentarches."

They all beamed happily. Unlike serving a lord it meant more money and a better uniform. "Carl, you will stand on the right of the front rank. Egbert, the right of the second and Edward the right of the third. Ethelred, you will stand on the left of the first rank and William to the rear of the three lines." They all knew that each position demanded different skills and they were all pleased in their own way. "The Komes and I will be in the centre. You will need to organise the warriors near you. I would do this but I barely know you." I looked at each of them in the eye. "Know this. I have given all of you promotion which means I trust you. But we are Saxons and I know the oath you took to the strategos will mean you will behave well."

Carl shook his head, "We took no oath. We were hired to fight."

I shook my head. "Saxons fighting for money. We must have an oath."

Varangian

William looked at the others and then at me. "We could swear an oath to you my lord and that would be more binding than gold."

I pondered that. What would the strategos think? I turned to Aidan. "How would that sit with the strategos, Aidan?"

He laughed, "They have no concept of an oath. Their loyalty is not to the man but the office. When an Emperor dies a new one receives the same support," he paused, "So long as he lives."

I looked at each face. They all nodded. "Then let us make an oath."

The horse archers were bemused as my men all chanted their oath, cut their palms and shook hands with me."

Andronikos came over afterwards and said, "It seemed a little barbaric to me but your men all took it seriously. What is the point of it?"

Aidan answered, "It means they will never leave the battlefield before their lord, even if he is dead."

"But that means they would all die with him."

I nodded, "As did the Housecarls of my father at Senlac Hill when the finest Housecarls ever, died to a man protecting their lord's body."

Varangian

Chapter 8

The army of Alexios Comnenus snaked its way along the road. We could see them from miles away as they raised a huge cloud of dust. From our forward positions, we could see the towers of the city and knew that they too would be able to witness this mighty army. Having seen what constituted a patrol I suspected that we would be outnumbered but the one thing I had noticed about the Byzantine army was that it was well equipped and disciplined. The Normans thought they were well disciplined but, as their attack against us had shown, they were not. The strategos and Nicephorus rode up the hill to greet us. Andronikos had sent back regular reports and they knew the situation.

The strategos was beaming when he dismounted and he embraced Andronikos and me. "I have made at least two worthy appointments. Well done." He held me at arm's length and looked up into my face. "So is it true you charged cavalry on foot?"

I shrugged modestly, "It seemed the right thing to do."

Nicephorus shook his head. "I should like to have seen that and I hear you slew over a hundred of their men."

I waved my arm at Andronikos, "We slew over a hundred. It was a good combination of horse and foot working together."

Alexios nodded, "Which is the Byzantine way but it seems Saxons learn quickly."

The Byzantine engineers set to work making defences for the siege lines. We were observers but it was fascinating to watch. They used huge shields such as we had against the Pechengs to protect the men who dug the deep ditches and then placed the excavated soil as a barrier. The shields were then buried in the mound to provide an instant wall. Next, they began to build the siege machines which had been brought by wagon and were assembled. All the while Andronikos' cavalry provided a screen to deter any sorties from the city but Roussel seemed happy enough to watch from within and bide his time. As soon as the ditch was dug then Andronikos bade us farewell as he and his cavalry left to surround the far side of the city and prevent reinforcements and escape.

For the next four days, our role was as a spectator. The siege engines were built and they began to hurl their missiles at the gates and the walls. The strategos was a cautious man and he did not wish to waste his men's lives; here men were expensive while at home the poor fyrd were thrown into battle like chaff in the wind. Eventually, I was summoned to the command tent. By now my Greek was passable and becoming better each day. Ridley too had made such progress and I left Aidan with him to improve my friend's skills.

"Ah Aelfraed, I think we are ready to begin the assault." Nicephorus, his second in command, was with him and they had a model of the town built in the tent. "We are going to use a ram here." He pointed to the gate. The archers from the Thema will cover the walls but I want a shield wall around them." I nodded. I suspected more was expected of us than human shields. "When the ram has penetrated the gate you and your men will force an entry supported by the archers. As soon as you have control of the gate then we will send the rest in."

I nodded and looked at the plan. "What of this gate?" There was a gate on the opposite side of the city.

"Andronikos and his men guard there."

"When we attacked the Normans in Jorvik many escaped through the gate which was furthest away from the gate we were attacking. Normans and Franks do not like to fight on foot. I would position some heavier armed men there."

"My cataphracts are of no use in an assault. I will support the archers."

"Good. Prepare your men. We will attack as soon as it is dark." That made sense for our numbers would be hidden. The men were excited as I briefed them. "Leave your spears and cloaks here we will not need them. This will be axe work. I will lead the first wedge. Egbert will lead the second and, if we need it, Edward the third. Once we are inside we have to secure the gate. My wedge will form the shield wall while the others secure the entrance."

We followed the ram out of our defences. The onagers were still hurling rocks to weaken the gate. Once the ram reached the gate they would shift their aim to the walls. "Keep your shields up. I want no dozy bugger peeping over the top!" Ridley and I led the men in two columns. We were better protected and I felt confident that we would reach the allotted position without injury. The archers on the walls concentrated their missiles at the ram and that allowed us to get closer than I had hoped. Night had cloaked us well. The Komes with the archers said, "Here is good."

"Shield wall!"

We quickly formed three ranks. I dropped to my knees and felt the reassuring presence of a shield behind my head. With three rows of shields, the archers were as well protected as possible. Flight after flight flew over our head and then it became more sporadic as the archers chose their targets. We could hear the steady beat of the ram striking the heavy wooden gate. To those inside it must have seemed like the sound of a coffin lid being hammered shut for the gate was giving. A figure emerged from the back of the ram and I saw a white hand waved. It was nearly time.

"Front rank! Wedge. Egbert, take charge of the rest."

We formed almost instantly and I set off at a trot. The first two hundred paces would be the hardest. I had my shield held before me and my axe in one hand. The rowing and hauling the boat up the portages had built up my muscles and I could, for a short period, use the axe one handed. It meant I could still protect myself. The brave men in the ram heard our feet thundering and they pushed their ram through the shattered gates. If we were slow then the unarmoured men would be slaughtered. That would not happen. I could hear their screams as the defenders fell upon them but then we were there. I saw a knight raise his mace to strike a cowering soldier and Death Bringer struck to cleave his head and arm from his body. The grateful soldier ran out of the gate to safety. "Shield wall." The wedge was unnecessary as there was no force to meet us. The defenders were now pouring along in ones and twos. I heard Egbert leading the men behind up the stairs and the shouts, screams and clash of weapons as they took the gate. The men before us seemed in no hurry to attack us and I moved us towards them. "Forwards!"

The effect was twofold, firstly more of Edward's men could fill in behind us and the enemy retreated, actually most of them routed. When we finally captured Roussel's capital we found out that the stories of our defeat of the Normans had been exaggerated but none were brave enough to try us. For us, it was the end of the fighting. We had no blood lust for we had lost no one and the defenders surrendered. It seemed strange to us until one soldier told us that Roussel and his knights had fled when the gate was assaulted. I just hoped that Nicephorus had been there to catch him!

That night we ate well and slept well for we were inside. The strategos did not exact vengeance on the people for Roussel had deserted them. We ate, with the other commanders, in the Governor's magnificent dining room. We were all in good humour until an irate and angry Nicephorus stormed into the room, drank off a small jug of wine and then slumped into the empty seat we had left for him. There was a silence and then he seemed to see us for the first time. He jumped to his feet and gave a short bow to Alexios. "Apologies, strategos. They escaped." He nodded at me. "You were right Aelfraed. They did come out but there were over two thousand of them and, although we killed many, they outran us in the dark. We had too few to pursue. I ordered Andronikos to follow them with a bandon. I have retained the rest."

"At least you killed some and where will he go?" We now know that he has less than two thousand men. Once he has been found we will take the Thema and the Saxons with your cataphracts and defeat him. We will not need the siege engines again."

Nicephorus relented a little and actually smiled. Alexios was a good leader who was always calm. I never played him at chess but I suspect he would have been as good as Aethelward, if not better. However, he was wrong. We did need the siege engines but by then they were two hundred and fifty miles away, still in Ankara. The siege engineers who were with us were an encumbrance and we left them and a detachment of the Thema to manage the city and we loaded our war gear into the wagons and set off in pursuit of Roussel. We were a hundred and fifty miles from Ankara when a weary Andronikos reached us. "He has gone to Amasya."

Nicephorus and Alexios exchanged a troubled look. "Perhaps the people will eject him?"

"No strategos. I followed him to the city walls and the people there have made him governor."

"What is the problem, my lord? We just do as we did in Ankara."

Alexios smiled and Nicephorus shook his head. "Amasya is on a high mountain and the approach is difficult. It would be very costly to assault. Added to that there is access to the sea so that he could escape there and cause us more trouble. No, this problem needs a little more thought but at least we know where we are going now."

"Should I send for the siege train?"

"No Nicephorus, we need to strike quickly and the siege train would take over a week to reach us here and we are still only halfway there. We will see what our minds can come up with."

As we trudged north along the dusty road I now understood my uncle a little more. I had assumed that he had been merely fighting in the east but he had been learning from the Strategoi who sometimes use other strategies to obtain their ends. The Norns were still weaving and had not forgotten me here in the mystic east, all of my training was coming into play.

After a couple of more days on the road, we saw the high citadel rising above us. I could now see what Alexios meant. Even without the local garrison, the Norman could rain destruction down upon us as we struggled up the single road. It would take cunning to affect an entry this time.

Varangian

We made camp at the bottom of the road leading to the city. There were mounted guards at the head of the road but we knew we could chase them away when we needed to. Alexios ordered a fortified camp and we held a meeting to decide what to do. Aidan was present although my Greek was now adequate for such meetings.

Alexios began, "We need to make the people throw him out."

"Throw him out to us rather than letting him escape."

"Quite Nicephorus and the question is why would the people do that?"

No one had an answer. I spoke up after a few moments' thought. "You say they love him." Andronikos nodded. "Then we must make them fear us even more."

"Go on Aelfraed, you intrigue me."

"Has this city fallen before?"

"Only after a costly assault."

"They will feel secure behind their walls. They will have seen that you have no siege train and they will be waiting for you to waste your men in a useless assault against their fortifications."

"Precisely!" Nicephorus was becoming impatient with my build up.

I ignored him and said, instead to Alexios. "Are there men in the army who know the city?"

"There should be." He waved over an aide and whispered something to him. The aide left. "Go on. I feel there is an idea behind these questions and unlike our friend Nicephorus I have a little more patience." Nicephorus gave an apologetic smile.

"Suppose we created a little terror inside the city walls?"

"Terror?"

"Yes. If we could somehow get six or seven warriors in at night time they might cause them to believe that there were traitors in their midst."

"What sorts of things do you have in mind?"

"A city in a siege situation needs plenty of food and water. If they were threatened then the city is not as secure. They must be housing horses; if those horses were released from their stables and ran amok then damage would be caused."

The aide returned and spoke quietly to Alexios. "There are some men who lived in Amasya so there is a chance but would this not mean the deaths of these men. If they could get in and they could cause this damage then how would they escape?"

"Oh, they would have to escape. There should be no connection to you and your army. Then when you go and demand that Roussel is handed over they might be more amenable."

Varangian

There was a silence as everyone considered the plan. Alexios nodded. "If we could do all as you say then there are no drawbacks to this plan and it would work but where would you get men who were not connected to my army?"

"My men. We use some of the Norman and Frank armour we retained after the battle so that, if we are seen, and heard they will assume we are Franks for our languages sound similar to the Greeks do they not?"

Andronikos grinned, "They both sound like someone bringing phlegm from their throat!"

Everyone laughed and Alexios, after a moment or two held up his hand. "But how would you get in and out?"

"Getting in is the easier part. There will be some way in and those who know the city amongst your men, if they were soldiers, will know those ways. Getting out will be the same way and, if our work is not discovered then it will be easy but if they are seeking us then it will be more difficult."

Nicephorus looked at me. "You intend to lead this?"

"I could not expect my men to do something which I would not do myself."

"It is a risk, Aelfraed."

"It is what warriors do every day, strategos. They take risks. The difference is I have calculated the risks here and they are acceptable."

"How many men would you take?"

"Five others and me."

"But not Ridley." It was a command and not a question.

"Why not? My lord, he always goes with me."

"If you were to fall then who would command my Saxons? No, it is either you or Ridley who command this task but not both."

Without hesitation, I replied, "Then I will lead."

Alexios looked at the commanders in turn, Nicephorus nodded as did Andronikos and the others. "Well, reluctantly, I give you my permission but if you find it will not work then return for I would rather another strategy be tried than lose my Droungarios of Saxons."

Ridley, of course, was not happy and tried to persuade me to let him lead. "No Ridley, it is my plan." I drew him to one side out of earshot of my other officers. "Who is better at improvising old friend, you or I? I would have taken you but the strategos forbade it."

"I preferred it when we made decisions and did not have to follow orders."

"Aye, as do I, but the Normans put an end to that did they not? This is our first payment on that debt."

Varangian

Andronikos brought the two men who had lived in Amasya and they drew a plan of the city. Egbert found me five men to accompany me. All of my officers had volunteered but I knew that, if I did not return, then Ridley would need them even more. Besides, this gave me the chance to observe my men first hand. We even had two who could speak Frank, Tadgh and Gurth had both served as mercenaries for a Frankish leader and they would be invaluable. The others were Alan, Sweyn and Alfred. We first changed into the captured clothes. Ridley had been thinking about it and said, "You will only need the helmet and tunic. The armour would only slow you down and you just need to pass for the enemy."

I clapped him on the back. "Sound thinking. And we will not need shields so just take the Frankish swords and daggers."

When dressed we could not be differentiated from those Normans and Franks we had fought. The men from Amasya had found us a way in. "Here, lord, there is a small gate. It is guarded but the sentries use it to relieve themselves and to let the garrison smuggle items in under the noses of their leaders."

I looked at Andronikos. "Would they speak Greek or Norman?"

"I will send one of these men with you. They were both keen to join you within."

I shook my head, "No, they can come to the door and get us in but they must not enter. We need no connection to Alexios for this plan to work. We have to make them think that their new guests cannot be trusted."

The two men nodded and agreed to come with us. They too dressed as Franks but they still looked like Byzantines close up but they would wait for us outside the gate and guard our exit. If we were seen fleeing then they would still look like us. To make it look as though we were men from Roussel's contingent who had planned this we would have eight horses tethered close by and our escape route would be towards the coast where Andronikos would wait with a bandon of cavalry.

Nicephorus cleared the guards at the head of the road before dusk. His frustration at losing Roussel was lessened as he, at last, had action and the guards fled back to the safety of the city. His men held the pass while we rode over the ridge and dropped to a spindly stand of trees eight hundred paces from the walls. It was pitch dark but there was the thin white mark of a rough trail. The two Greeks led us down the path. We halted in a small gully while we watched the men on the walls. They were not expecting an attack from this side for there were only two sentries on the whole length of the wall. We ran the last few paces to the gate and then my men split on either side; their daggers drawn.

Varangian

The two Greeks, who had poured wine down their tunics to make them smell of alcohol knocked noisily on the door and demanded, drunkenly to be let in. The door opened and the two Greeks feigned a backwards fall. The two guards came out laughing at their discomfort and, as they leaned forward to help them up we slipped out and slit their throats. We dragged the bodies back inside to make it look as though they were killed on the way out and then, leaving the two Greeks to watch the door, we entered the citadel of Roussel de Bailleul.

I had memorised the route to the well and led the way. This part of the fortress and city was deserted and we made swift progress. I hoped we would not meet any Franks for they would soon realise that we were intruders and I felt guilty that we would be killing the Greek soldiers but they had made the wrong decision in supporting this traitor, or at least their leaders had and, as in any conflict it is the poor soldier who pays the price for his leader's mistakes.

There were two Greeks guarding the well. They looked up when they heard our approach but relaxed when they recognised the uniforms. Their bodies were dumped in the well. That part of our plan had worked. We could have left then but I wanted the populace to be rid of their guests speedily. We headed towards the granary. I knew that it would be guarded but I relied on the fact that it would be Greeks who would do so. Again the guards allowed us to approach and paid the price. The grain was in huge silos and I wondered how best to spoil it. Alan spied the brazier and we emptied it into the grain which, as it was dry began to burn. Now we had to work speedily and we went to the stables. Here I was certain that we would find Frankish or Norman guards and I placed Tadgh and Gurth at the front.

There were four guards at the entrance and they viewed us suspiciously. Gurth said something and they relaxed a little. We approached a little closer and one of them spoke to Alan who shrugged. We were now less than five paces away and as I saw their leader, a sergeant from the look of him, begin to draw his sword, I shouted, "At them!" They were brave men but only one his sword drawn and our daggers were in our hands. All four fell but not without much screaming and shouting. Alan's arm was bleeding and my original plan would not now work. "Sweyn begin the fire. The rest of you release the horses and get on one, we will drive them through the city to the gates." I helped Alan to mount and Tadgh held Sweyn's horse for him. Sweyn had thrown the brazier on the hay which soon caught fire. We mounted and then shouted at the terrified horses to make them stampede.

I rode ahead of the men and horses to lead them to the gates. There were just two Greeks at the gates and they fled in fear as the wall of horses galloped towards them. I dismounted and began to lift the bar on the huge double gates. I could hear, in the background, the sound of alarm and arrows began to thud into the wood. Sweyn jumped down to help me for, even with my strength, I was struggling. The two of us managed to throw down the bar and, with the gates opened the horses fled to freedom. I felt a sharp pain in my shoulder as I mounted but as we struck the road I could see that all of my men were there. I just hoped that the two Greeks had heard the noise. As we headed for the camp I turned to Tadgh. "Ride to the other horses and bring our Greek friends."

Looking behind me I saw the flames flickering from the two fires. Unfortunately, our plan had not worked the way we had hoped and we were heading in the wrong direction, we were heading for the Byzantine camp. Alexios and Nicephorus were waiting for me. "What went wrong?"

"There were more guards than we expected and they raised the alarm." As I started to dismount I felt a sudden pain in my shoulder and I fell to my knees. Aidan and Ridley were close by and they raced to my side.

"You are wounded, my lord. You have an arrow in your back!"

"Fetch a surgeon. Lie down Aelfraed."

I shook my head, "Not until I know the others are safe."

Just then Tadgh and the Greeks galloped in leading their string of horses. Then I sat down. As I did so I had a sudden idea. I could see the concern on Alexios' face and I smiled. The arrow wound was nothing. I had had worse. "Do not worry strategos, I will not die and I have an answer to our problem. Tomorrow you take me and my men, bound to the gates and say you captured us. Tell the people you will exchange us for Roussel."

"That might work, but your wound?"

"We will make it even more convincing. I assume there is blood on the tunic?"

"It looks like a pig has been slaughtered."

"Good, then when Roussel is handed over we will have won." I gave them a sardonic smile, "Unless you do actually hand us over to them."

Alexios laughed, "No my friend, although I believe you are resourceful enough to escape if we did do that."

By the time dawn broke the surgeons had dressed my wound and I recognised Reuben's paste! When they offered me the white powder I declined for I knew I would need my wits about me at the exchange. We had to assume that they would think that we, as Norman rebels would not wish to stay with the Byzantine army and they would not expect us to return to their ranks. With my wounded shoulder and Tadgh's arm in a sling, we did look as though we had suffered.

Nicephorus rode up to the gate and made our demands. When he returned he was grinning. "It seems that we did not need to make the exchange. The city fathers want nothing more to do with Roussel. They have him and his lieutenants in chains and they say we can execute the prisoners for them." He turned to Alexios. "They apologise for making an error in judgement my lord."

Alexios laughed, "Well Saxon it seems your Byzantine plot has succeeded. You have learned our ways as well as our language."

I was glad that we did not have to continue with our ruse, I felt I had tempted *wyrd* just a little too much and the Norns' webs had pitfalls and traps within them. I was looking forward to meeting Roussel. He seemed to me to be a resourceful man. I think he was trying to emulate the Guiscard brothers in Italy and carve out his own kingdom as they had done. When he reached our camp he did not have the arrogant look of William of Perci or Guy of Evreux, the other Normans I had met. He seemed to have a pleasant disposition which is why I assume, that the people of two cities took to him so readily. He and his men made obeisance to Alexios and begged forgiveness for their indiscretions. Alexios was not moved by their pleas and turned to Nicephorus. "Escort them back to Constantinople and imprison them. I will let the Emperor deal with them. We will follow with the army."

As he was led off he halted close to me. He spoke in Greek to me, "Are you the Saxon who gave my men a bloody nose?"

"I am, Aelfraed Godwinson."

His face showed that he knew me. "Ah, the bastard who gave The Bastard the run around in England. And from your disguise, I assume that you were the ones who spoiled my stay in Amasya?"

I gave a slight bow, "I had a part in it."

He nodded. "It is a pity that we will not have time to talk of your life for I think we would have much in common."

As he was led away I hoped that was not true although, like me, the Norman appeared to be a survivor. Alexios watched him depart. "If the Emperor has sense he will execute that snake for he is slippery and full of guile." Then he smiled at me. "I am pleased that John brought you to meet me for you have already saved me the lives of many men but," he wagged an admonishing finger at me. "You are a Droungarios and I think one day perhaps a Tourmache or even a strategos so be a little more careful and take fewer risks."

Ridley and Aidan fussed over me and I knew that Ridley was unhappy about being left behind. As we trudged along the road back to the capital I took the opportunity of explaining our new life. I had to admit that it had taken turns which I had not expected but I knew that my life was being directed by someone other than me.

"Listen, old friend. Remember when you became Thegn of Coxold and you did not like to be away from me and my men."

"I remember."

"Well remember how you felt when the Normans slaughtered your people. They meant more to you at that moment than I did and that was right and proper. You are now Komes and command more men than the fyrd and your men at arms. Like your fyrd, you will come to care for them and when you take over from me as Droungarios you will have all of them under your wing. I will always be there, Ridley, but we cannot always fight side by side." I shrugged, "It is *wyrd*."

"I know, Aelfraed, but I would go back to the times when we fought for your father."

"Ah, but we can never go back."

Aidan gave a small cough. "Have you never thought of embracing the Church, my lords. You can find much comfort in God and Christ."

"I dare say Aidan but when you have seen the cruelty as we have you wonder if the God who allows that is your kind and thoughtful God."

"But you believe in God do you not?"

"I believe in a God but I think there are other forces directing us."

He shook his head. "I can see the pagan world in you two."

I waved a hand at the men behind us. "I think you will find it close to all of them. They would all rather die with a sword in their hand than a cross. You are welcome to be a priest to them Aidan but do not be surprised if they do not welcome your ideas. To a man of God, your God is understandable and reasonable but to a man of war, he is not. We do not turn the other cheek."

I did not mind Aidan's attempts to change me. It was his job just as my job was to fight. I think I did my job better for he never convinced us but I became even better at fighting and killing in this new Byzantine world.

Chapter 9

Constantinople 1076

By the time we had reached Constantinople my wounds had healed and both Ridley and I could speak Greek well. We could even speak some other languages and we bade farewell to Aidan as we landed. He would go back to the palace and his duties as a clerk. For a brief time, he had been a priest once more but he had failed to convert any of us to his ideas. My men were still the warriors they had always been. What delighted me was the swagger as they stepped off the transports. They had had the most fighting of any of the warriors involved and they had emerged with the most glory. While they had not been lacking in confidence when I took charge now they were brimming with I and it showed. I allowed Egbert, Edward and the others to lead them through the city. We were the first to return as we were the easiest to transport and they enjoyed the cheers of the crowds. Word had got out that the danger in the east had been averted and that the rebels had been captured. We had spent some time securing the province and Roussel had been returned for over a year with Nicephorus taking much of the credit for his capture. I suspected Nicephorus had spread that tale.

Ridley and I headed for Isaac as I was keen to know what had become of my comrades, Eric in particular. While on the road I had worried about the youth and, although I knew that Snorri and Ragnar would watch over him I still felt a certain responsibility to his father. The journey took much longer than on our previous visit; the people seemed happier and more optimistic. The streets were thronged. The threat from Roussel having been averted meant that life was easier. The name of Alexios was on everyone's tongue. Now that we understood their language it was easier to hear what they were saying.

Isaac's premises were in the Pera, close to the other traders and merchants such as the Venetians. Our last journey there had seemed swift and we were ready to the coolness of the interior when we arrived. He was delighted to see us. "I have heard, my lord, of your triumph. When you and your Saxons defeated the Normans there were great celebrations in the city."

I had forgotten what it was like to live in a civilised place where news could be delivered swiftly and one did have to rely on hearsay. "Thank you, Isaac, and we may be back for some time now. We will be receiving our back pay tomorrow and we will return to invest it with you."

"I am honoured that you trust me so."

"Where are Eric and the others?"

He smiled, "Eric is here, he works for me now in the mornings and he is free in the afternoon to continue his studies. Eric! We have guests."

When Eric emerged from the back I almost did not recognise him. Gone was the Danish boy and before me I stood a perfumed, Greek scholar dressed in fine silks and with oiled hair. He made a slight bow and then rushed to see us. He kissed us both on the cheeks. Perhaps because we were still road weary and soiled he smelled overly perfumed but he looked well. "No need to ask how you are doing, you have prospered."

"Isaac has been kind and with the money from the voyage we live quite comfortably."

"We?"

"Ragnar, Snorri and I share a house."

"Snorri did not go back to war?"

"No, it was not for him. I do not think his heart was ever in it."

I could not understand that; Snorri had been one of the best warriors who had ever fought beside me. He was the equal of Aedgart and Osbert which was the highest praise I could give. "What does he do?"

"He works with wood and Ragnar helps him. He is highly skilled and makes fine boxes and furniture which is much sought after."

"And you Eric, how do you fill your afternoons then?"

"I spend my time in the libraries. I can now read and write in Arabic as well as Greek and I have begun to write. It is wonderful here for there are many such as I who like poetry and song. It is different from home."

"But they had songs and sagas at your home in Hedeby."

He laughed and it was a high tinkling laugh that seemed to suit the perfume and the clothes. "No, that was barbaric with hairy men spilling their beer and chanting. Here it is more civilised."

I could see that Ridley was not convinced but the Norns had spun their threads and he was happy. *Wyrd* had sent him here. "We are here for a while. We will try to visit you."

He almost clapped his hands with delight. "Oh do. Come tomorrow evening for some food."

"Where do you live?"

"Just off the Makios Embolas near to the tower. When you pass the tower ask for the shop of Eric and Snorri."

As we headed back to the barracks Ridley looked perplexed. "He has changed."

"I suspect we all have."

"No, I mean, was it just me or did he smell like a woman?"

I laughed. "I don't know if you have noticed Ridley but many people in the east smell of perfume and they avoid us for I fear that we stink!"

He looked indignant. "I do not stink! But he seems a different person now."

"Did you like him still?"

"Of course but be seemed different."

"Do you remember in Jorvik, when you had your berserk moment?" He nodded. "Well, I was busy fending people away from Reuben because they thought that he was different. We cannot all be the same and I would not wish it so. If Osbert met us now he would say we were different."

"Not me!"

"Did you trim your beard, or comb your hair in Medelai?"

"Well no. We were living in the wild."

"For the past few months we have been on the road but you have begun, as have I, to look a little cleaner."

"Well, that is just because the other officers all do so."

"Exactly we want to fit in and Eric is doing the same. He is fitting in with the other poets and scholars. Change is not a bad thing Ridley."

He was silent for the rest of the journey. I knew Ridley and this was what he did. He ran the new ideas through his head and worked out the answers himself. He would see what I had seen but it would take him a longer walk to do so. Ironically the first thing we did back at the barracks was to go to the bathhouse and enjoy the rest of the afternoon in hot baths, cold plunge pools and then a massage and an oiling of the body. Andronikos had told us of the pleasures as had Egbert and Edward. I think Ridley was more impressed by the recommendation fellow Saxons than the Greek but he enjoyed it none the less. That evening we were shown, by the men, to our officer quarters. Ridley and I both had our own chamber complete with bed and chests for our war gear while the others shared one room. This was different from the crude camp in the forests north of Medelai and was a reflection of our new status and role.

The next day the Imperial Quartermaster came down to pay us our back pay. The cynical side of me thought that it was astute as they saved the money on those who died. We were, however, well paid and Ridley could not believe the purse he received. Edward explained that we received a bonus from the money levied from the captured cities and the ransomed knights; a totally different experience from that of fighting for your beliefs. We were given the rest of the day off as

Alexios wanted to brief the Emperor before meeting with his officers. We decided to buy some clothes that were not for war; clothes which would be cooler in the hot streets of Constantinople. Isaac advised us and we returned in the afternoon to pay him our money. He also agreed to buy us some wine for our quarters. Much as we both enjoyed ale and beer, the east was not the place to find such drinks and so we followed the trend of Byzantium and drank wine.

When we reached the home of our old friends I was impressed with it. The stonework was fine and there was a wonderful mosaic in the entrance. Ragnar had not affected the Eastern style of dress and he knelt to kiss my hands. I raised him to his feet. "No Ragnar, we are friends now, old friends. I am no longer your master."

He mimed that I would always be his master and I shook my head. He and Ridley embraced and then Ragnar led us through to the courtyard which had a small fountain dotted around with lemon trees, olive trees and oranges. Before reaching Miklagård I had never even seen one of these exotic fruits and now my friends cultivated them! Even the functional and practical Ridley was taken with the serene qualities of this oasis in a busy city. I almost did not recognise Snorri when he emerged from the upstairs with Eric. He had shaved his beard and his hair was cut in the style of the Byzantines with oil-slicked upon it. He was dressed in flowing robes and, like Eric, heavily perfumed. His eyes had not changed and I saw in them the real Snorri. He strode over to embrace me. "My lord, I am glad that you have returned from the east with so much success."

"And I am pleased that you too have found success."

He embraced Ridley and then said, "Success, peace and happiness."

"You no longer yearn for the shield wall?"

He laughed, "Yearn for heaving sweating bodies and the likelihood of death? No, my lord, I think not. Come sit and take some of this."

He poured us a drink chilled with ice and flavoured with lemons. It was refreshing. What a change from the lives all three of them had lived before they came to Constantinople and, as we sat at the table to eat I thought again about the Norns. I was happy for them to chatter on about their day to day lives while I thought back to the thread which bound us. Had I not fought with Calum, Earl of Fife and fled to Leith I would not have boarded the boat to Denmark. Eric would still be unhappy at his father's court, Ragnar would still be languishing with the thralls and Snorri would be dead in the land of the Pechengs. One life, two if you counted Ridley as a separate being, affected so many others.

Eric, who was always sensitive to others, sensed my distraction. "Come Aelfraed, what of your life and your adventures?"

"You have probably heard much on the streets but it has been interesting," I told them of our journey and Ridley added detail that I had forgotten.

Eric nodded. "That is interesting for Nicephorus who returned last year told a slightly different tale. Oh do not get me wrong, you and Alexios were given credit but the ideas, the strategy were claimed by Nicephorus Botaniantes." I could not speak in Isaac's shop for, although I trust him, there are others there in the pay of the various factions in the city. Nicephorus is now a strategos and is close to Emperor Michael who, it is said, tires of being Emperor."

I could not conceive of tiring of such power. "So you are saying he is more powerful than he was?"

"I am saying that he is a good man to stay on the right side of for he may be the next Emperor or if not he will decide who the next Emperor will be."

"He was just one of the staff when we left and now he has been promoted."

"His family have influence and he is ambitious." He shrugged, "When we read and study we also talk and many of the others have ears around the city."

"What happened, my lord, to your wish to serve with the Varangians?"

"A Norseman, Snorri. The leader fought at Stamford and hates all Saxons and me in particular. I was told in no uncertain terms that I would be dead if he or his men found me!"

"Will you be long in the city?"

"I know not. We have a meeting tomorrow with the other officers and I daresay we will find out then."

"Well, you are always welcome here. And if there is aught I can do for you…"

"Thank you, Eric, there is one thing, well two really. One is to find out how things are in England. I would like to know if my men still fight and I would know how Stig and the others fare."

"I will discover news of England but I can tell you of Stig. He is now an important leader. He has a hundred men who guard the boats. Jarl Gunnersson also commands more boats and they sail down the rivers together. Their success means that more merchants use them." I nodded, pleased. "A half smile played upon Eric's lips. "They have a new powerful boat called, '*The Aelfraed*' and Stig calls his men the men of the Red Horse."

I was touched and, as I looked up at Ridley I could see that he felt the same. "When you see them tell them that I am honoured."

"They will be sorry to have missed you but I am pleased beyond words that you have graced our home."

Snorri and Ragnar both nodded. "For myself, I can just say that this has been the most peace I have known for many a year, thank you."

The briefing the next day was for all the senior officers and I left Ridley to check on the equipment of our men and to begin their training. I did not know when we would be needed again but the briefing suggested sooner rather than later.

The strategos looked pleased with himself as he greeted us all. This time I was not the newcomer and all of the other commanders knew and respected me. We had fought together for over a year and you get to know the qualities of a man in that time. I had been close to Nicephorus but his early departure meant that I was now closer to the others. Andronikos, in particular, warmly greeted me. He had developed into a cunning commander of light horse and had made significant improvements to his men's arms and armour. "Welcome gentlemen. It seems that our success has put us in great demand. It seems there is unrest around Dyrrhachium and we are to be sent there to quell the insurrection." He glanced around the room as the murmur of conversation rose. He held his hands up and the room became silent once more. His voice seemed quiet as he continued, "I am afraid, Andronikos, that your horse will not be as useful in the mountains as they were in Asia and we will not have the benefit of cataphracts, although I am not sure of how much use they would be in the mountains." He smiled at me, "However I am sure that our Varangian Saxons will prove as resourceful there as in Asia."

I took his praise as a compliment but I was not sure how my men would cope with uneven terrain. A shield wall worked best when it was a continuous line on good ground but I also knew that my men were confident and, given time I could train them to perform individually as my warriors had in England in the woods above Medelai.

He became serious. "We have now lost all of our territories in Italy and Sicily to the Normans and I hear that Robert Guiscard is casting his greedy eye across the waters to Serbia. We need to ensure that the province is loyal and a buffer against the Norman threat." I felt the cold shiver run down my back as the Normans were mentioned. The Norns were sending me close to my Nemesis and that made me even more determined to have the finest force I could. "We have three days. We will be taking wagons but we need no siege train." I saw the disappointed look on Basil, the siege train commander's face. I nodded sympathetically. It would be hard to remain behind while comrades were off fighting for we had all become close. Alexios gestured for me to join him as the others pored over the map. "It seems the commander of the Varangians has dismissed other volunteers from England. There are fifty more men waiting for equipment and training." I brightened. That more than made up for our losses. "The title Varangian Inglinoi appears ever more appropriate."

Ridley and my other officers had wasted no time in training and equipping the new men. I watched them for a while and then, as the noon meal break approached, I asked my officers to join me. "We have three days to turn these into a fighting unit and we also need to train them to fight in smaller groups." Ridley nodded, he knew there would be a way but the others looked sceptical. "Do not worry about their ability to do so. They are resourceful. How else would they have managed to make it all the way here from England? After they have eaten split them into Kontoubernia. We need one man to lead each unit; he will be the Dekarchos and paid accordingly. Choose your men well for they will need to be able to command on their own. We will then train them to fight in pairs."

Edward looked puzzled, "In pairs, my lord? That seems a hard task."

"No, I have been talking with scholars and the other officers. There were warriors in the ancient past, the Theban Band of Thebes. They fought as pairs, protecting each other. "I pointed at Ridley. "Ridley and I have done so for years. Whenever the shield wall broke we protected each other." I risked a jibe, "except of course when my friend went berserk once." They all laughed for they loved that story. Ridley just reddened and I was pleased that he had learned to laugh at himself. "The Kontoubernia will then need to fight as a shield wall." I could see that they were uneasy. "We are going to fight in the mountains to the west. Ridley and I have fought in Wales which is similar but even that, apparently, is gentler. We will not have the luxury of even ground and the shield wall will not hold and the wedge will need to be more flexible. We have three days to train the men to move from shield wall to pairs, to small shield walls and wedges and back. Each of you may end up leading your own wedge if the occasion arises. I know that you can do this. All of you were trained as warriors and Housecarls; Ridley and I by the best, Sweyn. You will succeed, I know it."

They left, happier. Ridley joined me. "You are right, Aelfraed, and they will see it."

"I know but there is one more change that affects you. You and I will need to be able to take charge of half of the men." I pointed at the departing officers. "There are five of them which gives them command of, roughly a hundred men. You will command two hundred and I three hundred so that we are more flexible. Our cavalry will not be of much use and the Thema at ten thousand warriors is too big. I can see us having our work cut out."

The men responded well to the training and the new officers were delighted with their extra pay. The new men enjoyed the new armour they were given and the hobnailed shoes which replaced a whole variety of footwear. Once in the mountains, they would prove invaluable. We had no time to visit our friends again but as we marched from the city out of the Adrianople Gate I saw them in the crowds cheering us. I heard Snorri's voice ring out, "Remember Senlac Hill!" When my men heard that they began banging their shields and I saw Alexios turn around and give me a wry smile. The Varangian Inglinoi were never quiet, as Andronikos said, "You always knew where the Inglinoi were whether in camp, marching or on the battlefield!"

We headed west and this time our route was along better roads and was safer for we were still in the Empire and the lands which had been ruled by Rome and its descendants for over a thousand years. I explained to Ridley, as we marched along, what I had discovered about the area which was causing trouble. "It has only recently been recaptured and rejoined the Empire. The fact that it is close to the Normans in Italy is a cause of concern. Many of the people there are happy to be under Byzantine rule but there are men who seek power, a little like Roussel and take the recent losses at Manzikert as a sign of weakness."

I could see that Ridley was troubled. "But Aelfraed, are the people there not as we were in England, fighting an invader?"

"No Ridley. The land belonged to Rome since the time of the Caesars. It is the newcomers who are as the Normans; trying to seize a little power."

That reassured him and he looked happier as we trudged along the straight, cobbled roads built by the legions of Rome.

Once we neared the troubled area we took to a more defensive formation. We still had the same army which had destroyed the mercenary rebels. Not a huge army but a well-led one. We could see the burnt out farms and villages which reminded me of England and the Normans. The people we met were wary of us for they had grown up in a land not ruled by the Emperor and the new lawless phase made them look to themselves. Andronikos and his men had been scouting far ahead and they reported a rebel stronghold. It was in the mountains and they had an old Roman tower that had been added to make a sturdy fort. Alexios decided to use this as our first opportunity to show the rebels that they had to submit to Byzantine rule once more. The warriors used a variety of weapons and tactics. They were superb horsemen and the horse archers we had brought began to suffer increasingly damaging casualties. Alexios decided to keep them close to the main army which annoyed Andronikos but he accepted it was necessary. We also found that they were almost suicidal and fanatical for their unarmoured warriors would attack us at night wielding their wicked curved swords they called the rhomphaia. Sometimes it was used attached to a pole and caused great casualties amongst the cavalry. I was told, when we returned to Byzantium, that the Varangians all used the rhomphaia. I never cared for it as you could not use it effectively to stab but it was highly efficient as a slashing weapon.

I first met one when we camped close to the first fortress and they made a night attack. At the first scream from the dead guard, I was awake and grabbed Death Bringer. I leapt from my tent and saw a Thracian almost cut one of the sentries in two with his blade. He saw me, emerging from my tent and must have thought I was one of the effete Greek officers from one of the other regiments. He raced fearlessly at me with the long sword above his head. I held Death Bringer behind me while watching the sword. As soon as I saw it descend and that he was committed to the stroke I stepped aside and brought Death Bringer around to cut his body in two. The other raiders were all despatched but three of my men lay dead a grievous loss.

We had waited at the foot of the hill near the fort for a week and this had been the third attack; my men's morale was beginning to dink and, as the bodies were taken away, I stormed to the command tent. I should have halted but the sentry, who knew me, quickly stood aside to avoid being bowled over. Alexios was standing over the map with Andronikos. "Staring at the fucking map will not get the hill fort taken! When are we going to stop sitting on our arses and take this place?" I could converse in Greek but when I was angry I reverted to English and Andronikos only understood a couple of my words, he did, however, understand the meaning and he took a step back.

Alexios gave a small smile. He was always a calm and calculating man. "Ah, the impulsive Englishman who cannot get out of the habit of speaking his mind. I fear we will never make a Byzantine out of you."

I had calmed a little and I answered in Greek. "Perhaps Byzantine commanders do not mind their men being killed for no good purpose but I value each one of my men for they are hard to replace."

"Then you come at the right time for we were planning just such an attack although the manner of your arrival leaves much to be desired."

I gave a weak smile and felt myself redden, "Apologies, strategos. I speak too passionately."

Varangian

"It is part of you. I wish it was not but without it, you may not be the warrior you are. Now to the problem in hand. Andronikos?"

He grinned at me, "It is my fault we have delayed Inglinos; we have been scouting around the hill fort. It is well made for the base was constructed by Pompey's legions and it is soundly made. There are cliffs and steep slopes at all but the four gates and they are well protected by towers. Even if we had rams we could not use them for the roads are cunningly made and twist and turn but we will have to try and build them for there is no other way."

I went to the map and the sketch the cavalryman had made. "Is the gate wood or metal?"

"It is wood but studded with iron bolts. It is thick."

Alexios looked at me with curiosity written all over his face and I had the confident look of someone who has the solution. "Is the door as thick as a large oak tree," He looked confused, "Or a cedar from the east?"

"No, of course, it is less than half the thickness of a tree."

"Good, then I can get you in."

I went to the table and poured myself a goblet of wine which I drank in one. "Would you mind explaining how?"

"We divide my men into four groups and each one makes, what the Romans called a testudo. Then, when we are at the gates, we use our axes to cut them open."

"But the metal bolts?"

"The more bolts there are then the weaker the gate but I would guess that the bolts are at least a hand span apart." Andronikos nodded. "Then the axes strike in the gaps between them. We are accurate when we use them you know. It may look like blind swinging to you but we aim and we always strike where we aim. Of course, we would need your horsemen to keep them from shooting too many arrows or throwing too many stones."

Andronikos slapped the map table. "That might just work."

"And you, of course, would lead one of the attacks."

"Of course, strategos."

He sighed, "When will you learn it is a commander's duty to command."

"I thought it was a leader's duty to lead."

He laughed. "You are incorrigible. When do we attack?"

"Towards late afternoon?"

"That soon?"

"They would expect an attack in the morning or at night time. Soldiers, especially, with due respect, Imperial soldiers are predictable.

Let us be unpredictable. It means that we will have the cover of darkness for part of the attack and yet still have enough time to thin their ranks on the walls."

"I am decided. Andronikos, your men will divide into four also and guard the four gates. Aelfraed, you choose when to attack and I will follow with the Thema. Try not to lose too many men."

I looked at him in surprise. "It is my aim to lose not a single man, strategos!"

Ridley and the other officers were delighted to be in action again. I would lead the attack on the main gate and Ridley the one opposite. The two other gates would be attacked by Egbert and Edward. They each had one hundred men whilst Ridley and I, attacking the more heavily defended gates, took a hundred and thirty.

"Rotate your men hacking at the door and always go for the same point. There will be a bar on the other side and when that is broken a wedge can push it through. Our first task is to secure the gates for the Thema to follow and the second to capture the keep."

I almost laughed when they all just nodded and looked at me. They all knew precisely what to do and they would do it.

Varangian

Chapter 10

These days getting ready for war was easy for we had servants to help us dress and to keep our armour and weapons clean. I still sharpened my blades myself but Basil did a good job with the armour. The new armour was so much lighter than the old one I had had for years that I felt I could fight faster and respond quicker to danger. I stepped from my tent and shouted for assembly. My eager warriors were all there and quickly formed up into the four columns. Ridley and Egbert led off first for they would have the furthest to move, then Edward and finally me. I had decided that it did not matter if we all attacked at once or at different times. There were advantages in both but I did not want time and possibly men's lives wasted because someone was waiting for an order.

The road wound steeply and I could see how hard it would have been for a ram. Andronikos and his men were waiting in the tree line out of bow range as we trudge up. I halted. "Column of fours." The men formed up behind me and I pointed with my axe. "Droungarios, if you wait until my men had passed you then you should be able to ride closer and hit them."

He looked at me in amazement. "But they will loose at you."

I grinned, "Aye and their arrows and bolts will strike wood and iron. We are a little better protected than you! Forwards!"

The advantage we had was that we were going up a cobbled road so we could keep our shields up and watch the ground. That way we were totally armoured and would not deviate off course. We heard the whoosh of the missiles and then the thud, clank and ping as they hit shields and helmets. The men on the right had their shields on their right and those behind, in the middle held theirs above their heads. Had we had oblong shields we would have been totally encased but the round ones were effective as they were doubled in places. I knew when the cavalry had ridden up for the barrage lessened. When the road curved to the left I knew that we were close and I raised my head to peer over the rim of my shield. The gate was ten paces away. "Nearly there lads!"

I heard a cheer ripple down the column and then we were at the door. I shifted my shield above my head and the three men designated to begin hacking came forwards their shields held high up by others at the front. We had chosen them because they were the shorter men it was easier to protect them. They also had axes with the best heads for cutting wood and soon chips and splinters flew off. I felt a thud as a stone was dropped from the ramparts above. "They are using stones, brace yourselves at the front." The ones at the rear would be safer for they would want to stop the relentless chopping which was already showing results. "Next three axes, forwards!"

The next three attacked the gate with renewed vigour and I almost cheered myself when I saw daylight. It spurred the men on and soon they were hacking into the thick bar. I heard a cheer from overt to my right and hoped that Edward had secured his gate. "Almost there, be ready to push on my command."

"Through my lord!"

"Shields! Push"

With one mighty heave, the gates sprang open and rhomphaia armed warriors hurled themselves at us. "Shield wall!"

My well-trained men made a three deep wall and the wicked blades sliced harmlessly off the shields. Opening the shields a little we stabbed forwards with our swords; used to fighting by slashing and hacking the Thracians fell to a man. I turned to the men next to me. "Secure the gate." I could see men backing away from the eastern gate and knew that Edward was there. I raced north to the gate which Ridley would be assaulting. I knew it was foolish for I was alone but the blood lust was on me and I felt invincible. I sheathed my sword and took out Death Bringer. With my shield on my back, I ran through the hill fort. The Thracians were brave but their shields were thin and without metal and the rhomphaia, no matter how sharp, would not penetrate my tunic, corselet mail and leather. Their only chance would have been to go for my throat. They were all short men and I do not think they had the reach. I must have terrified them for I was a good head taller than they. The brave ones died, those with wives, fled. As I neared the north gate it burst open and my men roared in led by Ridley. I nodded my mental approval as he secured the gate and then, with eight men joined me.

"Well done. Let's get to the keep." It looked as though the keep had originally been a tower that had been recently strengthened. It was where the defenders would retreat when the ramparts fell. The sooner we could get there then the fewer men could hide within its walls. "Wedge!"

The ten of us formed a small wedge and carved a path through the retreating Thracians who tried to stop us. When we reached the door, which was up a short flight of stairs we heard it slam shut.

They were Ridley's men with him and he ordered three of them to attack the door. We held shields aloft as arrows rained down. They quickly discovered that crossbow bolts could not be released vertically and they began hurling the few rocks they had. I peered out from under the shields and saw the first of the Thema enter the fort. As we crashed through the door I saw, to my surprise, a Norman knight standing behind five other Norman men at arms. We did not wait but rushed at them. These were a familiar enemy. The knight slew one of Ridley's men and then retreated to the stairs. The others headed for a door at the rear. "Ridley, keep after them!"

I went alone up the stairs. I knew that they suit him and that Death Bringer would not be effective so I unslung my shield and drew my sword. The curve of the stairs prevented me from using my sword but allowed him to attack with impunity and I cursed the hobnails on my shoes as I clattered up. It was his smell that gave him away. A mixture of sweat, horse and garlic filled my nostrils and I held up my shield just as the sword sliced around, wielded by an invisible hand. I hacked upwards with my sword and hear the grunt of pain as the blow reverberated up his arm. I raced up trying to catch sight of him. The only advantage I had was that he had to turn his back on me to move quickly and he chose to do so. I saw the back of his leg and I stabbed forwards. I sliced through the muscle on his left leg and he gave a scream and kicked back with the wounded leg, caught me a bloody blow to the mouth. It allowed him to gain a few steps on me. I cursed and followed. When the stairs lightened I knew that we were close to the top and he stood in the doorway waiting for me. I gave him no opportunity to ready or steady himself and I put my shield forwards and threw myself at him. We crashed to the ground and I felt a blow to my back as a Thracian chopped down at me. The haft of Death Bringer halted the blow and I leapt to my feet and stabbed my assailant in the throat. The Norman was on his feet albeit a little slower than me.

He was warier now and wounded. The sword had cut deep and he was dragging his leg. I had learned how dangerous Norman swordsmen could be and his long kite shield protected half of his body. I used that to my advantage and hacked with all my not inconsiderable might at his shield. It was like being beaten with an iron bar and the left leg which supported that side was not whole. He could not get a blow in return and began to back up. I did not know how long I could keep up the intensity of blows but I was determined to try. He raised his shield to protect from another hammer blow and I switched the blow to slice across his right side. Again the sword smashed into his hand and his side and I saw him wince. He took another step back. I punched with my shield and then raised the sword for a final blow. He raised the shield for protection and leaned back. He tumbled from the top of the tower his strangled scream ending with a dull thud as he smashed into the ground.

There were five defenders left but they were all busy trying to hurl rocks to the men below. I stabbed one in the back and decapitated a second before they knew I was there. One fled down the stairs and the scream I heard told me that my men were coming to join me. The other two threw down their weapons and prostrated themselves before me.

Egbert's grinning face greeted me. "Didn't need us, my lord, eh?" He glanced around the dead bodies and shook his head. "And Komes Ridley is the one who went berserk!"

We checked that the dead were really dead and I peered over the crenellated top. Andronikos waved cheerfully up at me. "They have surrendered." He pointed to the dead Norman. "It appears you killed their leader." I waved back.

"Take these prisoners down with the others."

Egbert did so cheerfully. Prisoners meant slaves and slaves meant money. When I reached the bottom there was a blood-covered Ridley with five of the men who had followed him and, clinging to his arm was a girl. He gave me an apologetic shrug and went outside. I called over Cnut who had followed him and was a dekarchos. "What happened?"

"There were cells underground with prisoners. The ones we chased began to slaughter them. The Komes, well I have never seen anything like it. He tore into them and didn't seem to care if they hit him or not."

"Did they?"

"Not one of them my lord. All that blood he was covered in, well it is theirs. When they were dead, we saw the girl hiding behind a wall and crying. She wouldn't come near us, my lord, but she clung to the Komes like a limpet to a rock. He was a bloody marvel was the Komes."

When I went into the fresh air it was good to be away from the smell of blood. I was becoming effete. I missed my baths and the sweet smell of fine soap. Andronikos dismounted to greet me. "I see our friend Ridley has the spoils of war eh?"

"This is the first time I have seen him with a woman. I hope he can cope."

The strategos rode in and after surveying the carnage, dismounted to greet me. "Did we lose many men?"

"I have not had a chance to check yet but I do not think so. What about you and your men Andronikos, how many losses?"

"Less than twenty."

I pointed out the ungainly body of the dead Norman. "They were commanded by a Norman and they had prisoners in their cells. Ridley rescued one, a girl, but we have yet to speak with her. She may be able to shed light on the identity of the knight and the reason he was here."

"Good you have both done well. I will leave a Kentarchia of men from the Thema as a garrison. I would not like to have to take this place again. Go back to the camp and rest." He nodded at me. "It was a good plan to attack at dusk. We took it before dark and I think you are right. Being unpredictable sometimes helps."

Basil had found a bath for me and boiled some water. Before I had travelled east I would have wondered at taking a bath after a battle but now that I had done it, the whole process seemed so natural. I did not see Ridley but I knew that he would seek me out as soon as he could. I must have been more tired than I thought; I was no longer a young man, for I fell asleep. When I awoke the water was tepid and Basil was hovering like a mother hen with a chick. He tut-tutted as he dried me but the bath had worked and I felt like the stench of battle was gone from me.

"Well, Basil I am famished. Has the food been served yet?"

"They are just eating my lord; you are invited to dine at the tent of the strategos." He looked at me sternly. "You are not yet late."

"Which is your subtle way of telling me to hurry up. Well, I shall because I could eat a horse, with the skin on!"

He wrinkled his nose at the unpleasant image. The Byzantines were more delicate eaters than the Saxon. We liked our meat and lots of it! I quickly dressed and strode over to the stategos' tent. The sentry waved me in. The other officers were all there including Ridley and next to him was the fey woman I had seen clinging to him. She was no longer clinging but sat as close to him as was humanly possible. He gave a shrug and continued eating. He looked happy enough. I could see that she was pretty. I am always hopeless at guessing ages. My wife Gytha found it an amusing trait in me. She had jet black hair and the most amazing violet eyes. I was surprised that her guards had not violated her. It must have meant that she was important to them.

Alexios had saved a place for me at the head of the table and I sat next to him with Andronikos next to him. He spoke quietly. "While you slept," he shook his head as I started to apologise, "you deserved the rest and we did not need you." He gave a disarming smile, "There were no men to kill!" The Droungarios almost choked on his food with laughter. "As I was saying, while you slept, we managed to interview the girl. It turns out she is related to Nicephorus Botaniantes. It seems her father and his family lived around here and they were captured by the knight Roger of Evreux whom you slew." He saw my face. "You knew him before?"

"I believe I slew a relative of his Guy of Evreux, he was a nasty bastard too."

"Quite, well it seems that they were being hostage while they put pressure on Nicephorus to support the Normans in this part of the world."

"Would it have worked?"

"Of course not. He will be the next Emperor, mark my words, besides the Normans did not understand the nature of families here. Nicephorus was not close to the family and there was nothing in it for him. He is not stupid, why let the Normans in. Your tales of what happened in England our experience in Italy has warned us that you do not make a deal with a snake. The girl, Anna, was the only survivor and she seems somewhat taken with Ridley and will not leave his side. I may have to send him back with her to Nicephorus. How do you feel about that?"

"It might do him some good."

"Excellent. A Kontoubernia of your horse as an escort?"

"Of course, strategos."

I watched the two of them and saw that Ridley, surprisingly was at ease and the girl seemed enamoured of the rough Saxon, feeding him tidbits of food and giggling throughout the meal. "I will speak with him afterwards, strategos."

"Thank you and tomorrow we head for Dyrrhachium and see if that, too, is a nest of serpents." Dyrrhachium was the largest port on the Adriatic coast and vital to the security of the Empire. If that had been infiltrated then the Empire was in trouble.

I found Ridley with Anna outside his tent. He saw us coming. "This is Aelfraed Godwinson, the commander of the Varangian Inglinoi and the greatest warrior in England."

"Thank you, Ridley, but you need not praise me. The title your friend would have sufficed." I could see that he swelled with pride at that title. "And this must be Ann Botaniantes. I am sorry for your loss."

"I too would be dead if it were not for the bravery of this man. Truly I have never seen such a display. He is a hero!"

"I know that. Ridley, the strategos would like you to take Anna to her uncle tomorrow with an escort of archers." I could see that he was torn between his duty to me and his desire to be with Anna. "It is more of an order, Ridley." I saw him relax with relief.

"In that case, it will be my pleasure."

They left early the next day. We had found a chest of clothes for Anna and, luckily, she was a competent rider. I suspected that they were

Varangian

country nobility and not city ones as I couldn't see those in the city knowing one end of a horse from the other.

We had lost fifteen men in the attack which was not a disaster but more than I had hoped. I hoped that Ridley would not tarry in the capital for I needed him with me. You get used to someone's ways and good as Egbert and Edward were they were not familiar reliable and unflappable Ridley.

With the losses and the garrison, we were a smaller force now and we headed over the Roman road to the port of Dyrrhachium. The port was incredibly old and the Romans had used it as a stronghold in that part of the world. The Great Pompey had used it as a base during his war with Caesar and I knew that Alexios was worried what we would find when we reached there. The ever-reliable Andronikos took his Droungos to patrol the outskirts and we felt vulnerable as we trudged along the road without scouts and without cavalry. I had yet to see the Thema fight and I wondered why their commander never offered to volunteer them. Perhaps it was not the Byzantine way.

We were relieved to discover that the garrison still remained and that the Normans had not attempted, as yet, to infiltrate that town. It also meant that we had the pleasure of a city instead of leaky tents. The weather had not only been hot but also wet, a dreadful combination. The strategos intended to stay for a few days in the port and then sweep northwards to return to the city.

The journey from the coast was not a pleasant one. Although the winters in that part of the world are not as harsh as those in the north of England, once you were in the high passes, there was snow and there were terrifyingly fierce winds. We received a message from Constantinople that Ridley and Anna had reached the city but Nicephorus was entertaining Ridley over the winter. I envied my friend for I was chilled to the bone every night and my feet were soaked each day. Maddeningly there was little action for us. The news of our defeat of the Norman and his rebels made most of the erstwhile revolutionaries surrender without a fight. My men wanted to fight. They were warriors. The Thema and the cavalry seemed happy to be paid to tramp around the wild mountains of Thrace but not my men.

It was spring when they had their wish fulfilled and one of the chiefs in the more remote part of the hills decided that he would oppose us. I suppose he thought that we looked like easy pickings. There were less than five thousand of us for Alexios had sent some of the Thema to Dyrrhachium in order to strengthen the garrison there. The warlord had gathered a huge band of warriors from various tribes. Andronikos had told me that this land had been the homeland of Alexander the Great and the warriors had always been truculent. We found ourselves camped on a hill less than five miles from the warlord's camp. Andronikos had reported where they were but when we awoke we had a shock for there were over seven thousand tribesmen array for battle. They seriously outnumbered us in cavalry and our only salvation was their lack of archers.

Alexios calmly surveyed the enemy. "Aelfraed, place half of your men on the right, the rest will be on the left in front of Andronikos. Andronikos put half of your horse archers on the left behind the Inglinoi and the other half behind the others on the right." He then placed the half of the Thema who had either javelins or bows behind our camp ditch. The rest of the Thema he placed with us about four hundred paces from the enemy. He explained to the three of us, his senior commanders, what he intended. "They think that we will run and then they will slaughter us. I want the Thema to withdraw but you, Aelfraed, will hold your men. The horse archers can loose over your heads. When they reach the camp then the other bows and missiles will come to bear and we will have them encircled."

"Good plan, my lord, if they take the bait."

"They will. Trust me."

I did trust him but my men would be in the front line. I gathered my officers around me. "Put spearmen in the second rank to hold off any horses and to deter them from attacking. I will be on the right and I will stand on the right of the line." The most reliable and stoic officer I had was Edward. "Edward you take the left of the left line."

They were appalled. "But my lord, you will be taking the biggest risk. Who will guard your right side?"

"Do not worry about me, Egbert. I will have Death Bringer and it will take a brave man to come within an arm's length of me."

As I was on the right, Andronikos took charge of the left. His horse archers would be commanded by me and he would order Edward should the need arise. We marched forwards towards the enemy and they began to wail and to scream. I could see that the Thema looked less than confident and I began to bang my shield with my axe. Soon all of my men had taken it up and the beat echoed across the valley. Oddly the noise made the enemy stop their screaming and look at us in wonder. When they suddenly launched themselves forwards they reminded me of the fyrd, they were uncontrolled charging, roaring beasts. "Englishmen do not fear them, they are like the fyrd at home and we know what useless fighters they were." My men gave a confident cheer and I felt guilt for my fyrd had been reliable fighters but I knew that most of my men would remember the disaster at Senlac Hill.

I shouted over my shoulder in Greek. "Archers prepare."

They were more disciplined than my men and roared back, "Yes, Droungarios!"

I glanced to my left and saw the Thema, standing behind their wall of shields and spears begin to look uncomfortable. I hoped that their officers would be able to make a controlled retreat or this could be a disaster. When the Thracian horse was fifty paces away I yelled, "Loose!" Horses and men tumbled to the ground but this was a wild barbarian horde and the ones behind merely hurdled or jumped the fallen and roared towards us. The archers needed no command now and continued to loose volley after volley into their ranks and then the line struck us. "Brace!"

There were spears either side of my head and my men were determined to protect me so that their heads were three paces before me. I swung Death Bringer, quickly getting into the easy rhythm of old. As the enemy were shorter than me the axe head was at my chest height and, even though four warriors rushed at me I was confident. The warrior next to me, Aedgar, was also swinging his axe and the line of whirling blades before us made the enemy slow. None wished to risk the wall of death after the first to do so were despatched in a sea of blood and gore. Had they too had archers, then it would have been a different story but they had to get inside our swings to use their rhomphaia and they could not do that. The ones before us fell back to regroup as the braver, reckless warriors to the fore were felled. I glanced to my left and saw that the Thema was moving backwards. I yelled to the warrior on the left of our line, "Cnut! Angle back!"

"Yes, my lord", came the English voice. I hoped that Andronikos' horse would remember their instructions.

Inexorably the line began to shift and the warriors who were unwilling to face the one hundred axes to their left and right were funnelled and channelled towards the middle where the battle seemed to be going the Thracian way. The further forwards they went the more they all congregated in the centre. We were still hacking at their flanks. I yelled over my shoulder in Greek. "Archers move to the right!"

"Yes, Droungarios!"

"Shield wall! Forwards!" I could see that there were few men left to join the fray and now was the time to close the neck on this trap. I was reassured to feel a horse's flank on my right and I glanced up to see a grinning horse archer loosing as quickly as he could manage. They were all excellent riders with superb mounts and they were guiding their horses forwards with their knees and their heels. It was impressive. I heard a collective groan from my left and knew that the strategos had unleashed his hidden men. "Into them! They have nowhere left to go." I chopped through the shoulder and the arm of one warrior and then took out the next by decapitating him. Some of the horses were being targeted and I yelled, "Kontoubernia!" My well-trained men quickly formed into tens. They all knew what their role was and I said to those around me, "Wedge!"

I turned to head towards the rear of their line where I could relieve the pressure on the horse archers. Here were the warriors who had been a little more cautious and that showed as they saw Death Bringer's bloody head closing on them. They tried to flee but the archers had drawn their swords and the Thracians were being massacred in their droves. I stopped when I looked up into the grinning face of the Kentarches. He saluted with his sword.

"Have any escaped?"

"There are a few Droungarios who are fleeing north."

"Take your Kentarchia and pursue them. I will close the trap with the rest."

We turned around to see a sea of terrified faces running towards us. "Shield wall!" The men with me formed a shield wall and the archers who remained poured arrow after arrow into the men who were brave but had neither armour nor helmet. When Andronikos rode up to me I knew that we had won although, in truth, it was never in doubt. This was not the same as fighting the mailed Normans; there was no glory in this. It was just the slaughter of the badly led.

Andronikos dismounted. "Your men are magnificent, Aelfraed. Never again will I listen to those who say they are undisciplined barbarians. They obeyed every order."

"Just point me in the direction of those speakers old friend and they will never lie again!"

The Kentarches rode in. "They are all dead, we found their camp but the women and children had fled. Did I do right Droungarios?"

Andronikos nodded. "It is winter and many will die anyway. This will be a lesson for them. They will spread the word that we are not to be trifled with."

The rest of the day was spent dispatching the wounded Thracians and securing those who had surrendered. My men were in high spirits for to them it was more coin to add to their horde. When Alexios met us his face was sad, "Two of the Tourmache died and many of the Thema."

I looked at the Thracian dead. "But we won, strategos, and the enemy will not rise here again. It is the risk the warrior takes."

He shook his head. "No Aelfraed, here we train and pay our men well and do not like them to be wasted."

I did not know how to phrase my next sentence diplomatically in Greek and so I reverted to English. "Perhaps if they believed they were fighting for their lives then they might fight harder. I saw the faces of the Thema, lord, and they looked terrified. If you are terrified when you fight then you will lose."

"Perhaps," he looked at me with a strange look on his face. He was a thinker and pondered things for a long time. I did not see what he was thinking until two years later. "How would you have done things differently?"

"It was a good plan strategos and it worked."

"Do not flatter me, Aelfraed. You know me better than that." It was the first time that I had seen impatience with the man.

"Well, I think I would have told the Thema and the others what we intended. It is what we did with the archers and my men."

He nodded. "It is risky."

"Not if you trust your men and trust your officers. You have a good system strategos. Your ten man groups are effective. I have adopted them and I believe my men fight better because of your ideas but you need to instil trust at all levels so that, even if they are on their own, they know what to do."

"Interesting." With that, he strode off leaving Andronikos and me to count our dead.

Varangian

Chapter 11

It was a month later when the Imperial messenger found us mopping up the last rebels. He looked road weary for, even though spring had begun to arrive the rain and the melting snow made travel difficult.

"My lord, a message for you from the Emperor." He handed the document to Alexios who broke the seal and read it.

When he had read it he folded it up and spoke to the messenger. "Get yourself some food and a fresh horse and I will have my reply." As the courier left he turned to Andronikos and myself, "Come with me gentlemen this is a momentous occasion."

Intrigued we followed him. We watched as he wrote his reply and then seal the document which he placed in the leather cylinder the courier had carried. He called in the sentry. "Give this to the Imperial courier and then find the quartermaster and tell him to break camp. We need to travel back towards Dyrrhachium. The Emperor is bringing over the other Thema."

Curiosity was eating me up and, I suspect Andronikos. Alexios smiled, enjoying our fraught faces. "It seems we have a new Emperor, Nicephorus the third."

Andronikos reacted first. "You man Nicephorus Botaniantes? The man whose family were held for ransom?"

"The very same."

I hesitated but I needed to ask the question. "And the old Emperor?" I had never met Michael but heard that he was a good man.

"He has retired to a monastery and the new Emperor is to marry the Empress." My face displayed my incredulity making Alexios smile, "This is Byzantium my friend do not be surprised by anything. And I am the Commander of the armies of the west."

"Well done, my lord." We were both genuine with our congratulations. For my part, I had never had such a good leader since my father and Aethelward and Alexios had qualities which would have served Harold well.

"We are to head south and meet the new Emperor." Since we had left Dyrrhachium we had travelled far to the north winkling out the last of the unruly tribes. Even had we not been recalled it was difficult to see how we could have remained on campaign for long; our weapons, armour and supplies were in need of replenishment.

We trudged south for two days and were less than a hundred miles from Dyrrhachium when the scouts reported the presence of the

Emperor. It spurred us on for we were all looking forward to seeing the soldier who had served with us in Asia. It had only been a few months but he had made a great impression upon me. When we crested the rise and saw the camp I was amazed at the number of tents which I beheld. It seemed as though the new Emperor had brought every soldier he had. I wondered why. He could have waited for us to reach Constantinople and then greet his new commander. This suggested to me that there was trouble ahead. As we rode into the camp I was delighted to see Saxons and even more delighted when Ridley, resplendent in new armour waved at me. I wondered where he had been for the past few months but I supposed we would discover all soon. Glancing behind me at the sorry sight of the troops who followed us I felt that we looked like the remains of a defeated army rather than one which had subjugated the northern border regions. We had left many men dead on various fields and garrisoned other towns. Even had we not been recalled it is hard to see how we could have survived in the field for much longer.

Leaving the men in the charge of their officers the three of us, looking incredibly dirty and dishevelled approached the Emperor's tent clearly marked by the Varangian guards who stood outside. Nicephorus came out and we dropped to our knees. He came and raised us up, kissing first Alexios and then Andronikos and then me on the cheeks. "Come I owe much to you three for you have worked miracles here but come inside and take refreshment for I have dire tidings to impart."

Once inside his servant poured us wine and then left. "We have no time for pleasantries. You visited Dyrrhachium earlier in the year did you not?" Alexios nodded. "How were things there?"

"There was no threat from the Normans, my lord, and the garrison was well equipped to deal with an attack."

"And therein lies the problem. It was not the Normans we should have feared but the rebels." Alexios looked as though he was going to say something but the Emperor held up his hand. "Not the truculent tribes Alexios but Nicephorus Bryennios. He has suborned the local Thema and raised his standard in Dyrrhachium." He pointed towards the tent door. "These are the only troops we have in the west commander. I will take my Varangians back with me and you will need to defeat these rebels with what you have. The fate of the |Empire is now in your hands."

"And now, gentlemen, I would like a few moments alone with my new commander. Thank you again for your efforts on behalf of the Empire. We are grateful." I began to leave but he held my arm. "Thank you, Aelfraed Godwinson, for Ridley has told me it was your decision to capture the fort and without it, my niece would now be dead. I am in your debt." He smiled. "Your friend is both loyal and a powerful advocate on your behalf."

When we left Ridley came up and picked me up in a bear hug. The soldiers who waited around the camp were amazed. "I wondered what had become of you old friend. I thought, perhaps, you had gone back to England."

"I wanted to come back sooner but the Emperor made such a fuss and kept me there. Of course, he was not Emperor then but I think he kept me close by as a sort of bodyguard."

"I am pleased to see you."

Andronikos also hugged him. "As am I. We missed you. Especially on the battlefield."

Ridley became serious. "I see our ranks are depleted."

"We did not do so badly but we could do without another campaign now."

He brightened a little. "I have brought more recruits. Two hundred of them and the wagons have some spare armour and weapons."

"Good," I turned to Andronikos. "I will see to my men I suspect you will be doing the same?"

"I had better." He scanned the officers he could see who were nearby. "I am just wondering which old man they have brought out of retirement to be our Strategoi."

I shrugged. "It matters not, we will keep doing as we have done. Winning!"

I put my arm around Ridley, "It is good to see you old friend. That is the longest I have been without you in battle since we started as warriors."

"I know. I preferred it when we made the decisions for I did not want to be a bodyguard for no matter how elevated a man when I knew you and the men needed me. But," he suddenly looked sheepish, "there were compensations."

"Anna?"

He looked at me as though I had the gift of second sight. "Yes, but how did you know?"

"I remembered the silly look I had when I was with Gytha!"

He suddenly burst out, "And I am wed! We married last month."

He looked at me expectantly as though uncertain of my reaction. I was, of course, delighted for him. I clapped him on the back. "That is the best news I have heard in a long time. When we are back in civilisation we will have to celebrate. Now let us get these new men sorted and the equipment doled out. Edward! Officer's call!"

Varangian

It took all the rest of the afternoon to allocate the new men to existing Kontoubernia and equip the men with damaged weapons and armour. We then spent some time appointing the new officers. We were so engrossed that it was only the men before us standing to attention that alerted us to Nicephorus' presence behind me. We whirled and dropped to our knees. "Apologies you…"

He waved his hand as though a magician, "Stand, it matters not and you are doing as I would wish, preparing for war. I will see you both when you reach Constantinople when I can properly reward you. And, nephew, I will look after your wife in your absence." I almost burst out laughing at the confused expressions on Ridley's old comrade's faces. I mouthed 'later'. The Emperor mounted his horse. "We will return to the capital. Good hunting."

It was as they left that I saw the look of pure hatred upon the faces of Olef and his Varangians. As he passed he leaned down to speak to me quietly. "There is only one Varangian Guard," He waved a dismissive hand at my men, "These Saxons are no Varangians. We will have words when you reach the city."

I started back at him. "You will find me and my men ready with blows as well as words Viking!"

His hand went to his sword but he thought better of it. Each man glared at me as they rode past. Andronikos had seen it all. "I see you are still making friends and influencing people."

"He is an arrogant bastard who, as far as I can see has never pulled a sword from its scabbard in anger."

"That is as may be but they are the Emperor's bodyguards and you cannot fight with them on pain of death."

An old memory of Scotland came into my head and I said, enigmatically, "We shall see."

The last of the Varangians had barely left the camp when the new Commander of the West summoned us. "Aelfraed, Andronikos and Ridley your officers can continue, come to the command tent."

Once inside he bade us be seated. "Things are even worse than we thought, however, the good news first. The Strategoi."

Andronikos sighed, "Don't tell me, they have found some in a dusty cupboard and they have sent them west."

"Well surprisingly I rate them and I asked the Emperor for them although he had already suggested one of them to me anyway."

Andronikos realised he had gone too far. "Sorry commander. It has been a long campaign and I…."

"If you would let me finish, the new Strategoi are Aelfraed Godwinson and Andronikos Tassius."

Ridley clapped us both on the back and I turned to Andronikos. "What size shoes do you take old friend and would you like a hand to get them out of your mouth."

He grinned and reddened as Alexios continued. "Of course, we need a new Droungarios for the Varangian Inglinoi and I am pleased to say that is you, Ridley. I will leave it to you two to find Komes and Andronikos as you will be in command of the cavalry you will need a new Droungarios. Now the bad news. We are outnumbered. Not only have the local garrisons gone over to the rebels but they have Pecheng mercenaries on their side as well. We have one Thema of foot plus the remnants from our campaign, the Inglinoi, ten Kontoubernia of cataphracts, three Droungoi of horse archers, plus your remnants and a Droungoi of light cavalry. Not enough I fear and certainly not enough to assault the port of Dyrrhachium"

We spent the next hour going over the lists of officers and men we had at our disposal and planned a route to Dyrrhachium. I already had ideas in my head but I found that they became firmer as we trudged along the road. The Saxons were doubly delighted with my promotion and Ridley's. They saw it as a vindication of their success and prowess. They had grown since we had first walked into their barracks all those years ago and, as I looked at the moon rising over the hills and mountains thought that they would probably have been similar to Alexander's Macedonians who travelled across the known world following their star.

The first sight which greeted me the next day was a magnificently dressed Andronikos, dressed in full cataphracts armour. He looked a little embarrassed but he looked, somehow more like a general. I had refused any other armour for mine felt comfortable and they all knew who I was on the battlefield without a feather. Ridley, however, had not been idle in Constantinople. He handed me a leather covered tube and when I opened it I saw that he had had a Red Horse banner made for me. "I thought it was time we showed them all who we were." My men loved it and many remembered it from the battlefields of England where it had enjoyed so much success. "It will be a rallying point on the battlefield, eh?"

When we were ready to march, I took my place at the head of my men. I noticed Alexios and Andronikos laughing at me. "Am I incorrectly dressed?"

"You could say that." Andronikos whistled and an aide brought a black horse. "You are a strategos now. No more walking for you. You ride."

My men gave an ironic cheer as I reluctantly mounted. He was no Sweyn, but he was a magnificent beast and they were right, a general should be seen. The aide made sure I was seated well and then said, "My name is Isaac, sir, and I am your aide and standard bearer."

"Welcome, Isaac. I suspect I will have to get used to this now."

"Yes indeed, my lord. I am but one of your aides and servants." He gave a sympathetic nod to my men. "I believe they will miss you too, my lord."

"Never worry about that, Isaac. They will always be in the thick of the fighting, as will I." His face almost went white with shock. "I am afraid, my friend, that this strategos leads from the front." I leaned over and said quietly, "You will need a good sword and an even better shield."

We were lucky, the weather began to improve and our clothes dried out. Even more important the roads became much easier and we made good progress. Our new strategos of cavalry was able to use his light cavalry as scouts for losing horse archers was unthinkable if we had the Pechengs to worry about. I still remembered those fierce warriors from the river and how nearly we had come to grief. We would need a good plan to defeat them. I found that I could think as well riding as walking and I came up with a plan. As with all my thinking, the plan I presented to Alexios was not the plan which started in my mind but was the one that evolved.

"Our weakness is our lack of numbers is it not?"

"Yes, but how does that help?"

"We use that weakness. Let the enemy know how weak we are."

"Why?"

"They will try to attack us and then we ambush them. Remember the Thracians who outnumbered us? Well, they were overconfident but we won because we planned for that. We can do the same with this Bryennios. Make him attack but we choose the ground."

They all liked the plan but Andronikos asked, "How do we let them know that we are outnumbered?"

"That is up to your scouts. I want them to capture a couple of men and bring them to the camp. Let them see our numbers but keep your cataphracts hidden. We tell them we are sending them back to Dyrrhachium demanding the surrender of Bryennios."

"Which they won't do."

"We don't need them to although if they do then we have an amazing victory. They will be asked how many men we have and when they report how few we have then he will attack us. Your scouts can follow the captives back so that they will know when they leave the citadel."

As with all plans, this one depended upon human nature and the enemy doing what we hoped. Most of it worked out but, unfortunately, not all.

The first part was easy enough. Our scouts were looking for the rebel scouts; they were looking for our army. The four men were brought in to the camp; we discovered later that three had been killed in the skirmish. They were brought before the Commander. "You have been spared your lives so that you can take a message to your leaders. Tell them to surrender Nicephorus Bryennios unconditionally and hand over Dyrrhachium and the rest of the town will be allowed to live. They have seven days to comply."

The four men gratefully galloped towards safety, no doubt delighted to be alive. The troops who had been in the camp were the ones who had been campaigning over the winter and the cataphracts and fresh troops were hidden. We had given them a week in the hope that they would become overconfident and assume that we would wait in camp. As soon as they left we broke camp and head quickly to be within a day's ride of the city. Alexios called us all together for a briefing. "I have decided to use the Varangian Saxons and the cataphracts in the centre where they can hold the line. The Thema will be divided into two; one on each flank. The horse archers will be held in reserve to counter the Pechengs and the light cavalry will be placed with the cataphracts in the middle for they will be the last to arrive and I want them to lead Bryennios to our trap."

I looked at Andronikos who looked as appalled as I did. "But Commander, we need the horse archers close to the Thema to give them protection."

He shook his head. "No for the Pecheng warriors are the bigger threat. You, strategos, will command the centre for they will have to bear the brunt of the attack and I know how resolute you are in defence. Tourmache Cassius will command the left Droungoi and I will command the right. The strategos of horse will command the horse archers for I know that he knows how to get the best out them." He paused, "We need to nip this rebellion in the bud and do it quickly. Whenever they come we must destroy them quickly."

The plan looked sound and I could understand his need to watch out for the Pechengs but to keep our potent horse archers in reserve seemed too risky to me. The only saving grace was that I was, at least commanding the centre. Andronikos came over and confided to me that he too had reservations. Alexios seemed determined to prove that he was the supreme strategos but all of us benefit from some discussion. As we were choosing the battlefield I decided to improve my part of it

Varangian

as much as possible. My men were to be placed across the road close to the ford across the River Halmyros. On the other side of the river the commander placed both halves echeloned so that the enemy army would be drawn into my men and the river. He was using the scrubby trees and woods to disguise our numbers. The horse archers were arrayed behind me. As we waited, I was reminded of the battle close to Osmotherley except that it was I who played the Aethelward role at the rear of the army and our dispositions were not as secure as I would have liked.

The first scout arrived just before noon announcing that the whole rebel army was heading towards us and the Droungarios was drawing them on. I rode to the river and turned to face the men. "Today we are the anvil and we must be as the anvil and take whatever punishment is offered. Cataphracts, you will be the reserve but when I order you forwards you must be decisive for we are the smallest part of this army and yet the heaviest. So the heaviest burden will be upon us. No matter what the others do we cannot, we will not retreat one step. We stand and we fall where we are!"

To the surprise of the armoured cataphracts, my men began banging their shields and chanting, "Aelfraed! Aelfraed!"

I saw Ridley grin and he looked like a boy again. The dark days following the loss of his beloved Coxold were gone and Anna had given him a new lease of life.

The thunder of hooves alerted us to the arrival of the light horse. They rode straight into the river. The Droungarios reported. "They are behind us, there are fifteen thousand of them!"

He was excited but before I could calm him Ridley said, "Excellent! More for us to kill!" The men roared their laughter and cheered.

"Put your men on the flanks this side of the river."

When they crested the rise I could see that this was no tribe of barbarians. This was an army armed and armoured much as we were. They had spread out in a long line so that I could barely see the flanks. Alexios' plan was doomed from that moment. He had planned on attacking the flanks of the enemy but they outflanked him. I turned to shout to Andronikos. "Take the cataphracts and the light horse, you will need to attack the enemy flanks, and drive them in."

"You are right but that leaves you with barely six hundred men."

"It will have to do." He saluted as he rode off to divide his forces. I shouted. "Shield wall! Three lines." I dismounted and handed Isaac the reins. "Watch my horse for me, there is a good fellow." There was a huge cheer as I took my place next to Ridley.

Varangian

The enemy had reached the other side of the river and they were adjusting their lines to match ours. I could hear the fighting in the woods and hoped that the Commander was having a better time than the one I imagined him to be having. Suddenly everything happened at once. The line of spearmen trooped across the ford and the men of the Thema fled in terror across the water pursued by the enemy. I could see that Andronikos had divided the archers and cataphracts equally and he waited for as many of the army to retreat before attacking. When I saw Alexios and his staff fall back I knew that we had lost. As soon as they were across I heard Andronikos signal the attack from his cavalry; at the same time, the line of spearmen crashed through the water to hurl themselves at us. They must have thought that they would have an easy victory for there were two Tourmai, almost five thousand men attacking my six hundred but they had not met our axes before and the sharp blades tore through the spears leaving their owners struggling to get their swords out. We gave them no opportunity and hacked through their shields which were thin and poorly made. Their bodies were hacked into pieces by two hundred men. Andronikos had not left us alone for, on our flanks, were two Kentarchia of horse archers who dissuaded the rebels from trying to flank us. I could see the enemy flooding across the river in pursuit of the Thema but our situation meant that we had to just keep killing. They must have hoped we would tire of swinging the deadly axes but we did not. Whoever was commanding them realised the futility of their action and he withdrew his men back across the river. The waters flowed with brown slurry which was the blood of their dead. I took the opportunity of placing the front rank at the rear and bringing the rear rank, who had seen little action, to the fore and we waited. I turned to Ridley. "If I were the enemy I would use my archers now."

"Me too." He turned, "Ready with your shields. They may try to use arrows. They look like sneaky bastards don't they?"

They all laughed. They were confident. Sure enough, a flurry of arrows came but we had practised this often and we had a protective wall of shields above our head. Suddenly I heard Isaac's voice, as they readied for a charge. "Sir, a message from the commander!"

"Take charge, Droungarios." I made my way through the ranks. "I will be back so don't kill too many just yet."

There was one of the Commander's bloodied aides. "Strategos, the Commander has rallied the men and he wants you to pretend to retreat. He has set up another ambush down the road."

"And the archers?"

"They will also feign a retreat."

Varangian

I hoped he knew what he was doing this time. "Very well. Isaac ride to the strategos and tell him the retreat begins when I dip my standard."

I made my way back through the men and shouted, I was fairly certain that our words would not be understood by the Greeks across the river. "We are going to pretend to retreat. We do this in waves. The rear two ranks will retreat and form a line two hundred paces back. The front rank will then go one hundred paces behind them and so on. The signal will be the dipping of my standard." I sensed despair creeping in. "We have not lost. The Commander is using us as bait. Let us hope we can catch a big fish eh?" I could see the enemy readying for a charge and I said to the standard bearer, Karl, "Now!" He dipped the standard and I heard the sound of hobnails running along the cobbles.

"Steady lads." I was watching for movement. The river was forty paces wide and they would be slower running through that than we would be on the road. As soon as the first spear moved, I shouted, "Retreat!" We all slipped our shields onto our backs and walked quickly backwards. As we did so I saw Andronikos' archers loosing volley after volley into the advancing line as they rode backwards. I saw Edward and the others in their lines. They had left gaps for us to slip through. We kept going until I had counted one hundred and then we turned. The second rank passed through our ranks and I yelled, "Retreat!" Edward performed the same manoeuvre. I turned to Egbert. "Take your line back one hundred paces. The Commander should be there."

When Edward's men were behind us I could see that the enemy were less than forty paces behind them. "Let's give them a bloody nose, eh lads."

They were so keen to come to grips with the retreating axe men that they had not formed lines and we were a powerful shield wall. They fell back and I took the initiative. "Forwards!"

To their horror, we began to advance and I heard someone give the order in Greek, "Fall back!"

"Right lads, let's retreat slowly and get back to the others." As we went back our men began a relentless drumming of their swords on shields and we walked back in time. Even I had to admit that it was impressive.

When they came on again they had dressed their lines and we were presented with a solid line of shields and spears. Arrows rained down from archers behind them. This time they intended to end it. They hurled themselves at my front rank which had Egbert at the centre. I was confident that we could hold. Glancing behind me I saw Alexios moving forwards on one flank with the Thema and Andronikos on the other with the cavalry. "On my command I want each Kontoubernion to form a wedge and then we will advance." I paused and then roared, "Wedge!"

The rebels must have wondered what was happening as the line before them ceased to be continuous and became, instead, ten arrows. At the same time, the two attacks on our flanks thundered in and the confused enemy became a defeated enemy. They fell back and we relentlessly drove them all the way to the river. For the first time in years, I was not in the front rank but in the second, dispatching those who lay wounded on the floor. We continued across the river and kept going until we came to a rise above the city. By then we were too exhausted to continue so we formed a shield wall and waited. Isaac brought my horse and I gratefully mounted. From his back, I could see the remnants of Byrennios' army fleeing in all directions pursued by Andronikos and his cavalry. We had won.

I turned to look at my men. Ridley wandered over and joined Isaac and me. "I am so proud of them Ridley. Their discipline and their courage."

"I know Aelfraed, although we trained them they can still impress."

Isaac ventured, "How do they do that, strategos?"

"Do what?"

"March back so calmly away from the enemy and then turn and fight and then, and I will take this picture to my grave, to charge four times their number."

"These are Housecarls. The finest foot soldiers the world has ever seen and these are the last of them. When they die then the world will never see their like. They have travelled thousands of miles to be here and yet they fight for Byzantium as fiercely as for Harold and of England."

"Why are they the last, my lord?"

"Because the Normans now rule my land and the Housecarls all fled here. There are fewer left to make the journey but this is now their home."

We watched as some of the men went over to the standard which Karl still held unfurled, and they touched it and kissed it. This was what the Normans would never understand, this allegiance to an idea, a brotherhood of warriors willing to die for each other as I knew these men would die for me.

The horse archers brought in Nicephorus Bryennios bound and bloodied. They reported to me. "Leave him with me, thank you."

He looked down at me, from on top of his white horse. He had magnificent armour but I saw that one of the horsemen had purloined his sword and another helmet. He had the arrogant look I had last seen amongst the Normans. I immediately disliked him. "So you are the Inglinoi. The one my men were so afraid of. You do not look like much to me."

Ridley's hand went to his sword at the insult but I shook my head. "Appearances can be deceptive. Men have been making that mistake for as long as I have wielded Death Bringer."

He laughed, "Do you think you are in the tales of ancient Greece, naming your weapon?"

"It seems to me that Ancient Greece was full of heroes. I would rather follow heroes than politicians who line their pockets with the lives of others. If I had my way your head would adorn a pole but my Commander is a civilised man and I feel sure that you will still be around in the future to annoy so hear this and hearken to my words. Do not cross me again for I do not follow the rules you Greeks have. I am English and I serve my own justice. If I wished you dead, you would be!"

I didn't realise that my men had gathered around and the Greek speakers had been translating. There was a pause and then a huge roar as the men heard my words. I gestured at them. "And, as you can hear, my countrymen feel the same!" I waved at Isaac. "Secure this snake!"

Alexios arrived soon after and, for the first time I could see that he had been in combat for he was bloodied. He rode next to me and extended his arm. "Thank you, my friend, you were right about the archers and were it not for your men's stand we would have been chased back to the Emperor."

"No Commander, for the Pechengs were still a threat."

He laughed, "It seems they decided not to attack us but to loot the camp of this traitor." He stared at Bryennios. "Make sure you choose your allies better next time."

I snorted. "Kill him now and then there will be no next time!"

He shook his head and wagged his finger at Nicephorus. "You see, other nations are not as patient as we are. No, Aelfraed, we do not kill everyone here who has a different opinion to us."

I stared at the hateful, spiteful eyes of the bound rebel and said, "Then more fool you for he deserves to die or he will return to bite you on the arse!"

I cursed in English, Alexios and Andronikos burst out laughing but the rebel and Isaac looked confused. I saw Ridley translate and then Isaac allowed a small smile to play around his civilised lips.

After we had settled the rebel city and installed the Tourmache and the Thema as a garrison, we took ship back to Constantinople. The cavalry went across the land rather than risk their horses on a perilous sea voyage but we managed to fit the commander and his entourage and all of my men on three ships of the fleet and we enjoyed a pleasant voyage around the coast of Greece. I say pleasant for I compared it with my voyages across the German sea. This sea was not even the same element. It was blue, it was calm and it was warm. It was like sailing in a bath and I, for one, enjoyed it. We had been on campaign for two years and the rest of the two-week voyage did us good. We missed meat and we missed ale but we enjoyed the sagas and the songs. Eric would have made much of our battles and trials in our wars in the Balkans.

Chapter 12

Constantinople 1078

There were no crowds to greet us as we stepped from the transports. Alexios and Andronikos had garnered all the plaudits and praise when they had reached the city. Not that we wanted cheers and flowers from grateful Byzantines; we fought for each other and accolades from our commander was enough. We docked in the evening and we quickly made our way to the barracks. Ridley left me and went to seek his wife, the old days of the two of us sharing all our adventures was gone. His priority, quite rightly, was his new bride. I felt lonely and wondered if I should call upon Eric and Snorri. I decided against that and, instead, wandered around the barracks and palace. I first checked that my officers had seen to the men, Ridley's new quarters in the palace meant that I kept my Droungarios' chambers. When I had ascertained that all was well I wandered around the palace, enjoying the cool breezes which the original architects had built into their design.

There was a small fountain close to the Imperial Palace which had lemon and orange trees. It was pleasant to sit in the cool air with the perfume of the citrus fruits above me and I felt content. My mind wandered back to England and those I had left there both living and dead. How was my son? He would now be almost eleven years old. Had Gytha told him of me or was he now the son of the Earl of Fife? And what of the brothers, Osbert and Branton? Were they still waging a war against the Normans or did they have some woodland grave? My life had changed so much and yet I still felt that I had yet to fulfil my task, whatever that was.

"A warrior who contemplates; now that is unusual and noteworthy."

I turned to see a smiling John, Alexios' clerk. I had seen little of him in the last three years and yet he had not changed. He still looked the same, a little whiter and thinner but his eyes sparkled just the same. I rose but he waved me down and sat next to me. "Warriors do contemplate wise one but not on the battlefield. There we have to react and fight with our instincts."

"I think you do yourself a disservice, strategos, for I have heard that you do use your mind on the battlefield. I believe you play chess?"

"I do."

"Which explains your success on the battlefield. The Commander has told me that but for your stand at Kalavrye we would still have rebels in the west."

"It is what we do, my men and I; we stand."

"Hmn." We sat in silence for a while. "Do you enjoy serving in Byzantium?"

"As long as I can still wield my axe and lead my Saxons then I am happy."

"Ah, but I sense that you still have the need to fight Normans."

I gave him a quick look. "You are perceptive. Yes, I would for they are a greedy and voracious people. They wish to impose their way on the world." I waved my hand around me. "It is one reason why I like this place and your people. You allow people to choose how they want to live." I laughed, "But I cannot understand how your Emperors come and go with such speed."

His face became serious and he edged closer to me. "We have had many Emperors and there are many with a claim to the title of Emperor. You have to be in the right place at the right time to achieve your ends."

"As Emperor Nicephorus was."

He put his hand to my mouth, "Ssh! Walls have ears but what I will say is that the Commander and his family will need you and your support sooner rather than later and if I were you I would watch out for Olef and his thugs for the word is out that you have annoyed them too many times." He rose. "You have good friends in Eric and Snorri. Your friend makes good furniture and I enjoy Eric's songs. I often visit their home." His eyes bored into me and I could see the message they were imparting. Eric's was a safe place to talk.

"Yes, I will visit them soon for I miss them."

"They are a delightful couple and they sing your praises. You are lucky to have such loyal friends."

My walk back to the barracks was tinged with suspicion as every shadow became a killer waiting to murder me. When I reached the safety of my chambers I felt relieved. A battlefield was one thing but to worry about a knife in the back in your own home was another. I spoke to the sentry at the barrack's entrance before I retired. "Let me know if anything untoward occurs this night."

He looked at me with a puzzled expression, "Strategos?"

"It may be nothing but I have an uneasy feeling; humour me." I shrugged, "*Wyrd.*" He nodded for he understood what I now meant and I slept easier knowing that extra care was being taken by my sentries.

I awoke the next day without any knives sticking from my back but, before I could visit my friends I was summoned to a meeting with Alexios. Andronikos and the other senior commanders were there. As soon as I arrived I knew that there was trouble afoot.

Varangian

The Commander gave me a weak smile. "It seems strategos, that not all of the rebels were quashed after our battle. Nikephoros Basilakes decided to wait until we had left before raising another rebellion against the Emperor."

My heart sank to my boots. "Not another campaign to Dyrrhachium." I dreaded the long walk in the hot sun of summer.

"No, strategos. He has obliged us by raising the men of Thessalonica, which is less than seven day's march from here. It seems your rest is to be a short one."

I shrugged, "We had a pleasant sea voyage which rested us and I think they will be eager for war once more. I suspect that they will grumble about not being able to spend their back pay but after this campaign, they should have even more!"

Andronikos slapped me on the back. "Are all Englishmen as confident as you? You always believe you will win."

"Normally we do!"

In the end, it was just Ridley who grumbled for Anna was heavily pregnant and he was loathed to leave her. "She will have the best of care in the palace old friend and, in my experience men are of little use when babies are to be born!"

It was the same army that had won at Kalavrye. The other regiments had been brought up to full strength but we only had fifty recruits to replace the hundred and thirty men we had lost but we set off in good heart. Andronikos rode with Ridley and me some way ahead of Alexios who was closeted with close advisers. "It seems that there are many rebels who do not like the Emperor."

Andronikos shot me a worried look and then another at Ridley. Ridley saw it and grinned. "I may be related to the Emperor by marriage but I took a blood oath to Aelfraed! He knows where my loyalty lies."

"I am not being disloyal, Ridley. I just wonder about these rebels."

"And there are some rebels who are not yet open about their rebellion. This rebel waited to see which way the wind blew and the fact that our commander almost lost will have heartened him." He leaned over to me. "Keep your own counsel Aelfraed and be careful for those Norns you talk about are nothing compared with the intrigue and treachery at the court of the Emperor."

"What do you mean?"

"Have you met Anna Dalassene yet?"

"No, who is she?"

"The mother of the commander and she is a shrewd lady who is more of a politician than any man I know. When we return to the city you should meet her." And that was all he would say but I began to ask around and found that she was close to the wife of Michael who had been Emperor and that, in itself, spoke volumes. It was what Andronikos did not say which intrigued me. There were obviously plots and, perhaps, that was another reason why Olef and his Varangians were intended me harm; it was known that I was loyal to Alexios and could not be bought. It was a pity I had not had time to speak with Eric.

"And how is your lady, Ridley?"

"She wishes I was not putting myself in danger." He hesitated. "The Emperor offered to give me a post in the Varangian Guard."

I waited for the next statement but he remained silent. "And?"

"I did not want to leave you and the others and I did not want to serve with the arrogant Vikings but…"

"But you wanted to be near your lady when she gives birth." He nodded. "And that is understandable. Hopefully, this will not be a two-year campaign and you can make a better decision when we return to the city."

I was sad at the thought of our friendship being broken but I fully understood his reasons. I had lost my wife to another man when I chose to fight and campaign for long periods. Ridley could not help but have noticed. Changes looked to be on the horizon at every level.

The journey took us six days and Andronikos' scouts reported that the camp of Nikephoros Basilakes was less than a day away. We prepared our own defensive camp and Alexios held a staff meeting.

"So we are close enough to another rebel to be able to see him. The question is how do we ensnare him. Strategos how many men did your scouts say that he had?"

"We are outnumbered again, Commander. Two Themai and four Tourmai of horse, including horse archers."

Alexios gave a wry smile. "So we cannot surround him."

"What about his camp?"

Andronikos looked at me curiously. "What do you mean?"

"Is it like ours? Is it defended as the Romans did with ditch and ramparts?"

Andronikos smiled, "No it is not. I do not think he even knows we are here. Certainly, my men saw no scouts."

"So we could attack his camp…"

I interrupted the Commander, "At night, my lord when they will not see that they outnumber us and, if the strategos is correct, when they think there are no Imperial troops for miles. He must have rebelled thinking that we were still on the west."

"Send scouts out to make sure they have no knowledge of us and then we will attack tomorrow night. We will spend tomorrow closing with the camp and surrounding it. I will arrange signals to coordinate the attacks."

My Thema and Ridley's warriors were assigned the role of attacking from the east. It meant that we had the shortest approach to the attack. Alexios joined us while Andronikos took the cataphracts and the cavalry to the west. They left at noon and we arranged for the infantry to begin the attack. Once the alarm was raised we would loose an arrow into the air and the cavalry would attack but, as I said to Ridley, if the strategos of cavalry did not hear commotion then we would have failed. This would be the first time I had fought with the Thema and I gathered the Tourmache around me. "I know it is not your way but I want you to lead your men into this attack. There is much confusion during battles at night and your men are dressed and armed in a similar fashion to the enemy. I want you to tell your men to use a code word. If they are uncertain if they are fighting friend or foe they say Ridley and the answer will be Aelfraed."

They grinned and one said, "Clever, my lord, for no Greek would naturally use those words but all of our men know them."

"We have so few men that the last thing we need is for our men to kill their fellows. At least the Varangian Inglinoi, look like nothing else on the battlefield."

They left to brief their men feeling more confident. In my experience confidence in battle is worth a thousand men. And well led another thousand. I hoped that we would have both.

We assembled less than a thousand paces from the unprotected camp. They were a confident enemy or perhaps just careless. We edged forwards. I had chosen a hundred small wiry warriors from the Thema to slip and slither forwards and kill the hapless sentries who were just waiting for their relief and bed. They died soundlessly allowing my seven thousand men to move ever closer. I had an archer with me and my aide, reluctantly, carried the pot containing the fire to light his arrow. I do not think that Isaac thought he would be so close to the fighting when he was assigned as my aide. Once at the line of tents all my officers looked towards me. I waved Death Bringer forwards and we silently swept into the unsuspecting camp. Each Kontoubernion took a tent and, once inside, slaughtered the sleeping soldiers. I wondered how long they would remain silent but we were on the third row of tents before a scream rent the air. I turned to the archer, "Now!"

The screams, shouts and the sounds of clashing metal filled the air as the arrow soared high in the air. I watched the slaughter take place; I

Varangian

was strategos and I needed to be alert to danger but part of me did not like this slaughter of sleeping men. The code of the warrior wanted them to have the chance to defend themselves. I heard the thunder of hooves and the whoosh of arrows as Andronikos' cavalry thundered into the camp. The crash of the cataphracts marked the end of the battle as men, still half asleep and drowsy, threw their arms before them and dropped to the ground in obeisance. We had won and another rebel general was captured. It had been too easy. I looked behind me and I could only see the enemy dead. We had not even needed the code words so complete had been the victory. Nikephoros Basilakes was captured as he and the boy he was in bed with awoke to find Ridley's warriors laughing at them.

This time we were afforded a triumph and we marched proudly through the streets of Constantinople leading our captives bound and downcast. Alexios was heralded as the saviour of Byzantium and the Emperor himself greeted us to lavish upon us medals and honours. I took some satisfaction from the sour looks on the faces of Olef and his Varangian Guard who appeared to be the only ones not to be enamoured of us.

When we returned to the barracks the men were in high spirits. Our losses had been minimal and all of us had made a fortune from back pay and the sale of slaves. I hoped that they would hang on to their money, as Ridley and I did, but I suspected that many would waste their gains. Their philosophy was easy come, easy go. After I had bathed I arranged to meet Ridley at Isaac's to invest more of my money. I also wished to speak with Eric and discover what was going on with Byzantine politics.

Isaac asked us both what we intended for our money. "What do you suggest my friend. We are but warriors and know nothing of growing wealthy."

He nodded to Ridley. "As you are going to have a family soon I would suggest some property. Probably close the palace. You will need your privacy."

Ridley's face lit up when he heard that and it was obvious that the idea had not crossed his mind. I smiled at his pleasure for Ridley, of all people deserved to have some good fortune. "Would that be a good investment for me as well?"

"It would, my lord. Perhaps an estate? You would not need to be close to the city and there are some fine properties which would bring in a healthy income. We would just need to appoint a steward."

A flash of pain struck me as the memory of faithful Thomas and Sarah came to mind. Isaac the Jew was right. It would be good to have somewhere to escape the politics of Constantinople and I would have another Maiden Bower, "That is a good idea. Let me know when you have such a property."

"Will you both be in the city for a while?"

"As long as there are no more rebels for Alexios to deal with then yes." Isaac gave a sharp look but then his face became impassive. I wondered just what he knew about our Commander and his plans.

Eric and Snorri looked to be even more prosperous. They had a new name on their door and they now traded as Castor and Pollux. Ridley looked confused until I said that they were twin brothers from Greek mythology. The two of them looked very comfortable and Eric, in particular, had grown into a handsome man. He still had oiled hair and used perfume heavily. He greeted us both in the Greek fashion with a kiss on each cheek. At first, I had found this a strange custom but I was now used to it. Ragnar, as usual, knelt and kissed my hand. He would never forget the debt he owed me.

As we sat in the cool courtyard sipping the cool wine Eric told us the news and the gossip of the city. He made sure there were no servants close by and began but the first thing he did was to address Ridley. "Now that you are married into the Emperor's family, where sits your allegiance?"

I saw Ridley redden and start to rise and I restrained him. "It is not an insult old friend. Eric wants to know can he speak openly before you?"

"Well, of course, he can! I am still the same Ridley I always was!"

Snorri laughed. "I can see that and my friend meant no disrespect but there are spies everywhere. I know that your wife's body servant reports to the Emperor's spymaster Calisthenes each day."

Ridley looked shocked. "I will have her dismissed!"

Eric shook his head, "No, for then they would replace her with someone you did not know. This way you know not to say anything to your wife which she might repeat to the servant."

"I would suggest, for your wife's safety old friend that you only tell your wife the things that are every day. She might say something which she thinks is trivial and it might land you in a cell."

I could see that my comments had given him pause for thought. Eric began, "There is a faction trying to rid the city of the new Emperor. He is not popular. The Doukas family is less than happy with him. And the Emperor's wife Maria of Alania is trying to promote her son."

"That means we will be fighting rebels again and Alexios will have to protect the Emperor's back once more."

Eric laughed, "Hardly for one of the chief conspirators is Anna Dalassene, the Commander's own mother." He paused to let that sink in before he hit us with his next astounding news. "Alexios himself has been approached."

Ridley and I looked at each other in shock. We both knew that he had a claim to the throne but, having been in the city for a few years there appeared to be many who had a claim to the poison chalice that was the crown. "That is an interesting bundle of facts, Eric. Where does that leave us?"

"If I were you Aelfraed I would worry more about Olef for it is known that he has put a price on your head. Your men have made such a name for themselves that many are saying that they are the true Varangian Guard and Olef and his Vikings are just greedy mercenaries who have never even fought for the Empire whilst you and your men have saved it on at least two occasions. Once again you are the victim of your own success."

Snorri looked concerned. "Do not wander alone. Take some men with you and avoid the narrow secret places of the city."

They had both confirmed what John had told me and now that I knew that Alexios was a potential rebel it made my life even more perilous. I had no problem with supporting Alexios as a rebel for I had taken an oath to him, not to the Emperor. Had Olef accepted me it would have been a different story but this way I could follow my leader with a clear conscience.

"Thank you for that. On a different matter; Isaac is procuring me an estate out of the city. I will need a steward. If you know of anyone reliable I would be grateful." I spread my hands, "I know little of farms and farming. I really want it as somewhere I can escape to."

"We will but there is an obvious candidate, someone you could trust with your life, literally."

"Who is that?"

"Ragnar of course."

The old warrior nodded eagerly and I took his hand. "Then Ragnar shall be my new Steward, just let Isaac know, will you? I suspect I am going to be a little busy watching for knives in the night."

"Do not worry. I will watch your back for you."

"As you always do, Ridley."

The next day Alexios summoned his officers to a conference. I wondered if there were other rebels for us to defeat but he looked very serious. "We will take the army from the barracks and establish a camp north of here."

Andronikos and I looked at each other. "But the city is cool and tents at this time of year are a nightmare with the heat and the flies."

"True, Andronikos, but I wish us to train together in the field. Our last two battles have shown me that we need to work together more effectively and not have to learn on the battlefield."

It made sense to me. "When do we leave, Commander?"

"You have three days and, one more thing, do not tell the men where we are going, I would like this to be a secret."

Ridley in what he thought was a quiet voice but which everyone heard, "That won't be difficult as we have no idea ourselves anyway."

Even Alexios laughed and we all left to deal with the logistics of moving our men again. At least they had had a few days to waste or to invest their back pay. I summoned my aide. "Well, we will be on campaign again soon. Prepare a wagon and this time let us take some servants with us."

"Where are we going, my lord? I thought all the rebels were dealt with."

"When I know then you will know." He left and I was a little irritated by his questions. As an aide, it was his job to translate my orders into actions. I had decided to take servants as this would be a training camp and a little pampering would do no harm.

Before we could leave we had to endure a celebration of our successes. In the centre of the palace was a parade ground and we were asked to bring a Kentarchia from each of the regiments which had fought so that they could be presented with phalerae to mark their achievements. For me, it was a hard choice, which men had fought better? In my view, they all needed a reward or none. I felt it would be divisive but the Commander of the West was insistent and Ridley, Andronikos and I made the choice and had the three hundred chosen men ready for the parade.

The Emperor had a raised dais and he was seated under a golden panoply surrounded by his Varangians all decked out in their finest armour. I noticed that although it sparkled it did not look functional and my armour, magnificent, though I felt it was looked dowdy by comparison. The difference was that it had seen much action over the years. Of more interest to me were the two women on the platform, Maria, the Empress and Anna, Alexios' mother. Although Maria was but a few years older than Alexios and myself she looked younger and I could see why Nicephorus had cemented his position by marrying the wife of the former Emperor. Anna, however, had the sharp eyes of a plotter. She put me in mind of Ealdgyth, an older Ealdgyth obviously. She had the inquisitive look of an observer and a planner; when I met her, after the ceremony I was most impressed.

It was Anna who first spoke to me. "I believe I am in your debt, Englishman. I am told that you have been invaluable to my son and instrumental in all of his victories. It is good to see such virtues of loyalty." She quickly cast a disparaging look in Olef's direction.

The Empress joined us as Alexios and Ridley spoke with her husband. "My husband also speaks fondly of you, even though he only fought alongside you once you impressed him. Tell me, why did you leave your homeland to fight here, so far away?"

"We lost, majesty, and the Normans won!"

"An honest answer and I suspect a warning for us to fear the voracious Franks."

"Indeed it is."

Anna had a mischievous glint in her eye and she said, quietly, "I heard a rumour that you shared a bed with your father's wife, the Queen of England after he was killed." I felt myself redden and struggled to reply. I had been brought up not to lie but, equally, I could not dishonour Ealdgyth's memory. "I apologise, Aelfraed. I should not have been so impertinent for I see that you are an honourable man and an interesting one. I would value some conversation when we have time."

That was the end of our conversation but, again, I was reminded of Ealdgyth, in a different way from Maria, for both Anna and Ealdgyth shared a passion for intrigue and politics. I was pleased that I had met her.

The next few days were hectic and we barely had time to stand and think as we planned for the move to the secret camp. Had we been going to a place which all knew then it would have been easier but the Commander was being cautious. In the end that was wise, but at the time all of his officers cursed the secrecy. I arranged with Isaac, my aide to feast the officers of the army the night before we left. I had enough money to put on a lavish feast but I did not do it for the kudos but to reward men who had worked harder and longer than they needed to. My aide showed that he was up to the task and arranged everything, from the cooks to the food, from the servers to the wine and it went smoothly. I wondered if I had been too hard on him.

My Saxon officers could drink and they soon made it into a drinking and eating contest. I was too wise, as was Ridley, to fall into that trap. I had learned that the best strategy, in front of one's officers was to drink moderately and keep one's mouth shut. If they were foolish it could be laughed off but the senior officer had to have the men follow him. Isaac hovered nervously all night, attending when a goblet was half empty, sending for a servant when a platter looked to be empty; sending for a cleaner when wine was spilt. I realised that I had misjudged him and that, when we camped, I should take the time to get to know him.

"More wine, strategos?"

"No thank you, Isaac. I will need a clear head tomorrow besides which I am enjoying watching my men relax and enjoy themselves." The only officer who was not present was Alexios and I did not think he would mind allowing us the time to become a tighter team.

"I have a fine drink which I think you enjoy." He nodded to Ridley. "My lord told me that you had this wine from Lusitania with a Jorvik Jew."

How thoughtful of Ridley to remember. "In that case, and, as you have gone to so much trouble I will indulge myself."

"I have it in the cellar, I will just fetch it."

As he left Andronikos stood, a little unsteadily. "I would like to propose a toast to my friend, the strategos, Aelfraed. He is a fine man to follow but a nightmare to fight. I thank God that we are on the same side!"

The whole table stood and cheered and then drank down their drink. Ridley stood. "Give us a speech, strategos. Inspire us!"

I reluctantly stood, I hated speeches but they had touched me. As I stood Isaac returned with the rich red drink which he placed by my side. I nodded my thanks. "You are all fine officers and I can give no greater compliment than to say I would happily stand in a shield wall with any of you."

The Greeks looked a little confused but my Saxons took that as the greatest accolade they could receive.

"We have just begun to learn how we fight and how we stand together and I am grateful for the chance, with Strategos Andronikos, to lead you and support our Commander." They all banged the table.

Isaac came next to me. "Do not forget your wine, my lord, and the toast."

"Thank you, Isaac. How did I manage before without an aide?" I lifted the goblet. "Here is a toast to the finest officers in the Byzantine Empire." I pointed the goblet to all of them and then, remembering Reuben's advice to sip I took a mouthful of the warming liquor. It was, as I remembered it and it warmed as it went down. The men were still cheering as I raised it again but then the warmth changed to a sudden pain in my chest and I found that I could not breathe. The pain became intolerable as a fire surged through my body. My knees suddenly could not bear my weight and I found myself falling, unable to speak. I almost tried to laugh as I saw the horrified expressions of the others and then mercifully, all; went black.

Chapter 13

Constantinople Christmas 1080

I dreamt I was back in England and Nanna and Aethelward were beating off the huge dog which was trying to eat me. I could see my brothers and their father laughing at me as I tried to run away but my feet kept sticking in the mud. All the time I could hear the crackle of laughter from William the Bastard who changed, strangely, into Olef and he held a knife which kept coming closer and closer to my eye and then I heard Ealdgyth scream, "Stop!" I could see a faint light and I felt weak as though I had run for a hundred miles in mail. A cool breeze came from somewhere which made me think about falling back to sleep and then I felt a cool hand on my brow. Was I dead? Was this Heaven? If so, where were my comrades and friends who had died before me? Was the idea of heaven a lie?

I began to discern voices, muted, but clear, somewhere near my fuzzy head. "Bring the water again Snorri." It was Eric and unless he was dead too then I was alive still.

I struggled my eyes open and saw sunlight dappling a beautifully painted wall. I heard a grunt and felt the unmistakeably rough grip of Ragnar's hand. "He is awake." A hand lifted my head and I looked up as Eric poured water gently down my throat. "We thought we had lost you, my friend." I tried to say something but just a croak came out of my parched lips. Eric held up his hand, "No, let us talk. We will give you sustenance for it has been a long ten days that you have lain close to death and you will need to build up your body's strength. Ragnar, sit him up and then he can drink a little easier."

I was pulled upright and saw that I was in a room on the upper floor of Eric and Snorri's home. The three of them all peered into my face as though to discern if I would live. Eric nodded, "Good! Ragnar get some food, soup I think and Snorri, continue to give him water in small sips." Eric had certainly grown over the years. What a confident young man he had become.

"Well, where to begin. Ridley told us this first part for we were not at the feast. You were poisoned. Luckily for you it was but a sip and Ridley remembered the attempt on the Queen's life and he recognised the signs. It was Andronikos who saved your life. He mixed some charcoal with water and forced it down your throat and you brought up much of the poison."

I croaked a, "Who?"

Varangian

And Eric shook his head and held his perfumed hand over my mouth. "We will come to that. You are going nowhere and remember, I am a storyteller. Let me perform for you now." The gentle smile took away any harshness from his words. "Isaac the aide had poisoned you for Edward had seen him hand you the drink moments before you fell. It was obvious that he was the culprit. After they had tortured him they discovered that it had been Olef the Varangian who had secured him his post and he was in the pay of that Norse. He had been paid to kill you." My eyes asked the question that my throat could not. "He was killed and his head stuck on a spear outside the Varangian barracks." I smiled. The Norse would know that was a message from my men for the Greeks would never resort to such barbarism. "Your men all swore an oath of silence. As far as Olef and the others are concerned, you were poisoned and the poisoner caught. They brought you here under cover of darkness and we have tended to you for the last ten days. Alexios and his mother know that you live but they will be silent on the matter for your sake. If Olef finds out that you are alive then he will not be so subtle next time and you are in no condition to defend yourself well against me, let alone Olef."

Ragnar brought soup and fed me like a mother with a sick child. Each spoonful was carefully cooled and gently poured into my open mouth. It was touching to see such concern in the gentle giant's eyes.

Eric went away for something and Snorri continued the tale. "The army is away somewhere secret, they did not tell us, quite rightly in my view and the city is still talking of the disappearance of the Inglinos. Those close to the Emperor and Olef talk of your death but those in the streets believe you are alive still. There is a cult of people who believe that you will be the saviour of Constantinople." I shook my head in disbelief. Snorri too smiled, "I know, ridiculous isn't it but you have been associated with so many victories which have come from near defeat that you have attained mythical qualities. You and I are warriors and know that battles are won on the backs of brave men standing toe to toe but the citizens of the city believe that we bear charmed lives for we are favoured."

Eric returned with a letter. "Isaac the Jew knows that you live and he has purchased the estate you wanted. Here are the deeds. When you are well enough Ragnar will take you there and you can continue your recovery. I think that is all, no, of course, it isn't. The Empress has adopted Alexios as her son!" I almost spat my soup out in shock and my wide eyes showed my surprise. "I know, she is barely older than he but there is method behind the plan. She is protecting her son, by Michael the Fourth, but it also gives Alexios great power." Even though we were in the safety of their home Eric lowered his voice. "The conspiracy against the Emperor grows. I hope it will not lead to war for Isaac the Jew has heard that Robert Guiscard is casting covetous eyes on Illyria. Now sleep and when you wake you can talk." Ragnar forcefully pulled up the cover and wagging a finger at me mimed sleeping.

Three more days saw me a little stronger and able to walk around the upstairs rooms. I dared not venture downstairs in case I was seen. It was maddening to be trapped, even though the cage I was in was gilded, it was still a cage. On the fourth morning, all three of my friends came into my room. Eric looked very serious. "We have come up with a plan which may well help you to come downstairs and even get to your estates."

"Tell me! I will do anything!"

They looked at each other dubiously. "Shave and have your hair cut."

I understand their suggestion and it made sense but would I be a Saxon warrior without my hair and beard?

Snorri spread his hands, "I did it old friend and it did not change me." That was not true and we both knew it. The Snorri before me was not the wounded fierce warrior we had rescued from the river but he was right. My beard and long hair marked me as a Saxon.

Eric shrugged. "It will grow again. You just need to be able to get out of the city. People will recognise you."

I shrugged, "Very well then."

I had never seen myself with a beard and I was not certain what I would look without but they had a piece of polished metal which they brought in and I saw my reflection. They were right. I did not look like a Saxon anymore but neither did I look like a Greek. I was too big but I would not be recognised.

"Excellent. Now take a few more days to recover and we will risk a journey to the country."

I never did manage to get to the estate for events began to move faster than we had anticipated. The Emperor's spymasters were becoming increasingly concerned about Alexios' intentions. Even worse he had been summoned by the Emperor back to the city to receive instructions about the forthcoming invasion of the Seljuk. On reflection, he should have chosen that moment to stage his rebellion but instead, he did the honourable thing and returned to the city. Eric brought me a visitor a few days after he had deemed that I had regained my health, it was John. He beamed at me when he saw me. "I am pleased that you still live and that you have changed your appearance. But for your size, I would not have recognised you."

"It is good of you to come to see me."

"Sadly I come not to inquire about your health but to enlist your help. The Commander has need of you. Straboromanos has ordered extra guards around the palace and he fears that he will not be able to escape."

Eric protested, "But he has only just recovered from the poisoning. How does the Commander expect him to save him in his condition?"

"I am fine, Eric. I am a warrior and I have suffered worse than this and still survived. Tell me, John, what do I need to do?"

"First I have to get you into the palace. That will be easier now that you have shaved and cut your hair. We will colour your skin a little and you can pretend to be my slave. I have purchased some fine furniture from your friends here and you can carry it in. The guards will not look twice at a slave entering. They will be more concerned with others trying to escape."

"And how will he affect the escape of Alexios? There will be two of them trapped in the palace then rather than just one."

"It is more than just one now for the Commander's mother and others in his family are in there. We need to rescue the whole family."

That sounded like a tall order to me but Alexios was a clever man and I knew that he would have some sort of plan and I also knew that my part would be one that would involve my strength and my skills as a warrior." All three of them were unhappy at my decision but I was Alexios' man and, if he needed me, then I would be there for him.

"You will not be able to carry weapons into the palace."

"I know and once in it does not matter for I have my own weapons in the barracks."

I bade farewell to my friends. "Thank you for all your help. I know that I owe my life to you three and I shall not forget it. When this is over we shall spend some time on my estate and enjoy the peace."

Eric embraced me, "For myself, I would just have you returned to us whole!"

The furniture I carried was heavy and Ragnar had to help me to hoist it upon my shoulder. "You need to drop your shoulders and shuffle your feet as the slaves do and keep your head down." Snorri adjusted the load to hide me and then Ragnar went back into the shop and brought out a floppy hat which he deposited on my head. "Ha, that is perfect; it hides your face and makes you look like every other male slave in the city."

I shuffled behind John who seemed to have the ability to carve a path through crowds despite his diminutive size. He assiduously avoided conversation with me but I saw his head flicking from side to side as he scanned the crowds for danger. As we neared the palace sentries he did

Varangian

not slow up but waved his arm imperiously for them to stand aside. They saw the familiar clerk with his slave and calmly stood aside. Within a heartbeat, I was in the palace grounds. Getting out again would be the tricky part. He did not take me to Alexios' quarters but led me through the corridors to his own rooms. They were exactly the way I envisaged them with everything neatly laid out and all the belongings were both beautiful and well arranged. "Just put it down there. You must be tired carrying such a heavy piece of furniture."

"No, after mail armour and my weapons it was nothing. Now, how do I get to see Alexios?"

"Go in there I have a tunic of one of the servants of the palace. It was the largest one I could find; put it on and we will see if it works."

The costume was with Imperial purple borders and it did fit me, just. The shoulders were a little tight but it made me anonymous as there were many such servants dressed as I scurrying about the palace. Satisfied he nodded and left the room with me behind him. We went first to the kitchens where other servants were busy fetching and carrying. They were too busy to notice another servant and John confidently walked over to the jugs of wine and sniffing them chose the one he approved of. He then selected four of the best goblets and put everything on a tray. He nodded at me to pick them up and then he led me through the corridors to the quarters of Alexios and his mother. There was a guard at the door and I was not sure if he was there to protect Alexios or prevent his departure but he recognised John and relaxed as he opened the door for us. Once inside I could see that there was just the Commander and his mother.

As soon as I put the tray on the table I was embraced by Alexios. "I am glad to see that you are alive my friend and sorry that I have to put your life in jeopardy again."

"I am your man, sire and serve you in all things."

His mother looked over curiously at us. "I find this sense of honour amongst barbarians a strange concept."

Alexios said quickly, "They do not see themselves as barbarians, mother. Do not insult my friend."

"I understand your mother, Commander and I suppose that we are barbarians but I would not trade that for the treachery of Byzantine politics."

"There my son, he does not need you to defend himself; he can trade insults even with a formidable foe such as I." She smiled at me and I saw that she meant no malice. Now, how do we get my son from the city?"

"And protect my family."

"You are all under suspicion I take it?"

"Yes, all of us."

"So let us look at this in two steps. Step one would be to get your mother and the family out of the palace."

"Not the city?"

"That is probably a step too far. "

"You have an idea brewing in your head do you not?"

"Just the glimmer of one. The Hagia Sophia, it is a holy place?"

"Yes, the most holy in the city. And the Queen could go there could she not, with the family to pray for…" I had no idea what they would pray for; prayer had never been high on my list of achievements.

"They could say they need to make a visit to pray for the success of her son's expedition to Asia, my lord."

"Perfect, John. But how does that help me?"

"If you were to claim sanctuary in the church would it be allowed?"

The two of them looked at the bookish John who looked as though he knew the answer. "Straboromanos probably has men at the church and they would be paid to keep you out."

"It is a public place?"

"Of course."

"Then when you get to the church you pretend to be women on a pilgrimage and get into the church. Once you are in you make your way to the sanctuary and claim the right to safety."

"I can see how that would work but not how it would aid my son."

"We need to get your son out of the city and this way all attention will be on you and the family. Once in the Hagia Sophia, you make a fuss and demand that the Emperor himself guarantees your safety. Make up something about a plot to kill you and your son. The Commander and I will then go to the stables, take two horses and sneak out of the palace while everyone is seeking you. We could then ride to the army, which I assume is close by?"

"They are in a valley to the north of the city where the other Strategoi await my arrival."

They still looked dubious. "It is a game of chess commander. You are not yet the king on the board," I had deduced that he would be the next Emperor for everything had been leading to that inevitable conclusion, "You are the piece who is making for your opponent's line. The Emperor will be looking to secure the next most important piece, the Queen. It is known that you are close with the Empress and she would demand that you be given sanctuary. You are only in a weak position when you are here hidden in the palace which Straboromanos controls. The Commander and I are warriors, we can ride and fight our way out if needs be but the family cannot."

Alexios' mother nodded. "It is a good plan and even if it were not it is the only plan we have. Besides, I can improvise when I meet with the Emperor. I have a great ability, I can bring on tears instantly and men are always weak when a woman cries."

John nodded, "Then the first thing is to get the family together but there is one problem. The Emperor's nephew and his tutor. The tutor is one of Straboromanos' men and he would go directly to the Emperor if he got wind of your departure."

"I can deal with him. I will go along and tell them that I am to give a lesson on military tactics and the girls will not need that." Alexios looked at me. "You need to wait in John's chamber. I will come to you once the family has escaped."

And without further ado, the plan began. John took me back to my room, Alexios headed for the tutor and Alexios' mother gathered the women and children like a mother duck with her ducklings. She was a formidable woman who, had she been a man, would have been a mighty general. The hardest part for me was the waiting alone, for John had gone with the family to ensure their escape. It was Alexios who arrived, late in the afternoon. "I have spent the last three hours with the tutor, boring the boy with strategy. I would hope that they have made it to the church." He handed me a sword and a dagger. It would not do to go unarmed. We walked through the servant part of the complex as though we had every right to be there. The Commander received a few strange looks but we were not challenged. It would be a different matter once we were closer to the stables for every soldier knew Alexios by sight and, despite my disguise, once seen in the company of the Commander, they would soon know me and I was already a hunted man.

We were favoured by the darkening night. Unlike England where nightfall took a long time, here it happened quickly and that, too aided us. My clothes were now the liability for what was an Imperial servant doing around the barrack area? We knew we were nearing the stables when the foetid, sweaty smell of horse dung hit us. We peered around the corner of the stone building and there, standing guard were two men of the Hetaireia. Had I been with Ridley I would have been confident that we could take them but I had never seen my Commander in close fighting. I had the feeling that I would have to deal with them both myself. As much as I did not wish these two sentries to die, I had to make sure of their silence. I turned to Alexios. "You head for them and tell them you wish to look at your horse."

"Why would I do that?"

"Why not and you would not expect to have to explain your actions would you? Not to a common soldier." He could see the sense in that. "When they turn to take you in I will strike the one on the right and render him unconscious. You just stop the other one from shouting out and I will deal with him."

"You have done this before."

I grinned, "Many times, my lord!"

The two guards viewed the Commander of the Army of the West with suspicion but they stood stiffly to attention. "I would visit with my horse." He made to pass them but they looked at each other and then him in confusion.

"Your horse, my lord?"

"Yes! If I am to lead the Army on a glorious war against the infidel then I would make sure that he is in good condition."

"But..." one began to be silenced by a nudge in the ribs. They stood aside and started to enter, no doubt to make sure we did not grab a horse and escape. I saw the heavy wooden bucket they used to relieve themselves in at the door and I picked it up and swung it heavily at the side of the head of the right-hand guard. It was half full and heavy. The ceremonial helmet was just that and he slumped to the ground in a heap. Alexios had thrown the other to the ground and I took out my dagger, reversed the blade and, taking the man's helmet off smacked him sharply on the back of his head.

"Tie them up."

There were leather reins aplenty and we soon had the two of them trussed up. I tore some strips from their cloaks and gagged them. They would live and they would not be able to raise the alarm. We chose our own horses from the barracks. They were both good horses and we knew them. The last thing we needed was a skittish horse. Once mounted, we rode casually out of the stables although we knew that the first time we were seen the alarm would be raised for the palace gates were shut. I was still unsure about our ability to get out but, if it came to it I could kill any guards and we would be able to leave.

Suddenly I caught a movement out of the corner of my eye and John appeared. He rushed to us. "Your mother should have been an actress. She demanded a cross and Straboromanos had to fetch one and then she demanded that the Emperor himself should guarantee their safety. He is leaving now." We quickly dismounted and led the horses down an alley between two barracks. I heard the tramp of the Varangians as they flanked Nicephorus and headed for the gate.

"That's the end of that plan then."

Varangian

"No so, commander. Let us follow them, leading our horses." We walked forty paces behind the last guards. They did not turn around for the clatter of their hobnails masked any noise we might make. I was doubly glad that they were our horses for they did not whinny or make a noise. We gradually drew closer to them so that, as we neared the gate leading to the city, we were but twenty paces behind. The last Varangian exited and the sentries began to close the gates. Alexios waved his arm at them and their training took over. They stood to attention and we mounted at the gate. It was then that our luck left us. The last two Varangians turned, I assume to make sure the gates had closed and they saw us. They both drew their swords and raced at us. This was no time for honour and noble gestures. I drew my sword, galloped at the two men slashing my sword on either side of the horse. My horse took care of one and the other had half his face ripped open. I swung my horse around and we headed through the narrow streets. "Head for the port!"

"Why, Aelfraed? The other gates will be guarded. The sea is our only chance."

I did not mention that I had friends there and we had a better chance of survival on the quayside rather than at the gates.

No one followed us and we rode our luck. We reined in at the port. There were many ships tied up and, to my delight I saw one I recognised, The Maiden. "We are in luck." We dismounted and I led the horses away from The Maiden and tied them up outside one of the many taverns frequented by sailors. I doubted that the horses would remain there for long. It was a shame to lose two such magnificent beast but our lives were more important. We made our way along the shadows towards the Jarl's boat. I could see two figures at the gangplank, which meant they had just loaded and would be leaving on the morning tide. *Wyrd*.

As we approached, we were spotted and I heard Stig shout. "You two, we don't need any who like boys on this ship so fuck off!"

I continued walking and he drew his sword. "Is that any welcome for an old friend?"

It took him a moment and then Olaf recognised me. "It is Aelfraed although he looks plucked."

They both embraced me. "We have not time for that. Take us to the Captain, we are in trouble."

Stig rushed us aboard while Olaf kept watch. Our faces gave away our plight and Gunnar quickly took in our predicament. "The Emperor is hunting you?"

"He is."

Varangian

"I cannot afford to upset the Emperor."

"He will not know. All you need to do is to leave a little earlier and drop us up the coast a little ways." I sensed Alexios' anxious frustration and I put my arm around his shoulders. "This is the Commander of the Army of the West and, just up the coast is the army that will make him Emperor. Now which Emperor do you want to piss off, the old one or the new one?"

He laughed, "Life is always interesting with you, Aelfraed." He turned to Stig. "Tell the First Mate to get the rowers ready, but do it quietly and then pull up the gangplank. As soon as the First Mate is there he can slip one of the moorings so that we can have a speedy exit." He bowed to Alexios. "Apologies for my caution but I would hate to lose what I took a lifetime to get."

Alexios began to relax and he smiled. "As would I and I thank you, captain. This kind deed will not be forgotten."

The jarl inclined his head to me, "I owe this one so much already and this small deed does not even begin to repay him."

I was too anxious to listen. I wanted us away as quickly as we could manage it. The First Mate burst in. "Which dickhead wants us to sail in the middle of the night?"

Alexios looked shocked. I just said, "This dickhead."

"I might have known. Right, Captain, we'll be underway in a moment!"

He was as good as his word and I heard the clunk of the oars and felt the sensation of the ship as she moved away from the quay and headed for open water. The army was camped on the Black Sea and we would reach there no faster on horses. As dawn broke we could see Miklagård disappearing in the distance. With the family safe in Hagia Sofia, we could now act honourably and declare for Alexios. As we ate some dried venison and sipped ale he put me right on that one. "No, Aelfraed. I will not embroil the Empire in a bloody civil war that only suits the Turk and the Norman. No, when I return to the city I will be welcomed. My mother and the Empress will keep us informed of the best moment to return but until then we will move ever closer to the city. It will be a reminder of our power and my mother will also tell the city of the treachery of Olef and that you are not, as they feared, dead but alive having saved me from the machinations of Straboromanos."

I would be lying if I said I was not disappointed. I wanted to fight Olef and his Varangians and that would not happen but I would, at least, be reunited with my men. I asked Alexios about the Guard, "Tell me about the Varangians. When Nicephorus is removed do the guards become yours?"

"It is complicated. They are loyal to the Emperor so long as he is Emperor. After he is deposed they normally loot the treasury and then most swear allegiance to the new Emperor."

I was shocked, "And this is allowed?"

He spread his hands. "What Emperor wishes to anger the men who guard him?"

"The difference that you have your own Varangians and we will stop Olef and his bandits from robbing the treasury." No matter what Alexios said I swore to myself that I would make sure that the murderer who had never fought once for Nicephorus would profit from this. I could see that Alexios thought that this was a fact of life and inevitable. It was not.

We could see the fires from the army out at sea and the Jarl edged us to the shore. "Do you want Stig and the boys to accompany you?"

"No Gunnar, you have done enough and the Emperor has no men this far out."

Alexios extended his arm. "When I am Emperor, Captain I will find some way to increase your profit."

"If you protected the lower end of the Dnieper and controlled the Pechengs then I would indeed be a rich man."

"Consider it done."

We had to wade the last few paces to the shore and I had forgotten the flies that seemed to love the low lying areas. We might only be a mile or two from safety but it would seem further. I was bolstered by the fact that Alexios struggled more than I did. I must have recovered from the attempt on my life. We were found by a patrol of Andronikos' cavalry. "We thought you were imprisoned." He dismounted to give his mount to Alexios.

He had not recognised me at first and I spoke, "And what of me?"

He almost jumped out of his skin; it was as though he had seen a ghost. "We heard that you were dead."

"No, just close to it and then shorn like a sheep."

The officers were delighted when we arrived and we were washed fed and watered in rapid succession. We told the rapt audience of officers of our escape and the fortunate happenstance of the presence of Jarl Gunnerrson's ship. "*Wyrd*." Was the only comment from Ridley but he was right. Someone or something was keeping me safe and for a purpose.

A rider galloped into the camp bearing letters for Alexios. "They all looked to him in surprise. "But who knows you are here?"

"My mother and she must have known that we would escape."

He began to read the letter and Ridley drew me to one side. "What of Anna, my wife?"

"I did not see her but she will be safe for she is Nicephorus' family."

"But what happens when he is removed?"

"We will be in the city by then," I explained to him about the Varangian Guard and the raiding of the Treasury. "We will enter secretly with our men and some of Andronikos' trusted men. We will secure your wife and the Treasury and if Olef tries to take it then…"

Alexios gave a triumphant wave of his hand. "The Emperor has allowed my wife and family to go to the convent of Petrion. They will be guarded but as you can see she is able to send us messages and she is being given information by the Empress. Tomorrow we begin our slow march to Byzantium. Let us see him sweat while we gather troops."

Chapter 14

My face itched as we rode towards the city, much to the amusement of my hairy Saxons. I was determined to look as I once had and put up with the irritation. It made me somewhat short-tempered although my colleagues were delighted to have both Alexios and me back in the fold. We took the journey slowly for more Thema and Droungoi were joining us every day. Alexios was known as a soldier's general and was always more popular than Nicephorus. I was keen to get there quickly and prevent Olef from robbing the country of its treasure. We also heard from Alexios' mother that there were more western mercenaries in the city. I wondered where they had come from? Were they Normans? Perhaps more Saxons?

As we camped, less than a day away from the city I sought out Alexios. "You do not want a full-scale battle for the city do you?"

"Of course not, I told you I want no bloodshed."

"You may want that and Nicephorus may want that but Olef is a vicious Viking who just wants the treasure. Let me slip in with a thousand men and we will secure the treasury and the palace. With luck, they will then desert as soon as you arrive."

"I am not sure."

"There is one other way we could ensure a bloodless take over. I will speak with Nicephorus and give him your assurance that he will live."

His eyes lit up at that. "It is risky. How would you get in the city?"

"They are hiring mercenaries, we go in small groups to volunteer and others slip in during the day. Don't forget my men know the city and they know the barracks. They will be looking for an army, not a rabble. My men can play the rabble."

Although Alexios argued for a while he knew it was a no lose situation for him and it would ensure a peaceful entry to the city. Andronikos was disappointed that the Commander of the West refused to allow him to accompany me. He was there when I spoke to the men I would take with me. I made sure that they had all discarded any Imperial uniform and those who could speak other languages were selected to 'volunteer' for service. The others would be secreted in various parts of the city. Timing would be crucial and Alexios and the army would arrive outside of the city at dusk allowing us to open the gates during the night. He was keen for civilian casualties to be minimised and empty streets would ensure just that. I went ahead with the first group of volunteers. I chose a group who could all speak

Danish. Some of Andronikos' warriors would follow and then Ridley with more Danish speakers. We hoped this way to have thirty warriors inside the walls soon after dawn allowing the rest to trickle in. We all wore worn mail and carried old swords. I had the tale that we had come down the river seeking our fortune in the Varangian Guard. I hung at the back for my scraggly beard marked me as different. I hoped for a certain lack of rigour when we were enlisted. The threat of Alexios' army might make them look less closely at those willing to fight for them.

When we reached the gate the guards sent inside the palace and I wondered if Olef would come but it was not, it was Straboromanos, the spymaster who now appeared, from his clothes and demeanour, to be running the palace. He only knew me vaguely and I breathed a sigh of relief. Cnut made a convincing Dane and we were admitted. The parlous state of the defence was obvious when we were immediately sent to reinforce the guards at the northern gate. The threat of Alexios was working.

The men who were outside would all congregate outside the gates. When we had control they would be admitted. Most of my men were to go to our old barracks where we had plenty of good weapons and armour and we could be hidden. This was a nervous time for me as I had to remain hidden from Olef for the whole day. I hoped that he and the Emperor would be busy with more pressing matters than new recruits. We did not know any of the other guards at the gate, there were six of them. There was little point in disarming and disabling them until more of our men arrived. The plan had been to seep into the city in groups of tens to avoid arousing suspicion of the spies in the city. It was almost noon when I saw the first two groups in ferreting around the market stalls opposite the gates. I gave the smallest of nods and eight of them approached the guards. The men who approached were Andronikos' Greeks and I heard them offer to volunteer. One of the guards turned to fetch someone but Cnut said, "No, I will go. I need a piss anyway."

Once the six guards returned to their duty, standing in a line, blocking the gate, we were on them. The twenty men ran forwards and we struck them on the backs of their heads. They were quickly tied up. The market only saw some men rush the gate, a scuffle and then the six guards were there again. We had secured one gate. I left the six men to admit our fellows and we went quickly to our barracks. It was, as I had hoped, empty and we quickly armed ourselves more effectively. I left Cnut in charge and, with five others, made my way to the other gates. The main gate, to my relief, was held by Ridley's men and I sent them to the barracks under Ridley's command. "We have almost enough now but I shall visit the Treasury and see who guards that."

"Don't forget the noon change of the guards."

"Send a group of men to each gate to take care of the relief when they come. That will just leave us the change of evening guards."

We made our way through the deserted streets of the palace. Every available guard was either in a tower or on the walls. The outer wall of the city had been abandoned just to protect the palace. As we neared the stables I halted the men. There were Varangians on guard and not the Hetaireia. That meant Olef was planning to run. The wily Norse must have known that Nicephorus could not stand against Alexios and was preparing for flight already. As we approached the Treasury I knew what we would find, Varangians on guard. Olef had been clever, the Hetaireia were loyal troops and they had been sent to fight, as they would do, Alexios. As soon as the attack started then the Varangians would loot the Treasury and flee.

Once back at the barracks I summoned one of Andronikos' most trusted Kentarches. "Get back to the army. We need to attack closer to midnight than dawn or the treasure will be gone."

After he had gone I looked around. With the guards on the gates and the men inside we had about five hundred men. There were another four hundred outside. We would need to neutralise the Hetaireia. That is a hard task. We would lose many men.

Then I had a blindingly simple idea. We would relieve the guards and tell them that they had been ordered to guard the Treasury. This would rid the walls of the guards and prevent the Treasure from being pilfered. "But who will give the order? They know you are the strategos of Alexios."

"It is quite simple. I send a relative. Someone the Hetaireia knows is trusted by the Emperor."

"Who is that?"

"Why you of course; the saviour of his niece. We will fit you out in the uniform of a Tourmache of Hetaireia. They value the title as much as the man. All you will need is confidence."

As the afternoon wore out, Ridley and I secretly sought out our men and briefed them. I hoped that the message had got through to the Commander but the new plan meant that we could secure the gates with the warriors we had. I had selected the one hundred of my finest Saxons to go to the Treasury although I hoped that the Hetaireia would deter the pillaging which might ensue.

Straboromanos and some of his officers toured the gates and the walls. As my men were all kitted out in Hetaireia uniform he saw nothing amiss and he even smiled at the main gate. "If those rebels come they will receive a shock when they see how many men we have." He clapped Sweyn on the shoulders, "We will show them that our city is not to be taken easily, eh?"

As the sun began to set and the guards were changed, Ridley followed them to relieve the new guards. I was close by in case there was any trouble. The Kentarches saluted when he saw Ridley, "My lord?"

"New orders, from the Emperor. He is worried about the Treasury. Take your men and make sure that no one gets inside. Relieve the Varangians and they can return to their barracks. These new men can suffer the night watch." The order seemed reasonable and was delivered by a trusted member of the Emperor's family and they left. Leaving Ridley to complete the changeover I took my men towards the Treasury. We reached there soon after the Kentarches and his men had arrived. The Varangians there were less than happy but they were outnumbered and outranked. When the Hetaireia took their places I breathed a sigh of relief. The problem would now come when Olef discovered that he no longer held the Treasury.

"Now lads we are going up against the Varangians. Do not believe all the stories about them; they have not fought since they came to the city and are full of piss and wind. You are the warriors. We might be outnumbered but the rest of our men will be here soon. Remember your training and all will be well."

We reached the Varangian barracks just as Olef and his men emerged. From the sound of his voice and his demeanour he was less than happy with his subordinates' vacillations but when he saw us, lined up in a shield wall he almost erupted like a volcano. "Sound the alarm, traitors are within the walls!"

That did not worry me for the walls and gates were secure and by now all of our men would be ready to support Alexios' army when it arrived. Olef was so angry that he forgot to charge in a wedge. It had been some years since they had fought and it was not a reflex any more. Even though there were two hundred pouring towards us we were in a solid shield wall whilst they arrived piecemeal. I swung Death Bringer in its steady arc. I had recovered my strength since the poisoning but I knew that I could not stand all day. I would have to retire to the second rank at some time but I wanted Olef to know whom he fought. Amazingly he did not head towards me but to the right of our line; the stables. He was going to head to the stables and I wondered if the guards who were there had his plunder already? It mattered not. We would have to defeat these men first.

Varangian

Olef might not have fancied his chances against the last of the Housecarls but plenty others wanted the glory of killing Aelfraed. Cnut guarded my right and he murmured as they raced up, "Beginning your pardon, my lord but you are a popular little bugger aren't you?"

And then the slaughter began.

We had fought many times and there was a line of scything blades that took out the braver, reckless warriors who wanted glory. They came at us with swords that did not have the range of our axes and the first wave fell. I glanced to the right and saw that Olef and his officers were carving their way through my line. They had not been as reckless. The next line to attack us were more cautious but they met the same fate and I was beginning to think that this would be almost a bloodless battle for my men when I heard a groan and looked to see my line break and Olef and ten warriors race by to get to the stables.

"Cnut, take charge and when they are defeated come to the stables."

"Yes, my lord, but be careful!"

I disengaged and a warrior from the second rank took my place. As I reached the end of the line I shouted, "You eight, follow me." The eight had been running to plug the gap left by their dying fellows and we ran after the Varangians. "They are going to the stables. We stop them; anyway we can. Go for their horses!"

I heard a roar from the east and hoped that was the arrival of Alexios and the army. My more pressing concern was the Varangians. It was pride more than anything. It did not matter if Olef escaped, where would he go? I wanted to face him and show him that his vaunted Varangians were nothing compared to a Saxon Housecarl. We were almost too late for their horses galloped out as we turned the corner. There were twenty of them and we could not stop them all but we would make them pay. One of the riders rode directly at me and I swung Death Bringer timing the stroke to crash into the horse's jaw. Horse and rider crashed into the wall, the horse dead from my blow and the warrior from the collision with the wall. Another raised his sword to strike me but he was not battle ready and his swing was slow; mine was not and the sump of an arm flew behind him and he fell to the ground. I dispatched him with a blow to the head and then they were gone. Seven men and horses had been struck but the rest, including Olef had escaped. I prayed that the guards at the gates would halt them. Cnut brought his men after their enemy had fled. The clattering of hooves and the arrival of Andronikos and Alexios told me that we had won.

He dismounted and clasped my arms. "Well done. The Varangians?"

"Either dead or fled. Olef escaped us."

He dismissed it as trivial with a wave of his hand. "Come, let us let the Emperor know his reign is over."

My men were possessive about Alexios and the survivors surrounded him and me with a protective phalanx. The Hetaireia guards at the entrance looked at us and their hands went to their swords. "We have killed too many loyal men. You would die and for what? This is the new Emperor. Sheathe your weapons."

Alexios threw me a strange look as they did so. Later my men told me that the blood of the men I had slain covered my uniform from head to toe and I looked like a butcher from hell. My words might not have swayed them but my appearance did.

Nicephorus had emerged from his chambers at the commotion and when he saw Alexios he slumped, with a sigh, onto the throne. He gave the new Emperor a wry smile. "Enjoy it while you can for I held it for barely three years."

Alexios walked up to him and, moving him off the throne and sat down saying, "I will but I will make sure we last longer than three years."

"What of me?"

"Retire somewhere but if you raise a rebellion against me then you will die."

By the time the city and palace were secured my advance party was exhausted and we were forced by Andronikos to rest. When I awoke it was the middle of the next afternoon and I could hear distant cheering. I dressed and went to the gates of the palace. The streets were lined with people cheering Alexios as he took a celebratory walk in the streets. It was something Nicephorus had never done but Alexios was more popular and, importantly, knew the value of having the city on your side. Ridley saw me and walked over to me. "How did we do then?"

"We lost barely forty men. The Varangians fled west. **Apparently, they planned to join the Normans in Italy.**"

I shook my head. We had not killed the snake, we had merely made it hide. "And what are the Emperor's plans?"

"The cheering is because he announced that Empress Maria's son, Constantine, is to be co-Emperor with him."

"But he is barely a child! What is the point of that?"

Ridley grinned, "So there is no problem making him a co-Emperor then."

That reminded me of Ridley and his wife. "And Anna. How is she?"

"The midwives and doctors sent me away. The child is imminent."

"Well, you have lost your close relationship with the Emperor."

Varangian

He shrugged. "Alexios is a better Emperor already and besides I can go back to being a warrior again. With you."

The parade had drifted out of sight and we returned to the palace. John found us. He was now dressed in a fine outfit as befitted his status as adviser and confidante to the Emperor. "Well done, my lord and if you will both dress then the Emperor would like to see you when he returns from his little walk."

I put on my Strategos armour. It was the first time since I had been poisoned that I had donned it and I noticed that it fitted more loosely. I had lost weight, not surprising when I hadn't eaten for ten days. I would need to spend some time building up my strength. When I entered I found I was not the first to arrive. Anna, the Emperor's mother was there having been brought from the convent. She embraced me. "Our plan worked and the Empire will be grateful to you for your efforts."

"Now we just need to hold on to the Empire."

"That was cryptic? What do you mean?"

"I mean that we are already assaulted by Turks who think that we are weak and ripe for plunder and the Normans, I have heard, are looking to Illyria as their next conquest after Italy."

"We will need to build up the army then?"

"And where will we get the money, your majesty? Imperial soldiers do not come cheap."

"At least the treasury remains. Had we lost that then I dread to think of the consequences."

John and the other officials came in with a series of documents which they laid out on the table. I heard a noise in the corridor and the doors burst open as Alexios and his new entourage entered. There were many I knew but others were new to me. Obviously, they had been the ones watching and waiting to see which way the wind blew. I was not worried; Alexios was an excellent judge of character. He ascended the throne and his mother sat beside him. I saw Empress Maria hovering close by and saw the excited look in her eye. I suspect she viewed Alexios as the third Emperor she would have bedded.

John coughed and we all went silent. His piping voice sounded shrill to me as he attempted to make it louder but he was, as always, John and we all knew him and his ways well. "The Emperor Alexius I Comnenus wishes all to know that he is grateful for the efforts made on his behalf. He will now reward some of those who provided exemplary service. Stategos Aelfraed Godwinson. You are promoted to Commander of the Varangian Guard and the Hetaireia. Tourmache Ridley of Coxold you are promoted to Tourmache of Varangians. Andronikos Cassius, you are to be Commander of the Eastern Armies."

Varangian

Alexios waved us forwards and he kissed us each on the cheeks. He said quietly, "This is a new start for all of us. Our task now is to drive our enemies from our lands. Commander, you will drive the Turk back from whence he came. I will retain command of the west and take the army to rid our land of any Normans influence."

We all bowed. The fact that he had spoken quietly was to cement the fact that he trusted us but others would have to earn that trust.

When we returned, John continued, "The son of Emperor Michael, Constantine Doukas is to be co-Emperor and will live in the palace with his mother. The Emperor will also take a wife Irene Doukaina, and the wedding will take place next week." I saw Maria throw a murderous look at the Emperor. She had not expected that. When I saw the look of triumph on the face of Anna, the Emperor's mother I saw who had made the arrangements. Finally, to pay for the army there will be a new tax levied on churches and business in the city."

Although it was necessary, I did not know how that would turn out for the people of the city loved their new Emperor and it seemed strange to me that he alienated them by the taxes. Still, he was the politician and I was just the soldier but at least I would get to fight the Normans! While the Emperor dealt with petitions and the obsequious and fawning new friends the three of us wandered over to the window where the air was fresher and the atmosphere less unctuous.

"I do not know who has the harder task, me or you. At least you will be fighting with the Emperor and men you know."

"Many of the men we will be fighting alongside will also be new. The whole of the Varangian Guard will be new."

"Not to you!"

"True but the numbers are down and we will need to recruit."

Ridley laughed, "As soon as Jarl Gunnersson takes word back that they are commanded by you…"

"And you."

"Then they will flood the river to join you."

"To join *us,* Tourmache." I could see that Andronikos was worried. "With luck we will defeat the Normans, secure the west and join you."

He shook his head. "I think the Normans will take more defeating. Asia has been fought over for so long that it is never really settled but the west has been settled for many years. I hope you have strategies to defeat this man who has conquered a whole land with a handful of knights."

"He is old. He must be almost seventy."

"He shows no sign of tiredness and his son, the giant Bohemund is with him."

"He has never faced Housecarls."

"No, but he has defeated every other warrior who has come up against him."

With that sobering thought, Ridley and I headed for the city to meet with our friends. The three of them were delighted to see us. "Hopefully things will be easier in the city now that we have an Emperor who is more decisive."

"You may not be happy when you realise that he has raised the taxes."

Eric shrugged. "If we have peace then we will make more money anyway. Besides, money is not everything. We have a good life here and, thanks to your seed money, we are more than comfortable. We are able to help others out."

I smiled at Ragnar. "Well, Steward, we should be able to visit that estate of ours in the next few days." He mimed that he was happy. "Are you sure you can do without him?"

"We no longer need him as a guard and we have skilled workers to do other things. He means well but his skill is as a warrior but we have another present for you. We have found a Greek who can communicate from Ragnar's signs and make it into Greek speech. Ragnar understands Greek now. It will help him to work better with you and your people."

"I have no people. That will be Ragnar's task."

"And he will choose good ones believe me."

After we had enjoyed a pleasant drink Ridley made his apologies and returned to see if his son or daughter had arrived. "He is happy." It was not a question from Snorri it was a statement.

"Aye, they are good for each other and now that he is back with his warriors he is doubly happy. I feel that good things are headed Ridley's way."

"And you, Aelfraed, do you have happiness, fulfilment?"

"No, Snorri, but I do not think I was meant to have it. My life has been a series of struggles against obstacles thrown at me by the capricious Norns. I no longer plan for it is of no use. I wait to see what task I have next been given. I now go to the west to fight the Normans and after that…"

"We have peace and fulfilment. Why not you?"

"You two had fortune on your side. The Norns threw me into your home Eric and then it threw you into our boat, Snorri."

"You can hope."

"I gave up hope long ago for I have had too many disappointments but I feel that the estate will be good for me." I turned so that Ragnar could not see my lips. "If I should fail to return from one of these wars then the estate goes to Ragnar. " I waved a hand at the room. "You two have enough."

"That is kind of you and you have done more than enough for us anyway. He would be upset at the thought of you failing to return."

"I know but I probably will return. I am a hard man to kill."

Later as I was walking to meet with Isaac I thought back to those words. I could not remember a fight where I thought I would lose. Even when wounded at Stamford Bridge I had won the combat. I had never faced a man I did not think I could defeat. I suspected there was one, I just hadn't met him yet.

"Good to see you, my lord and I am pleased that you recovered."

"Thank you, Isaac, it was the care of my friends that did it."

"They are good men."

"Thank you for arranging my estate. Ragnar is to be my steward."

"A good choice he is a sound man."

"And if I die I want him to inherit the estate. Any monies which remain should be divided between the rest of my friends, Ridley, yourself, Eric, Snorri and the Jarl."

"That is kind but I hope we do not collect it for many years."

"In my profession, you can only see as far as the next battle. Speaking of the Jarl, pass the word amongst the captains that I am seeking Varangians, especially Saxons."

"We had heard that you had command of the bodyguards. That is a distinguished post."

I shrugged, "I will still be fighting in the front line so, for myself, there is no difference."

I would have spent another couple of hours chatting with Isaac and drinking the Lusitanian wine were it not for the sudden entrance of one of my men. Karl burst in, grinning, "It is the Tourmache, and he is a father. He has a daughter!"

"Thank you I will follow behind. Well, that will make a difference, a girl. I wonder if Ridley will try to teach her to stand in a shield wall?"

"Farewell, my friend."

The palace was filled with excited people. Anna was popular for she was a happy young woman. Her ordeal at the hands of the Normans and her rescue by Ridley had brought to mind the story of St. George and the two of them had attained a fairy tale quality about their life. It also seemed to mark the beginning of Alexios reign with a propitious event and Anna, the baby was always seen as a symbol of good luck and good fortune. The mother of the Emperor was flattered that it was named after her. The new Varangians, now resplendent in their magnificent uniforms, needed no urging to follow the Saxon tradition of wetting the baby's head. What it really meant was drinking until you became unconscious. I did not begrudge it them for they had been loyal and fought hard to get us where we were. I remained sober knowing that it was I who was in charge of the Hetaireia who would have to guard the Emperor while the Varangians drank.

Andronikos left with his army the following day. His faithful horse archers and cataphracts followed him and he sailed for Asia where he would command the Asian Themata. He would have his work cut out for they had largely been neglected by the last two Emperors but he had learned much from Alexios and I knew he would cope. What it did do was to make me more aware that I needed to grab the army and whip it into shape. Alexios was still Commander of the Western Army but he was busy organising his government and it was left to me as senior strategos to ensure that we were ready. John proved to be a valuable help and never seemed to need sleep. He was always bright and cheerful no matter how large the problems appeared to be.

"I have arranged a baggage train and guards. The soldiers are not the best but they will be enough to make sure that your baggage train is not robbed before it reaches you. I understand that it is archers and arrows which you will need against the Normans?"

"It is."

"Good I have begun the production of many arrows but you will need to find your archers. However, we have an ancient device from the time of the Caesars which we can manufacture. It is a Scorpion or bolt thrower. I guarantee that, no matter how well armoured a Norman Knight is, the missile will pierce him. We have ten of these." I had heard of them and Aethelward had told me of their power. It might make up for the lack of bows and good archers.

"What about caltrops?"

"They are being produced even as we speak. Now I have set the cartographers to making maps of the area for you. I could never understand how you could fight in a strange place and not have a map. I have remedied that oversight. Now, anything I have omitted?"

It was comprehensive but I still had requests. "We need more men to fill the ranks of the Varangians."

"Sadly we cannot make those in the numbers we make arrows. It depends upon volunteers."

"I have spread the word and you may find new recruits beginning to arrive. I do not know when we leave but I shall leave the wounded Varangians here to recover and they can train up the new men. It will speed up the process and then, when the wounded are healed they can bring the recruits to us. You will need to keep up a good supply."

"So I take it you will be not be as Olef was, and avoiding a fight?"

"We protect the Emperor and he is going to war; it is a perfect solution."

It suited me to be busy for Ridley was preoccupied with his daughter and the next couple of months flew by as I arranged for men to be trained and weapons ordered. The jarl had returned once during this time and he promised more men. It had been funny to watch Stig, torn between his desire to lead his band and his dream of fighting alongside the Varangians. They also brought news, how they got it I do not know, that Olef had fled to Italy and joined Robert Guiscard. *Wyrd*.

I had been with Cnut and Sweyn going over the lists of men when the messengers came. "My lord, you are required by the Emperor."

The court was subdued and I could see the other Strategoi and Tourmache there. Alexios looked up at me. "It is the Normans. They have landed in Illyria, Dyrrhachium is rumoured to have fallen and he and his sons are heading for Thessaly. Are you and the men ready?"

I grinned, "We are ready and that old man had better watch out for I have eight hundred Varangians who have a few scores to settle."

We went to war!

Chapter 15

I felt sorry for Ridley to be leaving his child so soon after its birth for that had been my lot and I had lost my son as a result. I did not think that would happen to my friend but I worried about him. Not that I had time to worry. Being in command of the five thousand men of the Hetaireia was a big enough headache but at least we had John's baggage train. What we did not have were the promised Scorpions. Priority had been given to the wagons which meant the Scorpions were not finished. Men would pay for that oversight with their lives. The Norman army and its allies were heading towards Thessaly which was on the western side of Greece. It was as close as they could get to Byzantium without attacking the city. More bad news was heaped upon us as word of a defeat for Andronikos in Asia reached us. It was not the best of conditions in which to march. The only bright spot was my Varangians who marched cheerfully along the summer roads. The baggage train carried their armour and, for them, it was a pleasant stroll. We had light cavalry scouts and a Thema in addition to a Bandon of cavalry. We hoped to pick up a Thema once we reached Thessaly. We had no ideas of numbers apart from the knights. It was rumoured that there were at least a thousand knights. It meant Alexios could not throw his cataphracts against the knights for they would be outnumbered five to one; not good odds. When we heard that Corfu had fallen our spirits sagged.

Our first good news was that the news that Dyrrhachium had fallen was exaggerated. It still held and we headed north-west to try to relieve the siege of that most valuable and important city. When we camped that night, I was invited to a private meeting with Alexios. I nodded to the two guards at the entrance to the tent and said, "No one within ten paces and your ears hear nothing."

They saluted their agreement. I had a fearsome reputation and I knew that they would not cross me. Once inside I joined Alexios at his map table. "There are things you need to know as my deputy. Should I fall during the battle you will need to pick up the pieces."

In many, this would have seemed morbid but not to soldiers and I did not use false flattery, "If you fall then it means my men will not have done their job."

"I have persuaded the Venetians to attack the Norman fleet. They have little reason to love the voracious Normans and it will prevent his army from being reinforced. I have also sent three hundred thousand gold pieces to the Holy Roman Emperor, Henry. He should be attacking the Pope in Italy in the next weeks. They are allies of the Normans and Robert will have to return to defend his ally. We just need to buy time. We will need to strike quickly and decisively."

I looked at the map of the city and the countryside. I remembered it from the last battle we had fought there. "We cannot defeat him unless we first defeat the knights. If we put the cataphracts on one wing and the light horse on the other then he will have to split his own cavalry and that means we might be able to defeat one wing and the switch to the other."

"There is only one Bandon of cataphracts."

"But we now have two Droungoi of Varangians. If we have one behind the cataphracts and one behind the light horse then the Hetaireia can still guard you and we have two Thema to hold the centre."

"We still do not know his numbers."

"We need horse archers for they make the best scouts and they are a deterrent. When this is over we will need to raise some more."

"If we get through this."

"We will Emperor, we will."

The day of the battle was a cool one for summer was well over and autumn upon us. I gave Ridley the place of honour on the right behind the cataphracts. He was reliable and would be a rock against which the Normans would flounder. The Thema were in front of the Imperial Guards and I took the left with the rest of the Varangians. Robert had a solid line of knights spread before us with infantry behind. I could see none of the dreaded crossbows and took this to be a good sign. The enemy were in three wings and the one facing the cataphracts was but three hundred strong which was the same as those on my flank. Alexios had the four hundred elite warriors facing him.

We began to advance. I was not sure if Robert had fought the heavy cataphracts before; they could only gallop quickly for a short distance but they were almost impossible to kill unless outnumbered. Their commander was a sound warrior who would judge his charge well. I had more of a problem with my one thousand light horses. Only one hundred had bows and the rest had javelins and shields. They would need to be used subtly.

The Normans began to trot. I yelled to the Droungarios, "Charge, throw a volley of javelins and then retreat behind me." At the same time, I saw the cataphracts thunder into action. The two hundred gleaming soldiers kept a solid line and they crashed into and through the Norman lines. I had little time to watch for the cavalry had hurled their missiles and were racing back pursued by angry Normans. "Shield wall." I had Boar Splitter for some of the men with me were new men and I was not confident about their ability to swing an axe in a shield wall. The Normans eagerly raced forwards and then the arrows began to fall, creating gaps in their lines. They did not reach us in a solid line but piecemeal and we dealt with them as such. I thrust my spear at the head of an approaching horse but the wily warrior jinked the head around. Unfortunately for him, it left a gap and I thrust my spear into his groin. As it entered I twisted and quickly pulled. He looked down as his entrails were ripped from his dying body. A shield wall is no place for complacency and I thrust again at the knight to my right who was trying to spear Edward. My spear went into the gap under his arm and as he died he fell to the left and dislodged another knight.

I heard a trumpet and the knights withdrew. My men cheered and some of them began to go forwards. "Back in line or I'll have your ears!" They all shuffled back into line. I could see on the right that the cataphracts had, indeed broken through and the Normans were routed. Our plan was working and then, to my horror, I saw Ridley and other Droungos charging after the fleeing Normans. I yelled a futile, "No!" but it would not have been heard.

The knights in the centre had not been committed and they wheeled and charged my poor Varangians who were caught in the open. Here and there small groups tried to form a shield wall but it was in vain. At that point, the knights from the Norman right and the infantry launched themselves, not at us but Alexios in the middle. I turned to the light horse. "Get to the right flank and try to cover their retreat. Hit and run! Hit and run!" I turned to the men around me. Plunging Boar Splitter into the ground I drew my axe, "Wedge!"

Alexios was struggling to maintain his line as the knights who had hacked Ridley and his men to pieces now joined the others. It was too much for the men of the Thema and they fled the field. Alexios and the Hetaireia would have all been slaughtered were it not for two things; the Normans had forgotten my four hundred men and the light horse were disrupting the Norman knights on the right.

My wedge plunged into the side of the Norman knights. We were on their right and there were no shields to stop us. We carved a bloody path through horse and knight relentlessly making our way to Alexios and the Imperial Guard. Inexorably we slowed down their advance and I saw that Alexios was moving them backwards. We had killed so many that we were exhausted and we were the ones at risk.

"Shield wall! Retreat!" My men performed this difficult manoeuvre well turning from an arrow to a line and then walking backwards. The Norman horses were blown and, when the cataphracts reformed the

Normans allowed us to leave the field, fearing even more casualties. They had won the battle but we had saved the army.

The baggage train was a mile behind the battlefield and we found that the Kentarches, the backbone of the army had rallied many of the Thema and they had made a crude fort from the wagons. It was little enough but it saved the army. As soon as we reached it the doctors began to deal with the wounds. I had the Imperial guard form a perimeter while we assessed the disaster. I had seen Alexios during the retreat and knew that he had survived. I would speak to him later but my first worry was that the Norman knights would attack us. "Make sure the wagons are tied together and the horses are in the middle!"

"Horsemen!"

Our nervous warriors immediately presented a wall of shields and spears but I was relieved to see that it was Basil and the light horse. They had been knocked about by the Normans but they had survived. Basil had received a blow to his head and had a dented helmet. A tendril of blood trickled down his cheek. "The city has fallen and the Normans have retired within its walls." His shoulders sagged with exhaustion, "They are not following." He waved with his arm and one of his men brought a horse with a body draped over it. "This is one of your Varangians, lord, he is wounded but alive."

I raced to the horse and saw, to my delight that it was Ridley. "Thank you, Basil, I am in your debt! Doctors!"

The doctors raced up and grabbed the limp, almost lifeless body. They waved my arms away, "This is healing business, not killing business, strategos!"

I did not mind their impertinence for they were right. Alexios took my arm, "At least he lives and now my friend we need to work out what we must do. This Robert, he has outfoxed us. Where to go?"

I thought of this Norman as a chess player. We had been playing a game of chess and we had been bloodied but how did we end up in this trap? Ridley's recklessness did not cost us the battle, it was our haste to get to the city. "Tell me, Emperor, why did we think that Robert was in Thessaly?"

"We had reports of Normans in the region."

"But it was not the army. He has been one step away from us each time. First, we think he has already captured the city and we moved south. Our distraction and the Venetians at Dyrrhachium meant he could take Corfu unopposed and that means he controls the whole of the west coast of the Empire."

"We know that Aelfraed, but it doesn't tell us where he will be going."

"It does. Thessaly. The place we started for. We can beat him to Thessaly and defend." I waved my arm around the camp. We are in no position to attack but we can hold until your plan for the Holy Roman Emperor comes to fruition. We can build up our armies and John can produce the Scorpions. It takes time to take a city, and we can bolster the garrisons with the Thema."

"It is a plan and, at the moment, the only one we have. I will send the Thema ahead to Larissa and my guards and the cavalry will escort the wounded there."

As he left to give his orders I hurried to the tents of the surgeons to see how Ridley and my other wounded warriors were. Edward was there already. He had suffered a slash to the arm and was bandaged. He approached me, "He is badly wounded my lord, he took a spear through his knee and he was hamstrung in the other. He will never stand in a shield wall again. His left arm was badly cut and he has a bad wound to the face," My face must have displayed my feelings for he added, "but he will live."

"Thank you, Edward. How many of our men survive?"

"We have three Kentarchia. Until Cnut and Sweyn return, I am the only officer." That was a measure of the bravery of my men and officers. They had not fled but stood their ground and died, they were warriors.

"You have done well. We escort the wounded to Larissa in the morning. Prepare the men and watch over Lord Ridley. I will see how many others are left."

A depressing walk around the camp revealed that there were only two thousand of the Hetaireia left alive and barely a Droungos of cavalry. We had been soundly beaten. The only force which had emerged almost intact was the one hundred and fifty cataphracts although a quarter of their men as losses was still too high a number. They too would remain with the column and they were the only threat we had against the Norman cavalry should they approach.

The Thema left as soon as they had rested, marching through the night to gain as much ground as they could. The surgeons reported that Ridley would live but it would be a long time before he would be able to walk again. I fell asleep as depressed as any time since before Fulford. Would I never get the better of the hated Normans? It was galling to win my own part of the battle but to see our army lose. I knew we could beat them but only if we fought them my way. I suddenly heard Aethelward laugh in my head at my arrogance but, in my head, I answered him. '*I am a strategos now uncle and I play the game.*'

I rode my horse next to Ridley's wagon which he shared with three other wounded warriors. He had been heavily drugged and did not awake. I took that as a good sign for it meant his body could rest. I also knew that the surgeons had used the pastes similar to the ones Reuben of Jorvik had given me and that my friend would heal and he would keep his limbs. He would become a cripple like Aethelward, but he would live!

We reached Larissa after five of the hardest days' travel I can remember. Ridley began to stir as we approached the walls. The Tourmache of the Thema had taken charge of the defence and I could see new ditches being dug and wagons entering with foods. The Governor of the town was a frightened looking little fat man who immediately began pestering Alexios with questions.

"Majesty, your man has begun to order my soldiers around and bring in supplies. Surely if you are here there is no danger?"

Alexios had a voice which seemed to calm people just by its sound and so it was with the Governor, "Governor, the Normans are coming but they are a nation of horseman. I will leave the Thema here to defend you whilst I go to Byzantium to raise an army to come to your aid. We are laying in food. If you wish to send your wives and daughters to Byzantium then we will escort them. We will defeat this enemy."

He suddenly seemed calmer and more amenable. We stayed there for one day only, merely enough time to collect the handful of wives, mainly the officials of the town. As we left the wagons were rolling in with supplies. Robert would have his hands full with a siege if he attempted it.

Ridley awoke as we left the vicinity of the soon to be beleaguered city. The wounded warrior next to him, Olaf shouted to me, "Strategos, the lord he is awake."

I rode to the rear of the wagon; we had left the front and rear open for fresh air to carry away the smell of blood. Olaf was supporting him. His face with the red, raw, scar running down it was now looking worse as the bruising made it also look black and blue. "I am sorry, Aelfraed. I let you down."

I was aware that the men were listening and this was not the time for recriminations, "We escaped the trap and your charge, reckless though it was, bought us time. Now rest. We are heading back to the city so that you can see your family and recuperate."

"This little wound," he pointed to his knee, "will not stop me fighting again!"

There was no point in depressing him so soon, "Just get well as soon as you can."

Varangian

There was a sombre atmosphere as the remnants of the army which had marched so proudly to war now slunk its way home. The sentries on the city walls looked shocked as the survivors of the vaunted Varangian Guard entered, barely a third of the number who had left. Their expressions told it all. If the Imperial Guards could not withstand the Normans then what chance did they stand? That was our lowest ebb. As soon as the wagons entered the barracks with their wounded the doctors and aides rushed to see to them. Anna was also there, her face filled with joy. We had sent riders back with news of the dead for I did not want the poor woman to be worried that he had died. I had written in my message of his wounds so that she knew what to expect. Ridley hated being on the litter but Anna grabbed his hand. "Strategos, this is a happy day! I have my husband back, he is alive and he cannot go to war again!" She kissed me on the lips. "Thank you, my lord."

Ridley almost screamed, "I will go to war again. This will not stop me."

I put my hand on his arm. "When you walk again, unaided then you can rejoin the army." Anna looked horrified but, unseen by Ridley I gave her a slight shake of the head and she mouthed her thanks. "The important thing is to get well. That is your wife's department. I have an army to rebuild."

"I am sorry, Aelfraed. I am a burden and you can do without my whining. I will concentrate on regaining my health."

I then went to see to the wounded with Edward. "Find out which ones will be fit to fight again and which ones will need a pension. Make a list of new and suitable officers and check the equipment."

"We will be fighting again soon?"

I looked at the sky. "Winter is coming soon and for once that will be our ally as it will slow down the siege. If our Venetian allies can maintain their blockade then the Normans will not have as many supplies but by the spring we will be fighting again Edward and it will be we who are at the heart of the army."

As I left to meet with Alexios and John I thought that what I had not said was that the Thema had not covered themselves in glory. They had not stood against the Normans and until they did then we would lose every battle we fought. I was praying that the Scorpions would be ready and more volunteers had arrived.

The normally ebullient and cheerful John looked downcast, as did Alexios when I entered their office later in the day. "More bad news my lord, Andronikos has lost another battle in Asia."

"So no help from that quarter." They had a map on the table. I pointed at the red dot, "If Larissa can hold out for the winter and the

Venetians continue to help us we may be able to attack them in Spring. Will the Scorpions be ready?"

"In the next month, they will be completed."

"Any more Saxons or Norse?"

"Three hundred but your friend Jarl Gunnersson tells me that many more are heading for the city by different routes. They seem to know your name, strategos."

Alexios smiled for the first time, "That is good news at least for your men and the men of the Hetaireia saved the day."

"And the cataphracts and light cavalry."

"You are right but the light cavalry only slows down the enemy they do not defeat them and we do not have enough cataphracts to make a difference."

"You need a better Thema. Arm them with longer spears, give them a bigger shield and incorporate more archers amongst their numbers."

"We could do all of that but how would that help us?"

"We need them to stand and soak up punishment. Shields and spears keep the knights at bay, arrows thin their numbers. When they tire then we attack with the few cataphracts we have and the Imperial Guard. There is no point using your best troops as assault troops until the enemy are tired and that is our advantage. They fight on horses and horses tire. Their horses wear no armour and we can kill them. If these Scorpions prove useful we can add those too." With positive ideas, the meeting ended fruitfully. Over the next few months, we worked hard to train new men and equip the Thema more effectively. Christmas was anything but a celebration. Too many men had been lost and the enemy too successful for cheer.

In January we received more bad news. I was summoned to a meeting of the Imperial staff. "Robert and his son have captured all of Thessaly apart from Larissa!"

I had to admire the Norman general. He had been thwarted by the fortification of the largest city but that still left him a whole province to ravage and he had done so. Alexios continued, "There are refugees thronging the roads. I have sent a Droungos of cavalry to guard the road."

"It does not change our task. While Larissa stands then we have a thorn in his side. As long as the Venetians are our ally he cannot reinforce and his men will have to be spread thinly guarding what he has. He will be busy building castles to protect his land. We still have until Easter to prepare. Our artillery is ready. We have new recruits and the Thema are better armed."

"You are right Aelfraed; we can still rid the land of Robert and his son Bohemund but we cannot afford to lose another battle. Each battle we now fight must be won. One more loss and the Empire will crumble."

I had taken to visiting Ridley each night to tell him of our progress. That and his family were his only highlights. "Then I shall be walking by then."

I had taken the precaution of bringing John with me and he was hovering outside. I waved him in. "John you have had many discussions with the doctors have you not and been examining the progress of my friend."

"I have."

"And what is the prognosis?"

John looked so sad as he sat on Ridley's bed and held his rough hand in his soft ones. "The spear to your leg shattered your kneecap. They can stiffen it with metal bands but it will not bend if we do that. Your other leg was hamstrung and will not bear your weight alone. The only way you would be able to walk would be to use a crutch. You will never be able to fight again. I am sorry but you know me, I speak the truth."

I saw the look of gratitude on Anna's face as she cuddled their daughter. Ridley slowly nodded and tears began to slip down his face. "But what am I to do? Do I lie on a bed growing fat and old?"

"I sincerely hope not old friend. I did not say you were leaving the Varangian Guard; you are too valuable for that. We need someone here who can train the men and prepare them for war. There is no one better suited than you. You can do that using a crutch, can you not? And you can take charge of the defence of the Hetaireia and the palace. When the Emperor is away with his guards there is no one to do that. Would that task suit?"

He smiled, "It would but are you not doing this to stop me moaning?"

"If it does that then all well and good but more important is that you do the role so that I can lead the men knowing that I will have many good and well-trained recruits to help us rid this land of the Normans."

I took the opportunity as the first signs of spring began to manifest themselves with a visit to my estate. It was a day's ride north of the city and I had put off the visit due to the needs of the army but I felt guilty that I had asked Ragnar to look after it and then ignored it. Once I was riding along the peaceful road north I found myself enjoying myself. For the first time since I could remember I was doing something which was peaceful. Even at Topcliffe, I had been making a defensive home.

Here I would not need to do that. I would sleep without armour and be able to relax in my own home. I had been given clear directions and a map by Snorri; my two friends had spent Christmas on the estate, away from the depression of the city and they both spoke highly of the house and the land. I found that I was becoming excited. I stopped along the way at a roadside seller of wine. I did not particularly want a beaker of wine but I did it because I could and it was a measure of the lack of urgency. He had no idea who I was for I had no sign of office upon me.

"Good day sir. A fine day for travelling. Have you come far?"

"From the city."

His face darkened, "They say the Norman monsters will take it soon."

I laughed, "They have as much chance of taking Byzantium as I have of growing tits!"

My laughter was infectious. "I am glad then, sir. Still, as long as those axe-wielding barbarians defend us I will be happy. They may be as ugly as my cow's arse but they are wonderfully tough men to stand between us and the enemy, eh sir?" He leaned in and tapped his nose, "I have heard sir, that the leader of them has bought an estate around here. That made us all feel happier let me tell you."

"Why is that?"

"It means if any enemy causes trouble around here they will have the invincible one to fight!"

As I rode away I smiled to myself. The ordinary people had no idea what warriors did to survive and to protect others. They had the stories after the battles, the stories from the winners, not from the dead. They were in blessed ignorance of the truth but I was glad of that for the truth would terrify them knowing that an enemy like the Pecheng, the Seljuk or the Norman was only kept away by the width of the wood of a shield and the sliver of steel that was a blade. It was little enough but it would have to do and as long as it was wielded by a true warrior then the Empire would be safe.

The house and lands were in a pleasant valley and the olive trees and vines rose on the terraces I descended. As a defensible position it was hopeless but as a home, it looked like perfection and I wondered what life would have been like had Gytha and Harold shared this with me? *Wyrd.* I could do nothing about the past and very little about the future. As I rode through the gate a farm worker approached me. "What can I do for you stranger?" He had a billhook in his hand and he sounded as though he would be ready to rid the world of me if I gave the wrong answer. I did not have to give an answer as Ragnar and two other servants rushed out. Ragnar clipped the poor farm worker on the back of the head and hit him so hard that he was knocked to the floor.

I almost laughed but I could not upset Ragnar. The smaller man said, "Apologies, Lord Aelfraed. We did not know you were coming and we had not prepared the workers. I am Andros and I work with the master."

I dismounted, "Do not worry Andros, Ragnar knows I do not easily upset." I embraced Ragnar. "Thank you for what you have done old friend. It looks perfect."

He mimed sleeping and I knew what he meant. "I can just stay for a couple of days and then I will be away to war but I wanted to see you and my new home." He made some hand gestures and Andros took my bags while the other servant took the horse. Ragnar had grown since I had seen him last. Gone was the quiet, almost sullen and shy cripple from the thrall hall in Hedeby and here was a confident manager of what looked like a well-run estate.

The inside was beautiful and cool and I could see that Isaac had bought a good property for there was much marble and well-painted murals. Whoever had built this had had taste. I was taken by Ragnar to a cool courtyard with a tinkling fountain and there was a jug of iced wine. As I sat down he clapped his hands and two servants came in with a bowl, a jug and water. They carefully washed and dried my hands and face then they removed my shoes and began to wash my feet. How civilised it felt. Andros came in. Ragnar mimed and I could see that the two of them understood each well, far better than I who only understood his basic gestures.

"The master asks what you would like to do first? I have the books if you would like to go over them? We could look around the estate?"

I looked at Ragnar when I spoke, "I have ridden enough today but I will look at the estate tomorrow and I in no mood for reading. Just tell me about the estate and how it goes." I liked the fact that Andros called Ragnar master, for he was master of the estate and I could never see me living there as much as it appealed to me. I was a warrior and the only time I would cease to be a warrior would be when I was either too badly injured like Ridley or dead. I suspected it would be the latter.

Andros smiled, "Good. As per your instructions, all profits are handled by Isaac the Jew. We visit him four times a year and he checks all the figures."

"You do not need to worry about my trust. Isaac and Ragnar have my complete trust and if they trust you then I am satisfied. "

He seemed taken aback by my frankness and then I remembered that he was a Byzantine Greek and openness and honesty were not their usual characteristics. "We had a good year last year and both olives and grapes were good crops. The master has enlarged the terraces and put in more vines and trees. In addition, we have created an orchard with lemons, oranges and figs. We have some good pasture and we have begun to rear horses as well as having cows for milk. Finally, the master introduced herds of sheep and goats for the high pastures so that we can provide our own meat."

I smiled and looked at Ragnar when I spoke, "Well done, my friend and I see that you yearn for your meat still." He grinned and rubbed his stomach. "I am surprised you do not grow barley for the ale." He put his head wistfully on the side.

The two days I spent at the estate were the happiest days I had in my whole time in Byzantium. Had I had a different fate or been a different man I could have been happy there. I could have found a woman and raised children and enjoyed watching things grow rather than just being a killer but my life had been formed long ago and the Norns had spun a different life and story.

I took Ragnar to one side so that Andros would not hear my words for they were just for Ragnar. I spoke in Danish and slowly so that he would know what I said. "I am grateful to you old friend for what you have done. My heart is full of joy at the home you have built for me. I may not be able to visit often but I will do so as often as I can for here, I am truly happy. Thank you."

We embraced for a long time. I felt real affection for the crippled and scarred old warrior for he and Ridley were my most faithful and loyal of all companions. I returned to the city feeling younger for the first time in years.

Chapter 16

Constantinople summer 1082

We had a larger army when we left Constantinople before the city was up. The Imperial Guard was almost at full strength although we still only had two Droungoi of Varangians. Edward commanded one and Cnut the other. Ridley had managed to hobble around the parade ground with the aid of a crutch and the pain of his wounds added to the lash of his tongue but the men were better trained and prepared because of that. The rest of the army was already on the road with the added artillery which we hoped would make the difference. We only had one Thema of troops but they had a better mixture of weapons which we hoped would stiffen the resolve of troops who had yet to prove their reliability. Alexios and John had managed to procure, somehow, more cataphracts and two hundred and fifty of these formidable horsemen rode with us as our shock tactic and finally, we had three Banda of light cavalry, including one whole Bandon of horse archers. We also left optimistically for Andronikos had finally won a victory against the Seljuk Turk. Perhaps God smiling on us again was the view of Alexios and others, for myself I thought it was the capricious Norns toying with us again.

When we reached the army, it was stretched out for miles and Alexios took the precaution of sending out a screen of two Banda of cavalry. The third was further afield seeking out some Normans. There were many of them for they were spread out across the whole of Thessaly. We suspected that the main army would be at Larissa and that was our present destination. Before we reached it, however, we had our first encounter with the Normans. The scouts reported a force of them close to Mount Olympus, near the coast at Heracleum. It was a worrying development for if they held Heracleum they controlled the western road to the capital. It was but a short deviation to reach it and Alexios sent all but a Kentarchia of light cavalry, along with the cataphracts to cut off their retreat. The scouts estimated a thousand men were there but only two hundred knights. It was the chance to put some steel into the Thema.

The Normans had not placed scouts north of the town and they awoke to find a large Byzantine army on their doorstep. The Normans are arrogant with a self-belief that is hard to understand unless you have fought them. They drew their army up with the knights in the middle, facing the Thema. Alexios placed the Varangians on the left and the

Hetaireia on the right. We had no reserves save for the secret weapon, which we wished to remain a secret.

We began to move forwards, the Varangians beating out time with their spears on their shields. I was seated on a horse behind them and I suddenly realised that this was the first battle I had begun without Boar Splitter which still lay on the battlefield where I had left it. The Normans were not going to let us walk up to them and fight and they charged. Alexios shouted, "Halt!"

The Tourmache of the front ranks called, "Spears and caltrops!" Each man threw down four caltrops as far ahead as they could and then the front two ranks braced their long spears into the ground and buried themselves behind their large oblong shields.

The archers in the third and fourth ranks drew back their bows and waited for the order to loose. I shouted to the men before me, "Shield wall but be ready for wedge when they run!" It was bravado but the men loved it and gave a cheer which must have disconcerted the charging Normans for their enemies were not fleeing and they were cheering!

I heard, "Loose!" and the sky filled with arrows.

The Tourmache yelled, "Hold!" as the horsemen drew alarmingly close to our men. The arrows struck and the horses which escaped the storm of arrows reared and screamed as they hit the caltrops.

This was the moment, "Wedge!" The men were in formation almost before I had turned to see if the Hetaireia had done the same, "Charge!"

The two flanks moved quickly forward and the Normans who faced us did not like the sight of a Varangian wedge of steel hurtling towards them, especially when half of their knights lay dead. They ran. Some of them did not run fast enough and they fell to the swords and axes of Varangians keen to redeem their honour. I wanted prisoners and I saw one of my men preparing to end the misery of a wounded warrior; I shouted, "Hold!" My men were well trained and the sword remained poised at his neck.

"Bind him! And see to his wound." As he was attended to I watched the Hetaireia joyfully pursuing the fleeing Normans. The knights were already through the town and I hoped that the Banda were still in position. "Who commands you?" He shook his head; I nodded to the soldier who held him. "Right hand, two fingers." The Varangian happily sliced off the two fingers. "I repeat, who commands you."

"William of Salerno!"

"Good and who commands the army?"

"Bohemund."

"Where is Robert Guiscard?"

Varangian

"I do not know for certain but we heard a rumour that the Holy Roman Emperor had attacked Italy."

"And where is Bohemund?"

He shook his head. "I held up my left hand and the soldier sliced off two fingers on the man's left hand. He screamed and then muttered, "Larissa."

"End it." The Varangian slit his throat, He would not have survived anyway, a soldier minus fingers on both hands was a beggar.

Alexios was delighted with the result. "The men showed more resilience."

"And I have some good news, Robert is back in Italy. It is just his son we deal with."

We entered Heracleum as triumphant heroes and the light cavalry brought us more good news, they had ambushed the retreating Normans and, although many had escaped, they had lost far more in doing so. It was not a huge victory but it was our first victory and that is always a momentous occasion. While the men and officers celebrated we planned our next move. Alexios took out the well-worn map. "Unless he has fortified the Tempe River crossing if we get across there we can be at Larissa with a two-day march." Now that we knew it was not the full Norman army we could be bolder with our moves. We still had the Scorpions and the Normans would be trapped between us and the walls of the city and we knew that there should be almost a whole Thema within the walls.

The next day we sent a Bandon of scouts to the walls of Thessaly. As we broke camp on the second day two riders galloped in to tell us that there was still an army before Larissa. There were a thousand knights and eight thousand other soldiers, including some Varangians. Olef had joined the enemy. It was a sizeable force we faced but, without Robert, beatable. When I told the men who was fighting against us my men could not wait to get at the enemy. The newer men had heard of the perfidious behaviour of the Norsemen and all vowed to have revenge.

The morning of the battle of Larissa we were all up well before dawn. There was a keenness and an eagerness for the battle which had been missing from all but my Varangians on the previous encounters with the enemy. We lined up with a single line of Thematic soldiers. They masked the ten Scorpions which stood behind them. On their flanks were the cataphracts, cavalries and Varangians in equal numbers. Alexios was tempting the enemy general who we assumed was Bohemund. He had seen the Thema flee the previous year and there was no reason to doubt that he would be able to do so again. Alexios had even chosen the battlefield to give him the illusion of favourable ground, for it was flat, but that suited our artillery more. As an incentive, Alexios had detached the horse archers and sent the Bandon to use the old Parthian tactic of shooting as they rode up and then turning backwards to fire as they retreated.

It worked and the knights only suffered the annoyance for half an hour. The pennants rose and the three columns of knights moved forwards with the four blocks of foot soldiers in between. The archers continued to loose arrows, almost goading the enemy on. When they reached a point a hundred paces from our line they split up and I heard the order to charge. The knights leaned forwards in their saddles eagerly anticipating an easy victory. Alexios roared, "Down!" and the front rank threw themselves to the floor.

The bolts whooshed as they were released and the teams of men quickly cranked them back to reload them. I had never seen them fired at real targets before and they impressed me immensely. The steel tipped weapons ripped through the first knight but did not stop, they punched through a second and third. I saw one go through a shield, a man and then a horse. They managed three volleys and then Alexios shouted, "Up!"

The men leapt to their feet presenting a solid line of shields and spears. The front three ranks were already decimated and the knights behind had to negotiate horses and men who lay in their path. The horse archers had wheeled left and right and now they pour their arrows into the flanks. The line hit my men solidly enough but we were ready with our own spears. The infantry stood little chance against my Varangians and I sought desperately to see where Olef and his men were. I spied them to our right. I turned to the cataphracts close to me, "Charge their knights!" The Droungarios grinned as he ordered his men into a line. I now had to make the room for him. Dismounting I took Death Bringer and my shield and forced my way through to the front rank who were dispatching the last of the front ranks of infantry. "Wedge! We are going there!" I gestured with Death Bringer and my men roared when they saw that the target was Olef. I hoped he heard my men's roar but it mattered not. I headed straight for the Norman knights who were still trying to get to the Scorpions. Bohemund or whoever led the knights knew that they could not retreat while the Scorpions remained or they would be slaughtered as they rode back.

I used Death Bringer one handed to slice down at the neck of the mount of the first knight in my path. It sliced through to the bone and then continued down to take the knight's leg off at the knee. Man and beast fell and, as I stepped over the dying pair, my men began to strike at enemies who were unprotected on their right sides. It was then that they began to flee and the ground between us and Olef thinned as men died. He saw me coming and I heard him shout, "Wedge!"

Their training was not as good as ours and they were slow, "Charge!" A wedge that is moving is harder to stop and we hit them with only the front ranks organised. We struck them obliquely and the Varangian before me never saw Death Bringer slice down, through his helmet and splitting his head. I punched with my shield and hit Olef in the side, stopping him from striking Aedgar next to me. The weight of our men pushed them back and over the legs of those who could not get out of the way. It was the worst thing that could happen to a wedge and the Norse Varangians fell and tumbled to the ground. My men were merciless, the edges of shields, axes and daggers rained down upon them. To either side of us the Thema had retreated to allow the Scorpions to pour their withering bolts into the packed enemy ranks but I only had eyes for Olef. I heard him roar and swing his axe, killing Ole, a young Dane who had joined us.

"This bastard is mine!"

"Saxon, today I will get great honour by killing the bastard who killed Hadrada and I will live in Valhalla as a hero."

We approached each other with shields held forwards and axes behind us. It was as though the rest of the two armies had disappeared. "The only thing a Norwegian is good for is shooting his mouth off; you are all piss poor at fighting and today, you cowardly renegade. You will die."

He feinted left and then swung his axe at my head. I ducked and swung my axe at his leg. He did not get out of the way quite quick enough and I saw the spurt of blood which told me I had nicked him. He screamed and spat at me in anger. "You cowardly dog! I will cut you into pieces and rip your heart out."

He swung all the way from behind him and I saw it coming. I braced my shield for the blow which was so hard it made my arm numb. My trusty iron-studded shield held and the blow had shaken him. I struck an overhand blow and he fended it off with his own shield but I saw a sliver of wood chip off and I punched him with my shield as he recoiled. Before he could strike again I swung my axe at his shield again. I saw the fresh white of wood as a chip the size of my finger flew off. Concern and worry filled his face and that is never good for a warrior must have confidence that he can and will win. When his axe struck my shield it did not have the same power and I saw that he was favouring his leg; he was weakening. The next blow from Death Bringer made a hole in the shield and I could see his glove. He backed away fearfully. I gave him no chance to recover and launched myself at him. I brought the blade all the way from my ankle, over my head to smash down on his shield with all the power I could muster. The blade sheared the shield in two and took his hand off at the wrist. He fell backwards screaming in pain. I stamped on his right arm and stood over him. "When you see Hadrada, tell him there was never a Norwegian born who could defeat an Englishman." I swung Death Bringer and his head rolled away with lifeless eyes staring at the walls of Larissa from which the garrison was streaming, killing the fleeing Normans.

I heard the relentless banging as the blood cleared my head and when I turned, my Varangians were banging their shields and chanting Aelfraed! Aelfraed!" At their feet lay the dead men whom Olef had led to their doom. On the horizon, I could see the remains of the Norman army fleeing westwards towards the coast. We had won and it had not been a skirmish or a minor battle, we had driven Norman knights from the battlefield. I wished that Ridley, Aethelward and my father could be with me for I had finally done what I had set out to do years ago, I had helped to beat the vaunted Norman knight.

We did not enter the city for it was crowded and, we had heard, had disease. Besides, it was pleasant to be outside under the stars with the men telling their own tales of the battle. Eric would have enjoyed writing the saga of Aelfraed and Olef but others made a fair attempt. As with every battle such as this the men came to reverently touch Death Bringer, as though they could garner some good fortune from it.

Alexios sent for me and I joined him in his tent where there was a jug of fine Cretan wine. He looked at me curiously as though trying to divine my mood. "It is strange Aelfraed I have seen you in combat before but I have never seen you fight like that. I doubt that any of the officers I know could show such skill."

"It is the way of your army. You have men who are great fighters but they are never promoted."

"They do not have the skills, as you have to make tactical decisions."

"Then teach them. My uncle was a strategos and he taught me. Not all men can be taught. I tried with Ridley but as he showed, his warrior instinct took over. If you want an army where the men respect their officers then train the best fighters to be good officers for you can never train a good officer to be a good fighter."

"Were you not afraid you would die?"

"I didn't really understand the question but I answered it anyway, "I was a better warrior than him. I knew I would win."

He shook his head. "And when you charged into their side, you knew you would win then?"

I knew that we had the advantage of attacking their weak side. I knew they were preoccupied with the Scorpions and I knew that if we hit them hard then they would crumble. If I thought I would die it would be hard to fight."

"And are you afraid of death?"

"I do not want to lose but I am not afraid of dying for then I shall meet my friends in the afterlife. Olef was not a good warrior but he died a worthy death and he will be with Hadrada and the others now talking of Aelfraed and Death Bringer."

"You frighten me Aelfraed and yet I would not be without you. The men, even my Greeks, regard you as a talisman. As long as you live then they will win."

That was the last major battle for a while. We chased Bohemund from city after city. It was like a game of cat and mouse. We would find a city with a small garrison and take it and then head directly for Bohemund's main army. Our light cavalry were superb scouts and we kept one step ahead of him. Gradually he worked his way back to Dyrrhachium, the place from which he had started. As we drew closer Alexios and I began to plan for our campaign in the East where Andronikos was still struggling to overcome the Seljuks. The scouts had reported that Bohemund was to the southeast of the city with his men and we made camp. A rider galloped in, his horse lathered and he exhausted. He handed over his package and almost collapsed.

Alexios read it and then he sagged in his chair. "It is the Pechengs. They have begun to raid our northern provinces. When we meet with Bohemund tomorrow we will then need to head north." It was the Norns again, tying me to this part of Greece and the Normans.

The next morning, we had even worse news. Bohemund and his garrison had slipped away in the night and were reported to be heading for Corfu which still remained in Norman hands. We headed into Dyrrhachium partly to see what effect the Normans had had and partly to give us some shelter after over a year in the field. Surprisingly the Normans had improved it with better defences and quarters. Alexios and I sat and ate dinner at a table, which was a novelty and we discussed how best to deal with the Pechengs.

"The news was that they were in Thrace and we know that country well. The local tribes there, the Bogomils and the Paulicians have allied themselves to the Pechengs so we have a rebellion and an invasion."

"The men are tired. Another march north might be their undoing. The cataphracts need a period of rest."

"I know Aelfraed and I cannot give them one yet. At least John has kept us supplied with weapons and armour."

"And the men that Ridley has sent have been a boon."

"I can give you a week strategos and no more and then we head north."

Except that we did not head north for we then received the worst news possible. Robert Guiscard was returning to Corfu with a hundred and fifty ships and even more knights. When Alexios read the news he was as low as I had ever seen him. "Look on the bright side. It is a shorter journey down to Corfu and the islands than to Thrace."

"But we have no ships and by the time they reach us he will be back on the mainland."

"Did I ever tell you about my father" He shook his head. "Harold Godwinson? My uncle Aethelward advised him to keep an army by the south coast to counter Duke William's invasion. It was a good plan and he did so. Then the barbarians allied with rebels in the north and my father took his army north and defeated the rebels but, by the time he marched south to fight the Normans that his army was so exhausted that they were defeated and his best men slain along with himself. So, Emperor Alexios, who is the greater danger, the Pechengs and the rebels, or the Normans?"

He smiled. "I think these Norns of yours are real for the stories are so similar… you are right of course, the greater danger is the Norman threat. I will send the local Thema north to threaten the Pechengs and we will go south and wait close to Corfu. Thanks to the Normans rebuilding and improvements, the garrison here should hold out of they are attacked."

The day before we left a scout rode in and approached me. "My lord, I was scouting for Normans close to the field where we fought and I found this." He unwrapped the broken half of Boar Splitter. "We heard that it was a mighty weapon and I thought that you would need it."

Even though it was broken I now felt whole. Wordlessly I reached into my satchel and brought out a bag of a hundred gold pieces and gave it to him. "My lord, this is too much, I did not do it for the reward."

"I know but the gold I give is not half of the value of this weapon."

"Will you repair it, my lord?"

I thought back to the hillside in Wales where I had first used it and I shook my head. "No. I will take it into battle with me but Boar Splitter is a spear no more." As he went I felt that this was truly wyrd, the spear had come back to me just as we were to confront my nemesis, the Normans.

And so a week later the army of Alexios Comnenus headed south for its final confrontation with the Norman threat. The further south we went the more convinced we became that this was the correct strategy. There were high mountains close to the coast near the islands he had conquered and if we could hold him there then we could do as the Spartans had done and thwart a much larger invader. We had reports that Guiscard had almost fifteen hundred knights which totally negated our cataphracts. Even more worrying was the fact that he had sixteen thousand men which outnumbered our force by four thousand men. It became imperative to reach the islands before he had landed. The light horse was sent ahead to observe the Normans while we plodded down through the mountains. The only good news was that the weather warmed as we neared our quarry. The Thema sent to halt the Pecheng threat had done just that by holding up in the forts along the border. Some of the land was ravaged but no territory was taken.

At last, we heard the news we wanted, the Normans had not landed. Their fleet was still between the islands of Corfu and Kefalonia. We halted close to the town of Margaritim. It was opposite the fleet and the men were hidden behind the walls and in the woods. We had to wait until Robert decided to attack. We actually needed him to attack for we needed a victory to enable us to deal with the Pecheng threat but for a week we waited.

Finally, they set sail, they must have boarded during the night for in the morning we saw the sails of his ships as they headed directly for us. Alexios quickly mobilised the army and within an hour, just as the Norman fleet was half a mile from the shore, we were all arrayed along the beach. The commander of the fleet must have realised that they would lose too many men in an opposed landing and they tried to slow down the ships and change direction. A number of ships fouled each other and two began to sink. Alexios despatched the horse archers to dispose of any survivors and we watched for Guiscard's next move. They headed south and, once again, although this time fully armoured, the army set off south watching the fleet to our right the whole time. Fickle fate then intervened in the favour of the Normans and a wind picked up so that they began to outpace us. The light cavalry was sent to follow them and we trudged on. By noon we were tiring and we came around a headland to see a messenger racing towards us but, in the distance, we could see that we had lost the race, the Normans were landing. The messenger confirmed the news. They had landed south of the river, just below the town of Glykeon.

My face must have fallen for Alexios leaned over to me. "Do not be downhearted, Aelfraed. We can see them and they needs must cross the river. We still have the advantage." Although he was right I knew how dangerous our adversary could be and I hoped that we could find terrain which suited us.

The town of Glykeon was on a small rise above the river. I could see why they had avoided the river for it looked swampy with glutinous marshes and a grey fuzz of insects. The opposite bank, close to where the Normans had landed and camped was the same. The town itself was in clean air some two hundred paces above the river. Some four hundred paces from the town there looked to be a ford, not a shallow one but from the tracks leading to it from either side, a well used one. As we set up our own camp and began to assemble the artillery, Alexios and I rode to view the ground over which we would be fighting.

Alexios pointed to the ford, "That is where they will cross." We looked at the land behind us, it was steep, too steep for the cavalry to risk riding up but perfect for our cataphracts to launch themselves down. "We will put the cataphracts and the light horse there to threaten their right. If they avoid the town and try to head inland then we can attack them from above."

I shook my head, "He will want to defeat you." I pointed up at the Imperial banner. "He knows you are here. He tried to put his own man on the throne and he wants you out of the way. He is an old man and this is his final throw of the dice. If we put my men close to the river with the Hetaireia and the Scorpions then we force him to attack towards the town and we can put the Thema archers behind the city walls. With their elevation and the spears of the others as a barrier we have our best chance and the Scorpions can scythe through their ranks."

Alexios considered the plan, "That might work and is as good a plan as any. I will place my banner in the centre to draw him there, away from the Thema."

"And I will stand with the Varangians and Hetaireia before you and to the right."

That night I went around the camp to speak personally to all the officers so that they knew precisely what we were to do. I sent out men to strew the ground, under cover of darkness, with caltrops and then I joined my Varangians around the campfires where we told tales of Stamford and Fulford. It was a good night and I saw, in my men's faces, that they feared nothing, especially not the Normans whom we had already defeated.

We were up before dawn and saw that it was a misty, foggy day. The men fed and there was the whining sound of the whetting stone as the blades were sharpened. I felt at my belt for Boar Splitter which nestled below my left arm. Today Death Bringer and Boar Splitter would bathe in Norman blood.

Varangian

When the mist cleared, we saw that Guiscard had been up early too and his army was arrayed on our side of the river. His knights could be seen in a block behind his infantry who faced us, in the town and then at right angles for the cavalry in the hills. The cunning old warrior, who sat astride a black stallion beneath his huge banner, was not risking his knights against the Scorpions. I could see the banners of the soldiers of Dalmatia and Ragusa were to the fore. He would waste his allies and save his own. William the Bastard had done the same when fighting my father, sacrificing the Bretons. It did not matter, they would all die this day. They waited until the sun rose properly and the ground dried a little more. That suited me for I could see the men waving their arms as flies and mosquitoes swarmed around their heads. The warriors would be irritated while ours were calm. My men began keening a song about Stamford. It was a lonely haunting song and its words carried across the valley making it even more melancholy but, oddly, calming the Varangians who waited for Guiscard.

The Croatian troops began their march towards us. I was not in the front rank for I needed to react to the enemy and their movements. The front ranks of the Imperial Guard bristled with spears. They did not attempt to try to climb the hill to face the archers and artillery and they remained a silent threat. As soon as the front ranks struck the caltrops their cohesion went, but they were brave men and came forward to face a withering volley from the archers in the town. Protected by huge shields they took fewer casualties than might have been expected but that very defence proved to be a hindrance as they reached my well-trained men. The Croatians did not see the spears which stabbed and jabbed unseen; they fell to the axes wielded by masters of their trade and they began to fall back through their dead and dying.

I was on a low wall behind my men and I could see beyond the retreating infantry. I looked for the signal for the knights to charge but it did not come. Instead, I saw him wave his pennant and a line of Dalmatian soldiers with crossbowmen began to trudge up the hill. Even from eight hundred paces away I heard the whoosh as the bolts were released and the screams as the bolts and the arrows began to take their toll but the crossbowmen had targeted the Scorpion crews and the number of bolts began to slow; allowing the Dalmatians to close with the Thema. The commander of the light cavalry ordered his men forwards and a volley of javelins sent the line backwards and we could see the ground littered with bodies and darkly stained with blood. Alexios saw the danger and sent two Droungoi of Thema to bolster the men on the hill.

Perhaps that was what Robert had been waiting for as he sent in his Norman men at arms. They walked steadily with a shortened version of the kite shield and they too were armed with spear and sword. The caltrops had served their purpose and now the infantry tramped steadily towards us, a line of mailed warriors facing another line of mailed veterans. This would be bloody. I left my place to stand in the third rank of my Varangians. My banner descended with me and my men began to beat their shields and chant my name. As they came into the archers' range, men began to fall but they were quickly replaced by the well-trained men in the second rank. These men had not fought and conquered Italy without showing that they had steel and determination in their bodies.

"Brace!" All of us put our shields into the backs of the man in front and placed our right leg behind us. The Normans hit our front ranks and then were pushed back. I could see the axes rising and falling and then rising again, bloodier. Here and there I saw a gap appear and then it was filled by another Varangian. The Normans were dying, but they were dying hard. I saw a gap before me and stepped into it. There was little point in trying to use Death Bringer and I took out the shortened Boar Splitter. One of the Normans saw a gap and raised his spear to stab one of the men in the front line. Boar Splitter darted out and went through his eye into his brain. As he slid to the ground the spearhead came free. I saw a gap between the two Varangians before me and I stabbed the short spear forwards. The cry of pain told me that I had struck someone. And so it went. They were brave men but we were protected by archers who shot at any who lowered their shields and eventually they began to retire. They had lost many men and although we had suffered fewer losses ours were the more telling for we had not as many men as the Normans who could afford a battle of attrition.

I looked to the left. The men on the hill still stood but I saw more bodies. Guiscard had attacked both lines at once. "Rotate!" The third ranks exchanged positions with the front rank which had fought long and hard. "Well done but the next ones will be the horse. Second ranks spears. Front rank axes." I made my way to the front rank and stood between Cnut and Edward. They both grinned at me and although I could see that they were covered in blood, it was not theirs. I glanced behind me and saw Alexios salute me. We both knew that the next attack would be directed towards him. Guiscard would go for the king in this deadly game of chess and I, the rook, would need to defend him. "Be prepared to go into a wedge on my command!"

The cheer told me that they had heard. Sure enough, the pennant dropped and the line of Normans moved inexorably towards us. This was the time when your bowels felt loose but you also felt a thrill of excitement. These were not cataphracts, these were just Norman knights. I had fought them and I had defeated them and I would do so again. I saw that Guiscard himself was leading the line which was impressively straight as it moved towards us. They picked up the pace and gathered speed. I could see that they held the lances overhand, not couched. "They will throw javelins. Second rank ready shields!" A thrown javelin was annoying because, although the flight was slow and you could follow it when there was a number you could be struck by one you didn't see.

They launched into the charge. "Steady!" A line of spears poked over our shoulders and it went a little darker as shields were raised. Then the javelins hit us. Some of my men fell to those with a shallow trajectory but most clattered off the shields and then they were upon us. Death Bringer scythed a line before me and I saw half a horse's head fly away. I saw a Norman knight crash to the floor and I split open his head. I saw a sword come down and I grabbed it in my left hand and pulled the knight from his horse. He flew over my head and I heard his screams as those in the third rank ended his life. We were winning! There was a clear space before us but I could see the enemy were having more luck against the Hetaireia and Alexios looked in danger. "Wedge!"

Edward took the place behind me on my left and Cnut to my right. I brought my shield around and held Death Bringer one-handed. A wedge of four hundred warriors is huge and the wall of shields to our right meant we were safe from attack. I edge to the left and led my Varangians into the flank of the horsemen. I knew that this would be bloody. Senlac Hill had been bloody. Stamford Bridge had been bloody. We were to fight enemies who knew not how to give up. Their shields faced us which meant their swords were on the wrong side and, initially, we cut through them like a knife through butter. I hacked, slashed and chopped. The flat of my weapon clubbed some men. I heard the breaking of bones and the screams of men dying. Blood spattered me. My tunic was covered in the gore and guts of my foes. We carved a path through two rows of knights and I saw the pennant and banner of Robert Guiscard and then their line turned to face us and we were amongst the finest Norman knights of the age. I hacked at the horse before me for I wanted to face Guiscard. Alexios was safe and we had done our duty; now the Varangians would rid the land of the Normans. A horse reared to my left and Edward and I raised our shields and pushed. The overbalanced horse fell backwards and we surged forwards. Suddenly Cnut was no longer next to me but I cared not for there was but one knight between me and my prey. I fended off the sword of the knight with my shield and swung my axe overhand, as it bit into his chest I felt a sharp pain in my side, I had been hit. In a battle such as this, blades came from all directions. Cnut was not there. He had gone to the Otherworld. I would continue for that was what we did. We fought on until we won or we died.

As the knight fell from my axe head, I saw Guiscard before me. His face was a mask of fury. I felt blood seep down the inside of my padded undershirt. I had fought with wounds before. It was on my left side. It was nothing. I could see Guiscard's white hair through his mail but I was not complacent; he had much experience. He had a long sword and he stabbed it towards my throat. I held my shield up. I felt a pain in my side and more blood spurted. He suddenly thrust the point of his sword over his horse and it struck me on the neck. It was a clever blow. It found a gap between my coif and my byrnie. I could feel the warm trickle of blood as it seeped down my chest. I held my dagger in my left hand with the shield and Malcolm Canmore's gift from years earlier stabbed forwards and struck Guiscard in the leg. It had a point and it penetrated mail links. It scraped off bone and into flesh. The bright blood told me I had struck home. At the same time, I swung my axe and caught his horse a glancing blow to his shoulder, the beast reared away. I saw I had cut through to bone and the terrified beast tried to evade me. Robert Guiscard was led away by his son. I recognised him by his size.

"We have them! Forward!" I was wounded but I spied hope. Their leader was hurt.

Two of his knights bravely faced us to stop our progress and others enveloped our flanks. As I sliced through the leg on one knight, I felt a sharp pain in my arm and I could not hold Death Bringer. I dropped it to the ground and pulled out the stump of Boar Splitter. The knight above me triumphantly raised his sword for the killing blow. I thrust upwards and felt Boar Splitter slide into his groin. I never saw the blow which struck my head but I heard the crash as my helmet was rent. The light began to fade and I found I could not hold myself up. As I slipped to the ground, I heard an almighty cheer. My men began to bang their shields but I could not see them. I guessed we had won but I was blind. I tried to shout but no words came out. I realised that the blood had ceased to flow and I no longer felt pain. It was quiet. My sight returned and I saw people moving across the battlefield but it was no longer a battlefield it was Medelai and Nanna was there with her arms open and her rosy cheeks shining and behind her walked Aethelward and my father with a woman who looked familiar and finally I saw Wolf, Osgar and Aedgart who faced me with grins as wide as a sunset.

Varangian

I heard Harold Godwinson say as blackness took me, "Welcome son, and welcome a hero."

Varangian
Epilogue

Constantinople

It is over thirty years since my friend Aelfraed Godwinson died. And today as we bury Alexios Comnenus it is time to put on paper the story of the greatest English warrior of his age. The Emperor was a great Emperor; there is not a doubt about that. He defeated the Pechengs and he drove the Seljuks from his land but his greatest achievement, the defeat of the Normans was not his. That was Aelfraed's doing. He and his Varangians drove the Normans from the field although all but three were killed. The sword which struck the fatal blow came from behind him for the rest of his oath brothers lay dead. The strike struck by my friend which sent Guiscard from the field although not mortal became infected as he and his men recovered in the swampy ground where he and five hundred of his knights died from fever. The cataphracts and their charge drove them from the field but it was the loss of their king which drove them back to Italy, never to return. Aelfraed had his victory.

They brought Aelfraed's body, packed in ice to the city where everyone turned out to watch it return to his final home. Jarl Gunnersson provided a boat and Aelfraed Godwinson, Commander of the Varangian Guard, the last Englishman was laid to rest with all his weapons and his armour beneath the hull of the boat. Gunnar explained that was the way the Anglo Saxons had buried their dead and it seemed fitting to send Aelfraed on his final voyage that way. The hull was covered with earth and, at the end, there were just a handful who remained while Eric sang the song of Aelfraed. I had fought my whole life next to this legend and I wondered what I would do next. His voice came into my head that I would continue to do as he had done and lead men who were still, at heart, housecarls. One day I might have a son and I would tell him of my friend. Perhaps we would return to England. This was not my home. I had followed Aelfraed for he was my leader and I was ever his follower. Now I would have to learn to lead. I hoped I could. What I did know was that I could never lead as he had done. He had been touched by God and I was honoured to have been his friend.

We all kept in touch over the years which was marked for me by my daughter growing, marrying and having children, by my training those men who still flocked to join the Varangians and hear the tales of Aelfraed and the others. Eric and Snorri became part of the city council while Ragnar prospered as a farmer but he mourned Aelfraed's death every year until he too died. The Jarl left the sea for Aelfraed's death had brought his own mortality that bit closer.

And me, Ridley of Coxold? Well, I write this because I wish to put matters straight, Anna Comnenus, the Emperor's daughter, has written her history of the event of that time. She is her father's daughter and always shows him in his glory. Alexios himself spoke often to me of the debt he owed Aelfraed but you will not see his name in the annals of the Empire. He is remembered only in the stories men tell around the table; the story of Aelfraed the Housecarl, who was loyal and brave, honest and faithful, the greatest enemy of the Normans and my friend. He never once failed to honour his word and he never once berated anyone for a mistake. To his men he was the ideal to which they aspired and to his friends, well he was Aelfraed and we loved him and now, as my life comes to an end, I look forward to the moment that he will greet me and then I shall be happy again.

Ridley of Coxold
Varangian
Constantinople

The End

Characters and places in the novel

Name	Explanation
aelfe	Saxon Elf
Aelfraed	Descendant of Alfred the Great's son
Aethelward	Aelfraed's uncle
Alexios Comnenus	Strategos and Emperor of Byzantium after 1081
Alfred	King of Wessex in the ninth century
Andronikos	Byzantine commander of light cavalry and latterly strategos
Andros	Interpreter and Ragnar's assistant at the farm
Anna Dalassene	The mother of Alexios
Bandon plural Banda	Unit of 200 men
Boatyard	Kiev
Branton	Osbert's brother, an archer
byrnie	Armoured coat
Calisthenes	Spymaster for Nicephorus III
Canute	King Sweyn's son
conroi	Knights who follow a leader
Danegeld	Bribe paid to Danes by English kings in the 8th-10th centuries
Dekarchos	Officer in command of ten men
Droungos	A unit, normally 500 men commanded by a Droungarios
Eric	King Sweyn's son
gammer	Old woman or mother
Gytha	Relative of the Earl of Hereford and wife of Aelfraed
Harald	King Sweyn's son
Hedeby	Denmark's capital
Hetaireia	Imperial bodyguard of the Byzantine Emperor
Inglinoi	English troops fighting for Byzantium
Irene Doukaina	Granddaughter of Caesar John Doukas- Emperor
Isaac Constanus	Aelfraed's Imperial Aide
Isaac the Jew	Jewish money lender
Jarl Gunnersson	Captain of The Maiden
John	Official at court
Kentarches	Officer in charge of 100 men
Kentarchia	100 men
Komes	Commander of two hundred men in the Byzantine army

Varangian

Kontoubernion plural Kontoubernia	A unit of ten cataphracts or ten soldiers
Kurya	Pecheng King
leat	An open stretch of water close to a river
Makios Embolas	A street in Constantinople
Malcolm Canmore	King of Scotland
Manzikert	The battle where the Byzantine Emperor was captured
Medelai	Middleham North Yorkshire
Miklagård	Constantinople
Nicephorus Botaniantes	Strategos and Emperor before Alexios
Nicephorus Bryennios	Rebel General
Nikephoros Basilakes	Rebel General
Olef	Commander of the Varangian guard
Osbert	Sergeant at arms of Aelfraed
Pechengs	Tribe of horsemen near southern Russia
Ragnar	Danish Warrior
Reuben	Jewish money lender
Ridley	Housecarl of the Earl
Roussel de Bailleul	Rebel Prince and Norman knight
Straboromanos	Head of the Imperial spies under Nicephorus
Strategos plural Strategoi	A Byzantine general
Sweyn	King of the Danes
Thema plural Themata	Ten-thousand-man Byzantine army
Thingman	Housecarls of the English Royal family until 1051
Thor	Sea captain
Tourmache	Byzantine commander of 2400 men
Wight	Spirit
wyrd	fate

Varangian

Historical note

Edgar the Aetheling did invite Sweyn II of Denmark to invade England; they captured York and then ravaged the countryside. When William came north he bought off Sweyn with the money he had raised through taxes and then punished the people of the north by slaughtering them! Sweyn then returned to Denmark. By 1080 Sweyn's son Canute was king of the Danes and then he was killed by his brother Harald who then became king. Sweyn had many illegitimate sons. I used Eric as one.

Alexios was a strategos and he did pursue Roussel who is a really interesting character. He did refuse to fight at Manzikert but was then forgiven and given command which is when he decided to become a ruler himself and rebelled. Alexios pursued him to Amasya where the people loved him and Alexios used a ploy to make them give him up. Aelfraed's clandestine operation is my version. Amazingly when Roussel was captured and imprisoned he was still allowed to lead men against Nicephorus Botaniantes who rebelled. He joined the enemy again! This time when the Seljuks captured him he was executed, having used most of his nine lives.

The Battle of Kalavrye took place almost as described in the book. Alexios was given command of the army and he tried to ambush Bryennios. The two wings collapsed and Alexios barely escaped with his own retinue. He regrouped his scattered troops and assaulted again. Meanwhile, the Pechengs had decided to loot their ally's camp and the Byzantines defeated the larger army by feigning a retreat. Bryennios was captured and the rebellion was quashed. Nikephoros Basilakes did rebel and Alexios defeated him through a night attack.

The war of Alexios and Robert was fought pretty much as described. The Varangians were massacred in the first battle and it ended the way it was described. As far as I know, there were no renegade Varangians with the Normans- this is a story after all. Alexios did bribe the Holy Roman Emperor to invade Italy and when Guiscard was away Alexios did recapture, from Bohemund, all the territory he had lost. When the Normans returned to Corfu they were faced by Alexios. The site of their battle is not known and the consensus of opinion was that it was a draw but Robert and five hundred knights did die of a fever and the Normans did not return until after Alexios was dead at the time of the First Crusade. Alexios was the only enemy Robert did not defeat. Alexios' daughter wrote a history of this time and most of the events I have used were written by her. History is always written by the victors.

My story is really about a Briton and in Aelfraed I see the archers of Crecy, Poitiers and Agincourt. The cavalry at Blenheim, the courageous riflemen of the Peninsular and the Guards at Waterloo; the 24th Foot at Rorke's Drift right up to the Cockleshell heroes who sailed up a river to complete a mission against all odds and who can forget the magnificent Paras at Arnhem. All of these are what I like to think of as the warriors who came from the Housecarls of Harold. Those men who fought and sacrificed for their country as comrades and long may we honour them.

Griff Hosker
January 2013

Varangian

Other books by Griff Hosker

If you enjoyed reading this book, then why not read another one by the author?

Ancient History

The Sword of Cartimandua Series
(Germania and Britannia 50 A.D. – 128 A.D.)
Ulpius Felix- Roman Warrior (prequel)
The Sword of Cartimandua
The Horse Warriors
Invasion Caledonia
Roman Retreat
Revolt of the Red Witch
Druid's Gold
Trajan's Hunters
The Last Frontier
Hero of Rome
Roman Hawk
Roman Treachery
Roman Wall
Roman Courage

The Wolf Warrior series
(Britain in the late 6th Century)
Saxon Dawn
Saxon Revenge
Saxon England
Saxon Blood
Saxon Slayer
Saxon Slaughter
Saxon Bane
Saxon Fall: Rise of the Warlord
Saxon Throne
Saxon Sword

Medieval History

Varangian

The Dragon Heart Series
Viking Slave *
Viking Warrior *
Viking Jarl *
Viking Kingdom *
Viking Wolf *
Viking War
Viking Sword
Viking Wrath
Viking Raid
Viking Legend
Viking Vengeance
Viking Dragon
Viking Treasure
Viking Enemy
Viking Witch
Viking Blood
Viking Weregeld
Viking Storm
Viking Warband
Viking Shadow
Viking Legacy
Viking Clan
Viking Bravery

The Norman Genesis Series
Hrolf the Viking *
Horseman *
The Battle for a Home *
Revenge of the Franks *
The Land of the Northmen
Ragnvald Hrolfsson
Brothers in Blood
Lord of Rouen
Drekar in the Seine
Duke of Normandy
The Duke and the King

Danelaw
(England and Denmark in the 11th Century)
Dragon Sword *
Oathsword *

Varangian

Bloodsword *
Danish Sword
The Sword of Cnut

New World Series
Blood on the Blade *
Across the Seas *
The Savage Wilderness *
The Bear and the Wolf *
Erik The Navigator *
Erik's Clan *
The Last Viking

The Vengeance Trail *

The Conquest Series
(Normandy and England 1050-1100)
Hastings
Conquest

The Aelfraed Series
(Britain and Byzantium 1050 A.D. - 1085 A.D.)
Housecarl *
Outlaw *
Varangian *

The Reconquista Chronicles
Castilian Knight *
El Campeador *
The Lord of Valencia *

The Anarchy Series England 1120-1180
English Knight *
Knight of the Empress *
Northern Knight *
Baron of the North *
Earl *
King Henry's Champion *
The King is Dead *
Warlord of the North
Enemy at the Gate

Varangian

The Fallen Crown
Warlord's War
Kingmaker
Henry II
Crusader
The Welsh Marches
Irish War
Poisonous Plots
The Princes' Revolt
Earl Marshal
The Perfect Knight

Border Knight
1182-1300
Sword for Hire *
Return of the Knight *
Baron's War *
Magna Carta *
Welsh Wars *
Henry III *
The Bloody Border *
Baron's Crusade
Sentinel of the North
War in the West
Debt of Honour
The Blood of the Warlord
The Fettered King
de Montfort's Crown

Sir John Hawkwood Series
France and Italy 1339- 1387
Crécy: The Age of the Archer *
Man At Arms *
The White Company *
Leader of Men *
Tuscan Warlord *
Condottiere

Lord Edward's Archer
Lord Edward's Archer *
King in Waiting *
An Archer's Crusade *

Varangian
Targets of Treachery *
The Great Cause *
Wallace's War *
The Hunt

Struggle for a Crown
1360- 1485
Blood on the Crown *
To Murder a King *
The Throne *
King Henry IV *
The Road to Agincourt *
St Crispin's Day *
The Battle for France *
The Last Knight *
Queen's Knight *

Tales from the Sword I
(Short stories from the Medieval period)

Tudor Warrior series
England and Scotland in the late 15th and early 16th century
Tudor Warrior *
Tudor Spy *
Flodden

Conquistador
England and America in the 16th Century
Conquistador *
The English Adventurer *

English Mercenary
The 30 Years War and the English Civil War
Horse and Pistol

Modern History

The Napoleonic Horseman Series
Chasseur à Cheval
Napoleon's Guard
British Light Dragoon

Varangian

Soldier Spy
1808: The Road to Coruña
Talavera
The Lines of Torres Vedras
Bloody Badajoz
The Road to France
Waterloo

The Lucky Jack American Civil War series
Rebel Raiders
Confederate Rangers
The Road to Gettysburg

Soldier of the Queen series
Soldier of the Queen
Redcoat's Rifle
Omdurman

The British Ace Series
1914
1915 Fokker Scourge
1916 Angels over the Somme
1917 Eagles Fall
1918 We will remember them
From Arctic Snow to Desert Sand
Wings over Persia

Combined Operations series
1940-1945
Commando *
Raider *
Behind Enemy Lines
Dieppe
Toehold in Europe
Sword Beach
Breakout
The Battle for Antwerp
King Tiger
Beyond the Rhine
Korea
Korean Winter

Varangian

Tales from the Sword II
(Short stories from the Modern period)

Books marked thus *, are also available in the audio format.
For more information on all of the books then please visit the author's website at www.griffhosker.com where there is a link to contact him or visit his Facebook page: GriffHosker at Sword Books or follow him on Twitter: @HoskerGriff or Sword (@swordbooksltd)
If you wish to be on mailing list then contact the author through his website.

Like what you have read?
Here is the opening of The English Knight, which is the first book in the Anarchy series and continues the story of Ridley and his son.

Prologue

Constantinople

I am Alfraed, son of Ridley, the leader of the English Varangian Guard in the Emperor's court in Constantinople. I was named after the last descendant of King Harold Godwinson who was killed at Battle Hill in 1066. Aelfraed had come with my father and fought for the Emperor Alexios. Aelfraed was dead these many years and the Emperor had recently died. My father had decided that, as he was getting older, we should return home back to the land which was now called England.

We stood aboard the Genoese ship which would take us to Frankia and I watched the land of my birth fade into the east. Constantinople, or Miklagård as my father's men named it, was the only place I knew. I did not want to go. I did not want to leave my pampered life. I had been happy in that exotic city. All my friends lived there. I had many friends and a wonderful life. I was familiar with all of its ways and now I was being dragged reluctantly to a new home in the west. It was unfair! I glanced at my father who was now white, shrunken and frail. He had once been the most powerful English Varangian serving the Emperor but now time and age had caught up with him. He had fought in his last battle. He had led his last warriors. I had to return with him to the home he had left so many years earlier. I owed my pampered and exquisite life of joy to him but he was taking me away from all of that.

He had been a sad, quiet and lonely man for these past twenty years. His wife, my mother, had died giving birth to me and he had withdrawn into himself. I think that he found it hard to talk with me. He was used to warriors. The only people he had ever loved were Aelfraed, my mother and me. The only time he spoke to me was to tell me the tales of the two of them as Housecarls fighting first the Welsh and then the Normans. I knew of all the battles in which they had fought and heard of every enemy they had slain. I knew of their journey down the Rus rivers where they had fought Pechengs until they had entered the service of the Emperor where they had fought the Normans. Once Aelfraed had fallen in battle it seemed that my father did not record the battles. They seemed not to matter. Only those where Aelfraed had led seemed worthy of remembrance. He was a modest man. I only knew of them through his oathsworn who followed him as he led the English Varangians to fight the Emperor's enemies. Six of them followed us now. Two were too old to fight, Ralph and Garth. Like my father their fighting days were done. They acted as companions and servants to my father. The other four would not have much longer to fight but they, like the others, were keen to return home to England to die. All of them were now Christian; the Emperor had insisted. Inside, however, I knew that the seven of them still held on to pagan ideas. They were forever touching amulets. The seven of them were a throwback to a bygone era. I did not feel like I had much in common with any of them.

 We were travelling in style for my father had acquired a vast fortune while serving the Emperor in Constantinople. He had maintained a friendship with two merchants whose lives he had saved and they had invested his money well. We were rich even by the standards of Constantinople.

 What concerned me was the home we were returning to. My father had been driven from England as an outlaw. He had neither land nor title. William the Bastard had taken Coxold, which my father had held, because of his opposition to him. He was now dead and my father deemed that Henry, who now ruled, might have forgiven his rebellion. We would travel through Frankia to Normandy where the King of England spent most of his time.

 And what of me? I was nothing like my father. I had my dark looks from my mother. I had my education from Byzantium. I could speak English, Norman, Norse, Greek and a little Italian. I could read Latin as well as Greek. Unlike my father I could ride a horse well; he just sat on one. I rode mine. I could use a lance and a sword. I had been considered one of the finest swordsmen in the city. All of that was behind me now. All of my friends were in Constantinople and I felt like I was just watching over seven old men to make sure that they did not fall overboard before we landed in Frankia.

 I trudged to the cabin I would share with the others. My life could not get any worse. What future did I have in a land I did not know amongst strangers and with all of my friends on the other side of the world? A world filled with barbarians and only one step away from a pagan hell of indescribable proportions. For the next weeks, my world would be bordered by the sea and the small Genoese ship which was taking me inexorably away from the place I wanted to live. Every day I woke to the torment of knowing that the life I had known was over.

Printed in Great Britain
by Amazon